THE GREAT BIG ENORMOUS BOOK of Tashi

To the City

Bluebeard's Castle

Royal Tomb

Haunted House

Village Square

Fields

Temple

Baron's House

Mountain of White Tigers

Cemetery

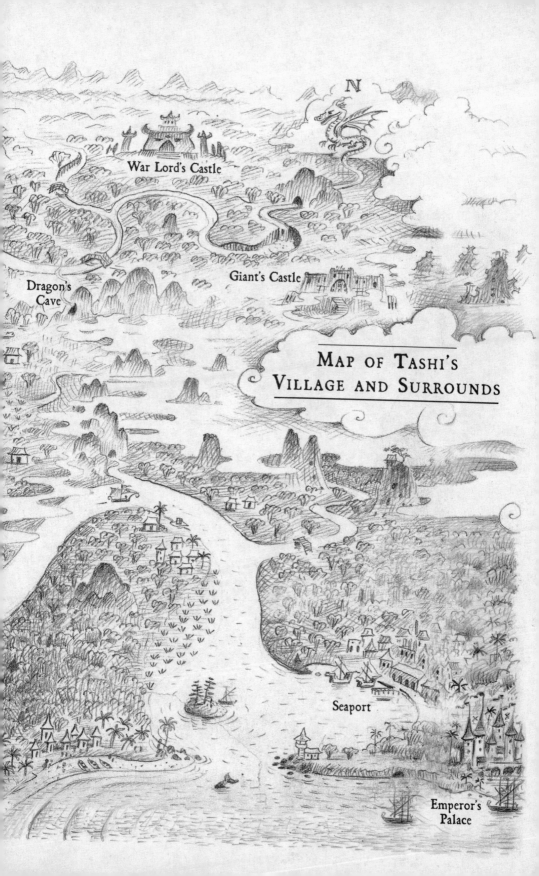

War Lord's Castle

Giant's Castle

Dragon's
Cave

MAP OF TASHI'S
VILLAGE AND SURROUNDS

Seaport

Emperor's
Palace

N

THE GREAT BIG ENORMOUS

BOOK of Tashi

written by
Anna Fienberg and
Barbara Fienberg
illustrated by Kim Gamble

ALLEN&UNWIN

When Anna Fienberg was little, her mother, Barbara, always read stories to her. At bedtime they would travel to all the secret places in the world, through books. The Tashi stories began when Barbara was telling Anna how she used to tell whoppers when she was a child. Creative fibs. Tall stories. And kids would crowd around her, dying to hear the latest tale. Together they talked about a character like Barbara – someone who told fantastic stories – and over many cups of tea they cooked up Tashi.

~

Anna Fienberg is a story teller with a special talent for fantasy and things magical. Kim Gamble is one of Australia's leading illustrators for children. For many years they have been working together to create such wonderful books as *The Magnificent Nose and Other Marvels*, *The Hottest Boy Who Ever Lived*, the *Tashi* series, the *Minton* picture books, *Joseph*, *There once was a boy called Tashi* and *The Amazing Tashi Activity Book*.

First published in 2010

Allen & Unwin
83 Alexander Street
Crows Nest NSW 2065
Australia
Phone: (61 2) 8425 0100
Fax: (61 2) 9906 2218
Email: info@allenandunwin.com
Web: www.allenandunwin.com

Cataloguing-in-Publication details are available
from the National Library of Australia
www.librariesaustralia.nla.gov.au

ISBN 978 174237 2914

Cover illustration by Kim Gamble
Cover and text design by Sandra Nobes
Set in Sabon by Tou-Can Design
This book was printed in November 2015 at McPherson's Printing Group,
76 Nelson Street, Maryborough, Victoria 3465, Australia.
www.mcphersonsprinting.com.au

15 14 13 12 11 10 9

MIX
Paper from
responsible sources
FSC
www.fsc.org   FSC® C001695

The paper in this book is FSC® certified.
FSC® promotes environmentally responsible,
socially beneficial and economically viable
management of the world's forests.

Contents

TASHI

'I have a new friend,' said Jack one night
at dinner.

'Oh, good,' said Mum. 'What's his name?'

'Tashi, and he comes from a place very far
away.'

'That's interesting,' said Dad.

'Yes,' said Jack. 'He came here on a swan.'

'A black or white swan?' asked Dad.

'It doesn't *matter*,' said Jack. 'You always ask the wrong questions!'

'How did Tashi get here on a swan then?' asked Mum.

'Well,' said Jack, 'it was like this. Tashi's parents were very poor. They wanted to come to this country, but they didn't have enough money for the air fare. So they had to sell Tashi to a war lord to buy the tickets.'

'How much did the tickets cost?' asked Dad.

'It doesn't *matter,*' said Jack. 'You always ask the wrong questions!'

'So why is Tashi here, and not with the war lord?' asked Mum.

'Well,' said Jack, 'it was like this. Soon after Tashi's mother and father left, he was crying for them down by a lake. A swan heard his cries and told him to jump on his back. The swan flew many days and nights until he arrived here, right at the front door of Tashi's parents' new house.'

'Did he arrive in the morning or the afternoon?'
asked Dad.

'It doesn't *matter*,' said Jack. 'And I'm not
telling you any more because
I'm going to bed.'

A week passed and Jack ate lunch with Tashi
every day. And every day he heard a marvellous
adventure.

He heard about the time Tashi found a ring at
the bottom of a pond, and when he put it on his
finger he became invisible.

He heard about the time Tashi met a little woman as small as a cricket, and she told him the future.

And he heard about the time Tashi said he
wanted a friend just like Jack, and look! the
fairy had granted his wish.

But at the end of the week he heard the best
adventure of all.

'Listen to what happened to Tashi yesterday,'
Jack said to Mum and Dad at dinner.

'Last night there was a knock at Tashi's door
and when he opened it, guess who was standing
there!'

'Who?' asked Mum.

'The war lord, come to take Tashi back! Tashi turned and ran through the house and out the back door into the garden. He hid under the wings of the swan.'

'Go on,' said Mum.

'Well, the angry war lord chased him out into the night and when he found the swan he shouted, "Where did young Tashi go?"

'The swan answered, "If you want to find
Tashi, you must go down to the pond. Drop
this pebble into the water, and when the ripples
are gone you will see where Tashi is hiding."'

'Did the war lord find the pond?' asked Mum.
'Well,' said Jack, 'it was like this. The war lord
did as the swan told him and dropped the
pebble into the pond. But when the water was
still again, he didn't see Tashi. Instead he saw
his own country, and his own palace, and he
saw all his enemies surrounding it, preparing to
attack.

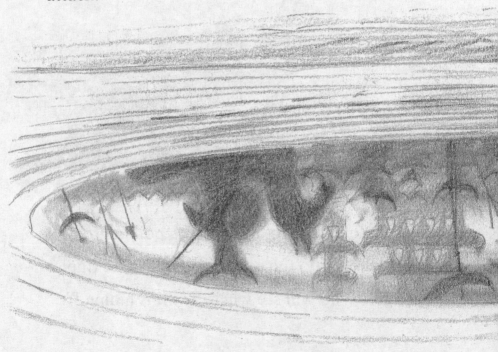

'The war lord was very upset by what he'd seen in the pond and he said to the swan, "I must go home at once!"

'"I will take you," said the swan. "Just climb on my back." And bending his head under his wing he whispered, "Goodbye Tashi, I am homesick for my country. Just stay in the long grass, and he won't see you. Goodbye."'

23

'Can I bring Tashi home tomorrow to play?'
asked Jack.

'Oh, yes,' said Mum and Dad. 'We're dying to
meet Tashi.'

Jack and Tashi sat at the kitchen table, drinking their juice.

'Would you like to play in the garden now?' asked Mum.

'Oh, yes!' said Tashi. 'I like gardens.'

'We could look for a dragon to kill,' Jack said
hopefully to Tashi.

'Are there any dragons left in the garden?'
asked Dad.

'You *always* say the wrong thing!' said Jack.

'He's right though,' said Tashi as they closed the door behind them. 'There aren't any dragons left in the whole world. Can you guess how I know?'

'How?' asked Jack.

'Well, it was like this. Come and I'll tell you about the time I tricked the last dragon of all.'

DRAGON BREATH

Jack took Tashi outside to the peppercorn tree.
They climbed up to Jack's special branch and
when they were sitting comfortably, Jack said,
'Did you really meet a dragon?'

'Yes,' said Tashi, 'it was like this. One day
Grandmother asked me to go to the river to
catch some fish for dinner.'

'Was this in your old country?' asked Jack.
'Of course,' said Tashi. 'Grandmother doesn't
believe in travel. Anyway, before I set off,
Grandmother warned me, "Whatever you do,
Tashi," she said, "don't go near the steep,
crumbly bank at the bend of the river. The edge
could give way and you could fall in. And," she
added, "keep your eyes open for dragons."'

'Dragons!' said Jack. 'What do you do if you meet a dragon?'

'Well, it was like this,' said Tashi. 'I walked across the field to the river and I caught five fish for dinner. I was just putting them into a couple of buckets of water to keep them fresh when I saw a cloud of smoke. It was rising from a cave, further up the mountain.'

'Ooah, did you run away home?' asked Jack.
'Not me,' said Tashi. 'I took my buckets and
climbed up the mountain and there, sitting at
the mouth of the cave, was the biggest dragon
I'd ever seen.'

'Have you seen many?' asked Jack.

'I've seen a few in my time,' said Tashi. 'But not so close. And *this* dragon made me very cross.

He was chomping away at a crispy, dragon-breath-roasted pig.

'"That's my father's pig you're eating," I said.

'"I don't care," said the dragon. "I needed something to cheer me up."

'"You can't eat other people's pigs just because you feel like it," I told him.

'"Yes, I can. That's what dragons do."

'So I sat down next to him and said, "Why do you need cheering up?"

'"Because I'm lonely," said the dragon. "There was a time when I had a huge noisy family. We'd spend the days swooping over the countryside, scaring the villagers out of their wits, stealing pigs and geese and grandfathers, and roasting them with our dragon breath.

Then we'd sing and roar all night till the sun
came up. Oh, those were the days!" The dragon
sighed then and I moved back a bit. "But Mum
and Dad grew old and died, and I ate up the
rest of the family. So now I'm the only dragon
left."

'He looked straight at me and his scaly dragon eyes grew slitty and smoky. "A few mouthfuls of little boy might make me feel better," he said.'

'Oh no!' said Jack. 'What happened then?'
'Well, it was like this. I quickly stood up, ready to run, and the water in my buckets slopped out over the side.

'"Look out!" cried the dragon. "Watch your step! Dragons don't like water, you know. We have to be careful of our fire."'

'*Aha!*' said Jack.

'Yes,' said Tashi. 'That gave me an idea. So I looked him in the eye and said, "You're not the last dragon, oh no you're not! I saw one only this morning down by the river. Come, I'll show you, it's just by the bend."

'Well, the dragon grew all hot with excitement and he followed me down the mountain to the bend in the river. And there it was all steep and crumbly.

'"He can't be here," said the dragon, looking around. "Dragons don't go into rivers."

'"This one does," I said. "Just look over the edge and you'll see him."

'The dragon leaned over and peered down into
the water. And he saw another dragon!
He breathed a great flaming breath. And the
other dragon breathed a great flaming breath.

He waved his huge scaly wing. And the other
dragon waved his huge scaly wing.

'And then the steep crumbly bank gave way and *whoosh!* the dragon slid *splash!* into the river.

'An enormous dragon-shaped cloud of steam rose up from the river, and the water sizzled as the dragon's fire was swallowed up.'

'Hurray!' cried Jack. 'And *then* did you run away home?'

'Yes,' said Tashi. 'I certainly did run home because I was late. And sure enough Grandmother said, "Well, you took your time catching those fish today, Tashi."'

'So that's the end of the story,' said Jack sadly.
'And now all the village was safe and no-one
had to worry any more.'

'Well, it wasn't quite like that,' said Tashi. 'You see, the dragon had just one friend. It was Chintu the giant, and he was as big as two houses put together.'

'*Oho!*' said Jack. 'And Chintu is for tomorrow, right?'

'Right!' said Tashi.

And the two boys slipped down from the tree
and wandered back into the house.

TASHI and the GIANTS

Jack ran all the way to school on Tuesday
morning. He was so early, the streets were
empty. Good. That meant he would have plenty
of time to hear Tashi's new story.

Tashi was Jack's new friend. He'd come from a land far away, where he'd met fire-breathing dragons and fearsome warlords. Today, Tashi had promised the story of Chintu, the giant.

Tashi was waiting for Jack on a seat by the cricket pitch.

'So,' said Jack, when he'd stopped puffing and they were sitting comfortably. 'Did you really meet a giant, Tashi?'

'Yes,' said Tashi. 'It was like this. Do you remember how I tricked the dragon, and put out his fire? Well, the dragon was furious, and he flew to the castle where his friend Chintu the giant lived. The dragon told him what I had done and Chintu boomed:

"*Fee fie fo fum*
    I'll catch that boy for you, by gum!"

'Chintu took one of his giant steps over to our village and hurled down great boulders, just as if they were bowling balls. Third Uncle's house was squashed flat as a fritter. Then the giant roared, "Bring Tashi out to me."'

'The giant looked terrible standing there, so tall
he cast a shadow over the whole village. He was
as big as a mountain—imagine, a mountain that
moved!—and tufts of hair stood up on his head
like spiky trees.'

'So what did you do?' Jack shuddered.

'Well, it was like this. My father, who is a very brave man, ran out into the street and cried, "Be gone, Chintu, we will never give Tashi up to you!"

'The giant was quiet for a moment. Then he answered, "If you don't bring Tashi to me, I will come back in the morning and crush every house in the village."

'The people all gathered in the square to discuss what to do. Some wanted to take me to the giant's house that night. Others were braver and said I should run away. While they were still arguing, I took the lantern and set out for Chintu's castle.

'I walked and walked until finally, there before
me was the giant's castle, towering up to the
sky. One path led up to a great door and
windows filled with light, but another led
down some winding stone steps.

'I took the lower path but the steps were so high I had to jump from each one as if they were small cliffs. After a while I spied an arched wooden door. It wasn't locked and I pushed it open. It gave a groaning creak and a voice called out, "Who's there? Is that you, Chintu, you fly-bitten lump of cowardly husband?" 'Now I saw a big stone-floored room and right

in the middle was an enormous cage. Inside the cage was another giant.'

'Ooh!' said Jack. 'Two giants! Didn't you want to run?'

'No,' said Tashi. 'Not me. See, it was like this. The giant in the cage was sitting at a table eating some noodles. She was terrible to look at. She had only four teeth, yellow as sandstone, and the gaps in between were as big as caves.

'Well, while I was staring at her she said in a huge voice, "Who are you?"

'So I told her that I was Tashi and what had happened and that I had come to persuade Chintu not to kill me. She gave a laugh like thunder and said, "You won't change his mind easily, it sets like concrete. I should know, he is my husband! He tricked me into this cage and locked me up, all because we had an argument about the best way to make dumplings. He likes to grind bones for them, but I say flour is much better. Now Tashi, you need me to help you."'

'And she needed you to help *her*!' Jack said excitedly.

'Right,' said Tashi. 'So when she pointed to the keys over on a stool, I reached up and dragged them over to her. Mrs Chintu snatched them up and turned one in the lock. "Now I'll show that lumbering worms-for-brains Chintu who is the cleverer of us two!"

'As she walked past, I scrambled up her skirts
and hung on to her belt. She picked up a
mighty club that was standing by the door
and then she tip-toed to some stairs that led up
and up through the middle of the castle.

'We came to a vast hall and there he was,
sitting on a bench like a mountain bent in the
middle. He was staring into the fire, bellowing
a horrible song:

"*Fee fie fo foy,*

   Tomorrow I'll go and get that boy,
   No matter if he's dead or jumping
   I'll grind his bones to make my dumpling."

'Mrs Chintu crept up behind him, grabbed his tufty hair in one hand and held up the club with the other. I slid down her back to the floor.

'"Chintu, you pig-headed grump of a husband, I can escape from your cages, *and* I make the best dumplings. Will you admit now that I am more than a match for you?"

'The giant rolled his great eyes and caught sight of me. "Who is that?" he roared.

'"That is the boy who chops our wood." And Mrs Chintu winked at me. "Now, let the boy decide who makes the best dumplings." She let go of Chintu's hair and gave me a hard look.
'"Very well," Chintu said, and he rubbed his huge hands together.

'Later, they put some sacks down on the floor for me to sleep on. As he was going to bed, Chintu whispered—it was like a thunderclap in my ear—"If you decide that *her* dumplings are better, your bones will make my next batch."

And as his wife went by, she said, "If you decide that *his* dumplings are better, I'll chop you up for my next pot of soup."

'All night I walked up and down the stone floor, thinking what to do. And then I had one of my cunning ideas. I crept downstairs to the kitchen and had a good look about.'

'What were you looking for, Tashi?' asked Jack.

'Well,' said Tashi, 'it was like this. The next
morning Mrs Chintu boiled her dumplings and
then Chintu boiled his. When the dumplings
were cooked they both spooned up one each,
as big as footballs.

'"We must put a blindfold on the boy so he doesn't know which dumpling he is eating," said Mrs Chintu, and her husband tied a handkerchief over my eyes.

'I took a bite of one dumpling and swallowed it slowly. Then I tried the other. They watched me fiercely.

'When I had finished I said, "These are the best dumplings I ever tasted, and they are exactly the same."

'"No they're not!" thundered Chintu.

'"Taste them yourself and see," I said.

'So they did and they were very surprised.
"The boy is right. They *are* the same," said
Mrs Chintu. "And they are the best dumplings
I ever tasted."

'So then I told them, "That's because I went
downstairs to the kitchen last night and I
mixed the ground bones and the flour together.
That's what makes the best dumplings—bones
and flour."

'"What a clever Tashi," cried Mrs Chintu.

'"Oho! So that's who you are," bellowed
Chintu, and he scooped me up in his great red
hands. "I promised my friend the dragon that I
would serve you up to him in a tasty fritter the
next time he came to breakfast."

'"Maybe so," said his wife, "but just try another dumpling first."

'The giant did, and when he had finished he thought for a minute. It was the longest minute of my life. Then the giant sighed and licked his lips. "Dragon can have a plate of these dumplings instead," he said. "They are exquisite. Be off with you now, Tashi."

'And so this time I walked out the great front door, as bold as you please. When I returned to the village they were still arguing about whether to give me up to Chintu or to let me run away. "I don't have to do either!" I cried, and I told them what had happened.

'"What a clever Tashi!" cried Grandmother.'

'So that's the end of the story,' said Jack sadly. 'And everyone was safe and happy again.'

'Yes,' said Tashi, 'that is, until the bandits arrived.'

The BANDITS

One night Jack was reading a book with his father.

'This story reminds me of the time Tashi was captured by some bandits,' said Jack.

'Oh good, another Tashi story,' said Dad. 'I suppose Tashi finished up as the Bandit Chief.' 'No, he didn't,' said Jack. 'It was like this. One wet and windy night a band of robbers rode into Tashi's village. They were looking for some shelter for the night.

'But next morning, just as they were leaving, the wife of the Bandit Chief saw Tashi. He reminded her of her son, who had sailed away on a pirate ship, and she said to her husband, "That boy looks just like our son, Mo Chi. Let's take him with us."

'So Tashi was picked up and thrown on to one
of the horses and away they went. He sneaked
a good look about him, but he was surrounded
by bandits, and it was impossible to escape. So
Tashi had to think up one of his cunning plans.

'The first night when the bandits were still
sitting around the fire after their dinner, the
Bandit Chief said to Tashi, "Come, boy, sing us
a song as Mo Chi did, of treasure and pirates
and fish that shine like coins in the sea."

'Tashi saw that this was his chance. So what do you think he did?'

'Sang like a nightingale,' said Dad.

'Wrong!' said Jack. 'He sang like a crow. The bandits all covered their ears and the Bandit Wife said, "Stop, stop! You sing like a crow.

You had better come over here and brush my hair like my son used to do." Tashi bowed politely but as he stepped around the fire, he filled the brush with thistles and burrs so that soon her hair was full of tangles.

"'Stop, stop!" cried the Bandit Wife, and her husband told her, "This boy is not like our son. He sings like a crow and he tangles your hair." Tashi put on a sorrowful face. "I will do better tomorrow," he promised.

'"You'd better," whispered the Chief's brother, Me Too, "or I'll boil you in snake oil."

'The next day when the bandits moved camp, they put all the rice into three big bags and gave them to Tashi to carry. When they came to a river, what do you think Tashi did?'

'Well,' said Dad, scratching his chin, 'he's such a clever boy, I expect he carried them over one by one, holding them up high.'

'Wrong!' said Jack. 'He dropped them all into the river. The bandits roared with rage. They called to Tashi to mind the horses. Then they jumped into the water and tried to recover the bags of rice that were sinking further down the river.'

'But Tashi reached them first, I suppose,'
said Dad.

'No, he didn't,' said Jack, 'and when the
bandits came back, all angry and dripping,
they found that he had lost all the horses. The
robbers began to whisper about the Bandit
Wife, and Me Too gave Tashi evil looks. It
took them a whole day to find the horses
again.

'Well, that night, the Bandit Chief said to his wife, "This boy is not like our son. He sings like a crow, he tangles your hair, he loses the rice and scatters the horses." Tashi put on a sorrowful face. "I will do better tomorrow," he promised.

'"You'd better," whispered Me Too, "or I'll pluck out your nose hairs, one by one."

'On the third day, the bandits decided to attack
the village where another band of robbers were
staying. Just before dawn they quietly
surrounded the camp—and what do you think
Tashi did then?'
'He rode into the village and captured the
chief,' guessed Dad.

'Wrong!' cried Jack. 'They were just preparing to attack, when Tashi accidentally let off his gun.

'The enemy was warned and Tashi's bandits had to gallop away for their lives.

When they were at a safe distance they stopped. The Chief's brother wanted to punish Tashi—he said he'd tie him up and smother him in honey and let man-eating ants loose upon him—but the Bandit Wife said, "No, let him come back to camp with me. He can help me roast the ducks we stole yesterday and we will have a feast ready for you when you return."

'So she and Tashi worked all day, plucking, chopping and turning the ducks on the spit, and mouth-watering smells greeted the bandits as they drew near the camp that evening. And what do you think Tashi did then?'

'Washed his hands for dinner,' said Dad.

'Wrong!' said Jack. 'Just as the robbers jumped
down from their horses, Tashi stumbled and
knocked a big pot of cold water over the
almost-cooked ducks and put out the fire.

'"Enough!" shouted the Bandit Chief to his
wife. "This boy is not like our son. He sings
like a crow, he tangles your hair, he loses the
rice, he scatters the horses, he warns our
enemies—and now he has spoilt our dinner.
This is too much." And he turned to Tashi.

"You must go home to your village now, Tashi. You are a clumsy, useless boy with no more brain than the ducks you ruined."

'Tashi smiled inside, but he put on a sorrowful face and turned to the Bandit Wife. "I'm sorry that I wasn't like your son," he said, but she was already on her way down to the river to fetch some more water.

'Tashi turned to go when a rough hand pulled him back.

'"You don't deserve to go free, Duck Spoiler," snarled Me Too. "Say goodbye to this world and hullo to the next because I'm going to make an end of you."

'But as he turned to pick up his deadly nose-hair plucker, Tashi shook himself free and tore off into the forest. He could hear the bandit crashing through the trees after him, but if he could just make it to the river, he thought he would have a chance.

'He was almost there when he heard a splash.
He looked up to see the Bandit Wife had
slipped on a stone and had fallen into the water.

'"Help!" she cried when she saw Tashi. "Help
me, I can't swim!"

'Tashi hesitated. He could ignore her, and dive in and swim away. But he couldn't leave her to drown, even though she was a bandit. So he swam over to her and pulled her ashore.

'By now all the bandits were lined up along
the bank and the Chief ran up to Tashi.
"Thank you, Tashi. I take back all those hard
words I said about you. Fate did send you to
us after all."

'Me Too groaned and gnashed his teeth.

'"Brother," said the Bandit Chief, "you can see Tashi safely home."

'"Oh no, thanks," said Tashi quickly, "I know the way," and he nipped off up the bank of the river, quicker than the wind.'

'So,' said Dad sadly, 'that's the end of the story
and Tashi arrived safely back at his village.'

'Wrong!' said Jack. 'He did arrive back at the
village and there were great celebrations. But
at the end of the night, when everyone was
going sleepily to bed, Third Uncle noticed that
a ghost-light was shining in the forest.'

'And that's another Tashi story, I'll bet!'
cried Dad.

'Right!' said Jack. 'But we'll save it for dinner
when Mum gets home.'

TASHI and the GHOSTS

'Guess what Tashi is having for dinner tonight,' said Jack, as he spooned up the last strawberry.

123

'Roast leg of lion caught fresh from the jungle,' Jack's father said keenly.

'Wrong!' Jack laughed.

'Grilled tail of snake caught fresh from the desert,' his mother said proudly.

'Double wrong! He's having Ghost Pie, from a special recipe that he learned from—'

'Ghosts!' cried Mum and Dad together.
'Right!' said Jack. 'And would you like to
know how he came by this spooky recipe?'
'Yes indeed,' said Mum.

'Can't wait,' said Dad, getting comfortable
on the sofa. 'So tell us. After Tashi tricked
those giants and teased the bandits, how did
he meet these *ghosts*?'

'Well, it was like this,' said Jack. 'The very night that Tashi escaped from the bandits' camp and ran home to his village, Third Uncle saw a ghost light shining in the forest.'

'What does a ghost light look like? How would I know if I saw one?' asked Mum nervously.

'Like a street lamp, without the post?'
guessed Dad.

Jack shook his head. 'No, Tashi said it was
more like a small moon, sending out rays of
light into the trees, like white spider threads.'

'Ooh, can you get tangled up in them?' shivered Mum.

'In a way,' said Jack. 'Ghost monsters can be sticky, and they tend to hang around, Tashi says. Well, the next night there were more ghost lights. They came closer, and closer, and Tashi called his parents to see. Soon the news spread through the village and everyone was peeping behind their curtains at the phantom lights flitting through the forest.

'In the morning the people hurried to the
square to talk about the ghosts. Some
wanted to pack their belongings and move
right away. Others wanted to burn down
the forest so the ghosts would have no
place to live. Finally they decided to ask
Wise-As-An-Owl what he thought would
be the best plan.'

'*My* plan would be to ignore them,' said Dad. 'If the ghosts got no attention, they'd probably go away.'

'I don't think that works with ghosts, Dad,' said Jack. 'Anyway, Wise-As-An-Owl told the men to organise a great beating of saucepan lids outside their houses that night as soon as it grew dark. They did, and sure enough, the ghosts slipped away, back into the forest.

'But the next night the ghosts came back. They drifted up like smoke, nearer and nearer, until they were pressing their faces against the windows. Their mouths were huge and gluey, and the air in the houses began to grow stale and thin as they sucked at the keyholes and under the doors. Everybody in the village burst out into the streets, coughing and choking. Men and women thundered around making a great crashing noise with saucepans and garbage lids and firecrackers. The ghosts melted away but Tashi was sure that they weren't gone for long.'

'They'd have gone forever if people had ignored them,' muttered Dad. 'Who comes back for no attention?'

'Well,' continued Jack, 'in the morning Tashi went to see his father's Younger Brother. He lives up on a hill overlooking the village and spends his nights studying the stars through a great telescope that he built years ago.

'Tashi told him about the ghost monsters who were frightening the villagers and he cried, "Of course, I know why they have come now. Look, Tashi," and he took out his charts of the stars and his Book of Calculations. "You see, look here. In three days' time there will be an eclipse of the moon."'

'I'll bet Tashi didn't know what *that* was,' Dad laughed. He was already looking for the dictionary.

'Yes,' said Jack patiently. 'It's what happens when the moon is blacked out for a while by the shadow of the earth. Well, Younger Brother said to Tashi, "Last time there was an eclipse, the river flooded and your father's pigs were drowned. And the time before that we had a plague of locusts that ate the village fields bare. You'll see, with this next eclipse there will be a haunting of ghosts."

'At that, Tashi thought "*Aha!*", and he began to form one of his cunning plans. He waited two more days and sure enough the saucepan lids did no good at all. Each night after the people went to bed, the ghosts floated back to the village. On the third night, a brave dog rushed out of his house but as he drew breath to bark, he sucked in a tendril of grey ghost, and it was terrible to see. He choked and gasped and his fine black coat grew pale and wispy until he was just a shadow, melting into the stones.

'The villagers drew their curtains against the sight of it, but Tashi crept out into the forest. At first he could see only the small moons of light, tangling amongst the leaves. But as he tip-toed into the dark heart of the forest, he saw the ghosts themselves.

'And there were hundreds of them—
hopping ghosts, prowling ghosts, gliding
ghosts. They were like white dripping
shadows, fat and thin, tall and tiny,
whipping all around him.

'Suddenly Tashi felt a cold weight on his head. "Oh no, a jumping ghost," he thought, and he tried to pull it off. But it slid down over his eyes and nose like sticky egg white, and he could hardly see or breathe. "Oh no, a jumping *and* slithering ghost," he groaned, as it trickled down his back and clamped his arms.

'"Let me go!" Tashi screamed, and as he
screamed he sucked in a bit of cold eggy
ghost. He felt as if he were choking, and
then more and more ghosts pressed their
bodies against him. Like thickening fog they
crowded around and Tashi didn't want to
breathe for fear of sucking in those damp
whirling phantoms.

'And then a huge glowing ghost as big as a
ship loomed over him. Its eyes were empty,
and it was the meanest-looking ghost Tashi
had ever seen.'

'Has Tashi seen many ghosts before this?'
asked Dad.

'Yes, he's seen a few in his time, he says.
Well, this mean-looking, leader ghost asked
Tashi why he had come into the forest at
night.

'"I've come to warn you," Tashi hissed at him, blowing out wisps of ghost as he spoke. "If you don't leave our village at once, you will all suffer."

'The huge ghost laughed. The sound rippled like wind through the forest. "And how exactly will we suffer?"

'"Well," Tashi told him, "my friend the Red-Whiskered Dragon-Ghost will come and punish you if you hurt me or frighten the people in my village."

'There was a low buzz as the ghosts
swarmed together, discussing Tashi's news.
The smaller ghosts were trembling, and
their outlines were fading a little with fear.
But the leader ghost was scornful. "Why
should we believe *you*? No one could hurt
us!"

'"Oh, I can easily prove it," Tashi said. "Just look at the moon up there. See how round and full it is? Now I will call my friend, the Red-Whiskered Dragon-Ghost, and he will open his huge jaws and eat the moon right up. When the moonlight disappears you will know how great he is and you will be afraid."

'Tashi called out into the night, "O mighty Red-Whiskered Dragon-Ghost, when I count to three, please open your jaws and take your first gigantic bite out of the moon!"

'Tashi counted *o-n-e* very, very slowly. He was worrying, deep inside himself—what if Younger Brother was wrong with his calculations? Could an eclipse be late?

'He counted *t-w-o* even more slowly. Was the moon shrinking a little?

'"Are you ready, ghost monsters?" Tashi cried, and then he shouted, "*THREE!*" just as the black shadow of the earth moved across the moon and sliced off a great piece.

'The ghosts watched as the moon grew smaller and smaller until there was not even a needlepoint of light in the dark sky. The moon had been swallowed up.

'The ghosts moaned with fear and their sighs blew through the trees like a gale of ice. "Please," they cried to Tashi, "tell your friend to give us back the moon. Tell him to spit it out again!"

'Tashi was silent for a moment, letting the ghosts feel the awful weight of a sky without light. Their own little moons of ghost-light were paler now, swamped by the darkness of the night.

'"All right," Tashi said finally, "I will ask him to grant you your wish—if you do two things. First, you must all leave this part of the earth, and never come back. Every now and again, the Red-Whiskered Dragon-Ghost will gobble up the moon for a short time, just to remind you never to frighten my village and its people again."

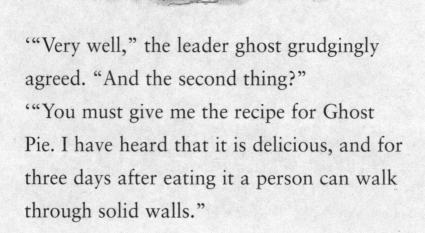

'"Very well," the leader ghost grudgingly agreed. "And the second thing?"

'"You must give me the recipe for Ghost Pie. I have heard that it is delicious, and for three days after eating it a person can walk through solid walls."

'The ghost leader let out a roar of rage. The little ghosts quivered and faded into the trees. They were shrinking with every moment, hanging like cloudy raindrops from the forest leaves.

'"Ghost Pie is one of our greatest secrets," the leader ghost spat. He waved for some of the older ghosts to come closer. They whispered together and then the leader ghost turned to Tashi. "We will do as you say, young Tashi, if you promise never to reveal the ingredients to any other *living* soul."'

'Aha!' cried Dad, slapping his knee. 'So when are we going to have a taste of pie?'

'Tashi says we can all come over to dinner next Saturday to try it, as long as we don't ask any questions about how it is made,' said Jack.

'It's a promise,' beamed Dad. He stood up and stretched. 'Oh well,' he said, 'I suppose that's the end of the story, and Tashi's had no more trouble with ghosts then.'

'That's right,' smiled Jack, 'but only one moon went by before he was in a sticky situation with a truly wicked Baron!'

The MOUNTAIN of WHITE TIGERS

The doorbell rang.

'I'll go,' Jack called, because he knew who it would be. Tashi was spending the day with him, and they were going for a ferry ride. Jack had said to come early, in time for breakfast.

But when Tashi walked in, Mum peered at his face with a worried frown. 'You look a bit pale this morning, Tashi,' she said. 'Yes, I know,' sighed Tashi. I've been up burping Ghost Pie all night.'

'Pancakes coming!' cried Dad from the kitchen.
Tashi turned a little paler.

When they were all sitting around the table in the garden, and Tashi had managed three pancakes after all, Jack decided that he'd waited long enough. 'How did you meet this Wicked Baron?'

'Well, it was like this,' said Tashi. 'One day
I went to visit Li Tam, my favourite auntie.
I always like going to her place because she
has the most interesting house in the village.
The rooms are all decorated with painted
scrolls and she lets me touch the delicate
bowls and vases and hand-carved swords.'

'Does Li Tam do a lot of sword-fighting?'
asked Dad.

Jack rolled his eyes, but Tashi just smiled.
'No, the swords belonged to her father.
Anyway,' he went on, 'this particular day I
didn't even get a chance to knock on the
door, when it was flung open and out
stormed Li Tam's landlord, the wicked
Baron.'

'Aha!' cried Mum and Dad.

'Yes, he was grinding his gold teeth, and he pushed me out of the way. I picked myself up and as I dusted my pants off, I wondered why the Baron looked so angry.'

'Was he a friend of Li Tam's?' asked Dad.

'Oh no!' said Tashi. 'He was no one's friend. The only thing he loved was gold. You see, this Baron had once been poor, but he had tricked an old banker out of his riches, and then he had stolen some money here and hired a few pirates there, until he had a huge fortune.'

'Where did he keep all his gold?' asked Mum.

'Well, it was a great mystery,' said Tashi. 'The people in the village were certain that he had hidden it away in a deep cave. But no one could be quite sure because the cave lay at the top of The Mountain of White Tigers.'

'I've never seen a white tiger,' said Dad, 'but I've heard they are the fiercest kind.'

'Yes,' said Tashi. 'Anyway, Li Tam was very
upset after the Baron stormed out. She told
me that he had called to tell her that she
would have to leave her home at once
because he had been offered a good price
for it. And Li Tam had cried out, "Why
must you have *my* house? You own the
whole village!" But the Baron had ordered
her to pack her bags by the end of the week.

'"Look at this then!" Li Tam had told him,
and she'd pulled a piece of paper from the
hidden drawer in her cupboard. On it was
written a promise from the old banker that
she could stay in the house for as long as
she pleased.

'The Baron's face had grown red and that is
why he'd stormed out, knocking me over as
he went. But Li Tam was worried. "Tashi,"
she said to me, "I just know he won't stop
at this. He'll try to find a way to push me
out of my home."

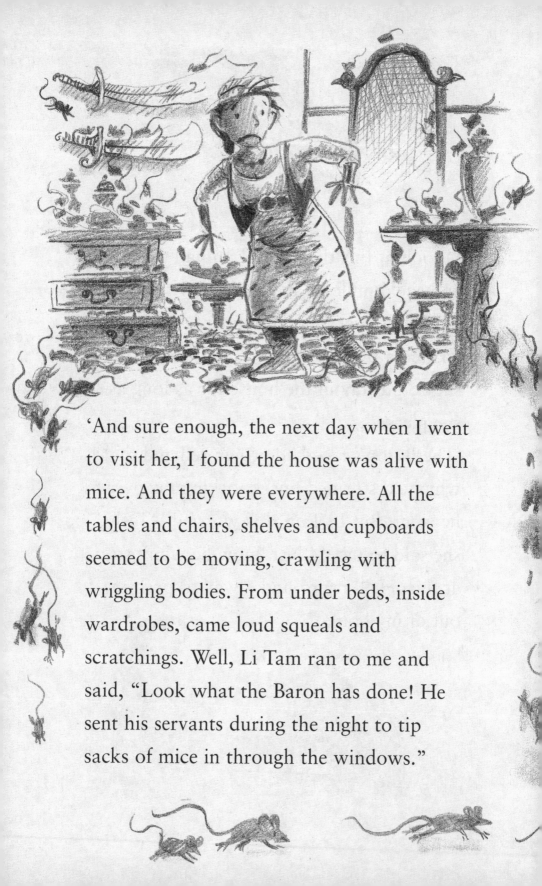

'And sure enough, the next day when I went
to visit her, I found the house was alive with
mice. And they were everywhere. All the
tables and chairs, shelves and cupboards
seemed to be moving, crawling with
wriggling bodies. From under beds, inside
wardrobes, came loud squeals and
scratchings. Well, Li Tam ran to me and
said, "Look what the Baron has done! He
sent his servants during the night to tip
sacks of mice in through the windows."

'"Don't worry, Auntie," I said, "I will fix it." I ran home for a bag of rice cakes. I crumbled them up and laid a trail of crumbs from Li Tam's house right up to the Baron's kitchen door. The mice scrambled after me, gobbling up the crumbs as they went. And soon it was the *Baron* who had a houseful of mice.

'He was furious—roaring like a bull with a bellyache!—and when he saw the villagers laughing at him behind their hands, he charged right into the square on market day and shouted to them, "Tomorrow is the day you pay your rent money. From now on, all your rent will be three times as much as before. Be sure to have the money ready!" The people were shocked. "What will we do?" they wailed. "We have nothing more to give!"

'When I ran to tell Li Tam she said, "Oh, Tashi, if only we had the money to buy our own houses, then we would never have to worry about the wicked Baron again."'
'Aha!' cried Mum and Dad and Jack together.

'Aha!' agreed Tashi. 'That's when I felt one of my clever ideas coming on. So that night, when the last light went out, I crept through the streets to the Baron's house and tapped on the kitchen window. Third Aunt, who was the Baron's cook, opened the door.

"'Auntie, please let me in,'" I whispered. I ran over to the table where I'd often sat on baking mornings and pulled away the rug that lay under it. There was a little door over a flight of steps leading down into darkness.

'"You can't go down there, Tashi," said Third Aunt. "That passage leads all the way to the Mountain of White Tigers, and no one has ever returned from there."

'"The Baron must have," I said, "so I expect I will manage it, too." Still, as I peered into the blackness below, I did feel just a little afraid.'

'I don't wonder,' shivered Dad. 'Sometimes I feel a little afraid just going to put the garbage out at night.'

'Well,' said Tashi, 'I stopped looking into the dark and I whispered, "Hand me your lamp, please, Auntie. I'll be back before the Baron comes down to his breakfast in the morning."

'The passage twisted and turned, winding like a rabbit's burrow deep into the earth. I held my lamp high, but I could only see a short way in front of me, and the blackness ahead looked like the end of the world.

'I must admit that once or twice I did think of going back. I had no idea how long I'd been walking, or how much time I had left.

'But at last I felt the ground slope upwards,
and I could feel my heart start thumping
hard as I climbed up the steep path—and
suddenly, at the top, I stopped. The path
was blocked. I held up my lamp and saw a
door, with a gold latch. I pulled at it and
whoosh!—the door swung open.

'I stepped out onto the Mountain of
White Tigers.

'My face tingled in the snowy air and I
looked nervously into the night. The lamp
showed me a path, but on each side of it
were tall black trees, and behind those trees
who knew *what* was waiting!

'But I couldn't bear to go back empty-handed. And just then, I heard a growl, deep as thunder. I peered into the dark, but I could see nothing, only hear a grinding of teeth, like stones scraping. The growling became roaring, and my ears were ringing with the noise, and then, right in front of me, a white shape came out from behind a tree, and then another and another. The tigers were coming!

'They came so close to me that I could see their whiskers, silver in the moonlight, and their great red eyes, glowing like fires. They were even fiercer than I had been told, and their teeth were even sharper in their dark wet mouths, but I was ready for them. Second Aunt had warned me that the one thing white tigers fear is fire.

'I took a big breath and swung my bright burning lamp round and around my head. I charged down the path roaring, "Aargh! Aargh!" till my lungs were bursting.

'The tigers stopped and stared at me. They must have thought I was a whirling demon, with circles of light streaking about their heads. They bared their teeth, growling like drums rolling. But I saw them flinch, their white coats shivering over their muscles, and slowly, one by one, they turned away, gliding back through the trees. Oh, I was so happy watching those white shapes disappearing! I ran on and there, looming up above me, was the mouth of the cave.

'The entrance was blocked by a huge stone boulder. I tried to squeeze through but the gap was too small.'

'Did you have to turn back then, Tashi?'
Jack held his breath.

'I thought for a moment I'd have to,' Tashi
nodded. 'But then I remembered that I'd
popped a piece of Ghost Pie into my pocket
before leaving home. I quickly nibbled a bit
and pushed at the boulder again. This time
my hand slid right through it and the rest of
me followed as easily as stepping through
shadows.

'I ran inside *whooping*! There were sacks
and sacks of shiny, golden coins! Puffing
and panting, I loaded them into a huge
knapsack I had with me, and hauled it onto
my back to carry.'

'I wish *I'd* been there to help you!' Jack said
wistfully.

'Me too,' said Tashi. 'That knapsack made
my knees buckle. And then, coming out of
the cave, I had to whirl my lamp round my
head and roar as well, just in case there
were still tigers lurking in the trees.'
'So how did you crawl back through the
tunnel with all that gold on your back?'
asked Mum.

'Well, it was like this,' said Tashi. 'I took the sack off my back and put it on the ground. Then I rolled it along with my feet. It was easier that way, but very slow. And of course I was getting very worried about the time.

'I crept back up the stairs and into the kitchen as it was growing light. Third Aunt was just putting a match to the kitchen fire, and she almost dropped the poker when she saw me.

'"What a clever Tashi," she cried, when she spied the gold.

'Well, I thanked her, but I wasn't finished yet, oh no! I crept to each house in the village and whispered a few words, passing a little sack of gold through the windows.

'Next morning all the people were in the square when the Wicked Baron arrived for his rent. Wise-As-An-Owl stepped forward. "Baron," he began, "our children who went away to other parts for work have done well and sent gold home to their families. Now we would like to buy our houses."

'And all the villagers stepped up and poured the gold onto the table before the Baron. What a sight it was! The mountain of coins glittered so brightly in the morning sun that I had to turn my eyes away! But The Baron stared. He couldn't *stop* looking! Still, he was hesitating. He liked getting money every month from his rents, but he couldn't resist the sight of all those shining, winking coins. "Very well," he agreed, and I could tell he was itching to gather up the coins and run his fingers through them. "I'll sign right now," and he took the papers that Wise-As-An-Owl had ready for him.

'That night there was a great feast with music and dancing to celebrate the new freedom of the village. My grandmother and Second Aunt were singing so loudly, that only I heard the faint bellow of rage coming from the Mountain of White Tigers.'

'Oh well,' said Dad, 'that wicked Baron got what he deserved, eh, Tashi? And I suppose all the village people were happy and contented from that day on.'

'Oh yes,' agreed Tashi, 'and so was I, until I came face to face with the Genie. But now we'd better go—if we don't run all the way we'll miss the ferry! Are you coming, Jack?' And the two boys raced out the door, as if the Genie itself were after them.

TASHI and the GENIE

Jack and Tashi ran up the wharf and
hurtled onto the ferry. They flung themselves
down on a seat outside, just as the boat
chugged off.

Tashi watched the white water foam behind
them. The sun was warm and gentle on
their faces. Jack closed his eyes.

'What a magical day!' they heard a woman say as she brushed past them. Jack's eyes snapped open.

'Talking of magic,' he said to Tashi, 'let's hear about the time you saw that genie. What did he look like? How did you meet him?'

'Well,' said Tashi, taking a breath of sea air,
'it was like this. One day, not long before I
came to this country, I was in the shed
looking for some nails. Grandmother called
me, saying she wanted a few eggs. I
gathered about four or five from under the
hens and then looked around for a dish to
put them in. I spied an old, cracked one on
a top shelf, covered with a dirty piece of
carpet. But there was something very
strange about this bowl.'
'Ooh,' squealed Jack.
'I know, I know
what was in it!'

'Yes,' nodded Tashi. 'When I lifted the
carpet I saw a bubbling grey mist inside;
soft rumbling snores were coming from it.
The snores turned to a splutter when I
poked it. A voice groaned, "Oh not again!
Not already!" And the mist swirled and
rose up in the air. Two big sleepy eyes
squinted down at me. "And only twenty-five
years and ten minutes since my last master
let me go!" it said. Well, I was *very* excited.'

'Who *wouldn't* be,' Jack agreed.

'"You're a genie!" I shouted.

189

'"What if I am?" said he.

'"Why aren't you in a bottle?" I asked. "Or a lamp, like normal genies?"

'The genie looked shifty. "Oh, my master went off in too much of a hurry to put me back in my lamp. So I just crept into this bowl, hoping for some peace and quiet."'

Tashi winked at Jack. 'I happened to know a lot about genies, because my grandmother was always telling me what to do if I met one. So I looked him in the eye and said, "Now that I've found you, don't you have to grant me three wishes?"

'The genie groaned. "Wishes, wishes! People don't realise they are usually better off leaving things the way they are." But he pulled himself up to his full height and straightened his turban. "What is your command, master?" he bowed.

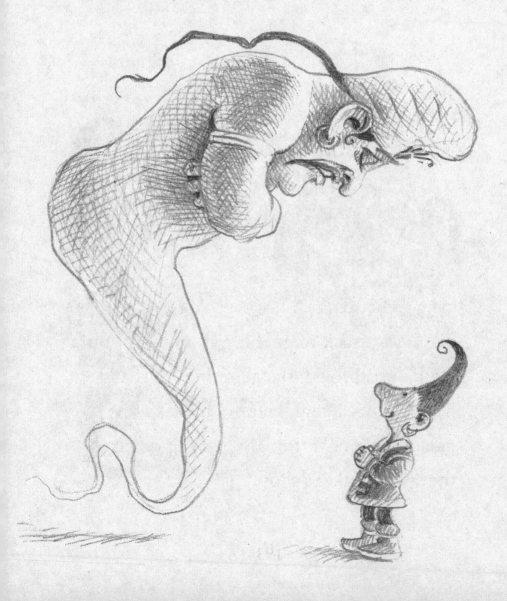

'I thought for a moment. "I would like an enormous sack of gold." Imagine, I could build a splendid palace, for all my family to live in.

'The genie snapped his fingers and— *TA RA*—a sack of gold lay at my feet! I ran my hands through the glittering coins and held one up. Hmm, before I build the palace, I thought, I might just run down to the sweet-maker's shop.'

'Good idea!' cried Jack. 'You could buy a *million* sweets, to last you till you're a hundred and ten!'

'Yes, but when Second Cousin at the shop took my coin, she looked at it carefully and rubbed it on her sleeve. The gold rubbed right off. "This coin is no good, Tashi," she told me. "It's only copper."

'I stamped back to the shed and angrily shook the genie out of his dish. "Those coins are only copper!" I shouted.

'The genie yawned. "Really? All of them? How tragic." He stretched. "Maybe a few at the bottom will be gold. What I need now is a glass of tea before I do any more work."'

'What a lousy, lazy genie!' exploded Jack.
'Yes,' agreed Tashi. 'And it gets worse. By
the time I'd brought his tea, I'd thought of
my second wish. "What about a flying
carpet?" I asked. Oh, if only I'd known.
The genie looked at me doubtfully. "Flying
carpets are not my best thing," he said. But
I was firm with him, so he snapped his
fingers, and there, floating at my knees, was
a glittering carpet. It was the most
magnificent thing I had ever seen. All
smooth and polished as skin, it was
patterned with hundreds of tiny peacocks,
with eyes glowing like jewels.

'The carpet trembled as I climbed on. The genie showed me how to tug at the corners to steer it. And then we were off, the carpet and I, out of the shed, over the house and across the village square. All the people were amazed, as they looked up and saw me waving at them.'

'I bet they were!' cried Jack. 'My dad would have fainted with shock. So, did you get to see Africa? Or Spain?'

'No,' Tashi frowned. 'It was like this. I had just turned in the direction of Africa, in fact, when the carpet suddenly dipped and bucked like a wild horse. My knees slipped right to the edge! I threw myself face down on the carpet, grabbing hold of the fringe.

'The carpet heaved up and down, and side to side, trying to throw me off. A hundred times it kicked me in the belly, but I clung on. The world was swirling around me like soup in a pot, and then I saw we were heading straight for the willow tree beside my house. I came crashing down through the branches. When I got my breath back, I marched off to find the genie.

'"Well, you certainly aren't very good at
your job, are you?" I scolded as I brushed
the leaves from my hair.'

'Is that all you could say?' yelled Jack. 'I
would have called him a fumble-bumble
beetle-brain at the very least.'

'Yes, but I still wanted my third wish,' Tashi sighed. 'Oh, if only I'd known. Well, the genie just yawned at me and said, "What is your third—and last—wish, master?"

'I thought carefully. One thing I had often longed for was to meet Uncle Tiki Pu, my father's Younger Brother. He had run away to the city while he was still a boy, but my father had told me stories of his pranks and jokes. "Yes, that's it!" I said. "I would like to meet my Uncle Tiki Pu."

'It was suddenly very quiet in the shed. The genie rose up and clicked his fingers. Nothing happened. "You will find him in your bedroom," said the genie, and slithered back into his bowl. I ran to my bedroom and there was my uncle, stretched out on my bed.

'"Ah, Tashi," he said, "it's about time someone came to find me. My life has been very hard in the city." Before I could say that I was sorry to hear it, and how pleased the family would be to have him back home again, Uncle Tiki Pu went on. "This bed is very hard, however."

'I looked around the room. "Where will *I* sleep, Uncle?"

'"Who knows?" he answered in a bored voice. "Get me something to eat, Tashi, a little roast duck and ginger will do. And tell your mother when she comes home that these clothes need washing."

'He pointed to a pile of his clothes beside my toy box. The lid was open and inside my box were jars of hair oil and tins of tobacco instead of my train set and kite and rock collection.

'"Where are my things?" I cried.

'"Oh, I threw them out the window," he told me. "How else could I make room for my belongings?"

'I ran outside and gathered up my toys. Two wheels had fallen off my little red train. "What about *my* belongings?" I called through the window.

'"Don't worry about them," replied Uncle
Tiki Pu. "You won't be living here much
longer. This house is too small for all of us
now that I've come back. You can have my
old job in the city, Tashi. But mind you take
a rug to sleep on because they don't give
you any bedding there, and the stony
ground is crawling with giant spiders that
bite. See, I've got the wounds to prove it."

'And he lifted his holey old singlet to show big red lumps all over his tummy, like cherry tomatoes.

'"Do they give you food in the city?" I could hardly bear to ask.

'"No, there's never enough, so you have to hunt for it. That's where the spiders come in handy. If you squish them first, they're not bad in a fritter. Oh, and watch out for alligators—they swim in the drains. Well, goodbye and good luck! You'll need it, ha ha!" And he laughed a wicked laugh.'

Tashi stopped for a moment, because he couldn't help shivering at the terrible memory of his uncle, and also because Jack was jumping up and down on his seat in outrage. The woman who had said 'What a magical day!' was staring.

'I know,' said Tashi. 'I know, I couldn't believe it either, that a member of my family could be so evil. My head was pounding, and I ran straight to see the genie.'
'How could *he* help, that old *beetle*-brain?'

'Well,' said Tashi. 'It was like this. I picked
up his bowl and tried to wake the genie
again. I shook him and begged him to get
rid of Uncle Tiki Pu, but he just closed his
eyes tightly and said, "Go away, Tashi.
You've had your three wishes and that's
that." Suddenly I put the bowl
down and smiled. I had just
had a cunning idea. I
remembered another thing
Grandmother always
told me about genies.

'I hurried back to my room and said to Uncle Tiki Pu, "You are quite right. This house is very small and poky. How would you like to live in a palace instead?"

'Uncle Tiki Pu sat up with a bounce. "Just what I've always wanted!" he cried. "How did you *know*?"

'"Come with me," I told him, "and I will show you how to do it."

'I opened the door of the shed and led him to the genie's bowl. Uncle let out a howl of joy when he saw what was curled up inside, but when the genie rose into the air, his eyes weren't sleepy any more. They were bright and sly.

'"I am your new master, so listen carefully, Genie," Uncle Tiki Pu began. "For my first wish—"

'The genie interrupted him. "There will be no wishes for you, my friend. You really should have been more careful. Don't you know that every seventh time a genie is disturbed, *he* becomes the master, and the one who wakes him must be the slave?" He glided over and arranged himself on Uncle Tiki Pu's shoulders. "Take me to the city," he commanded, "and be quick about it."

'Uncle Tiki Pu's face was bulging with rage
and his knees sagged, but he staggered out
of the shed with his load. As he sailed past,
the genie turned and gave me a big wink.
'"Look out for alligators!" I called.'

Jack was quiet for a moment, thinking. He watched people stand up and stretch as the ferry slowed, nearing the city.

'I hope nothing with teeth lives in *our* drains,' he said. 'Well, Tashi, that's amazing! Did you really fly on a magic carpet?'

For an answer, Tashi opened the top buttons of his jacket, showing Jack the gold coin hanging on a cord around his neck. 'How else would I have this?' he said.

And the two boys stepped off the ferry and strolled over to the ice-cream stand at the end of the wharf.

TASHI and the STOLEN CHILDREN

Jack burst into the kitchen. 'Tashi's back!' he cried.

'Oh, good,' said Dad. 'Has he been away?'

'Yes, I *told* you,' said Jack, 'don't you remember? He went back to the old country to see his grandmother for the New Year holiday. And while he was there, something terrible happened.'

'His grandmother ran away with the circus?' suggested Dad.

'No,' said Jack. 'She can't juggle. But listen, you know the war lord who came looking for Tashi last year?'

'Yes, I do remember him,' said Dad. 'He was the only war lord in Wilson Street last summer, so I won't forget him in a hurry.'

'Yes, and guess what,' Jack began, but Mum interrupted him.

'Come and have some afternoon tea, while you tell us,' she said, and brought a tray into the living room.

'Well,' said Jack, when they were settled comfortably. 'It was like this. When Tashi arrived back in his village, it was all quiet. *Strangely* quiet. None of his old friends

were playing in the square, and he could
hear someone crying. His grandfather told
him that the war lord had just made a raid
through the village. He'd captured nearly all
the young men for his army—and he had
kidnapped six children as well!'

'What did he take the *children* for?'
asked Mum.

'So that the men would fight bravely and
not run away home,' Jack told her. 'If they
didn't fight, he was going to punish
the children.'

'He deserves to be fried in a fritter, that war
lord!' exploded Dad.

'Yes,' agreed Jack. 'Well, just then the Wan twins came running back into the village square.

'They had hidden while the soldiers seized the young men. Then they'd followed the war party to see where their uncles were being taken.

'The twins said that the children had been put in the dungeon of the war lord's palace. The twins searched and climbed and tapped and dug, but they could find no way in. They said the children were lost forever.

'Everybody in the square listened to the
Wan twins' story, and a dreadful moaning
began. The sound of sadness rose and
swelled like a wave. Parents and aunties and
cousins hung onto each other as if they were
drowning. Then, one by one, people turned
to Tashi. He had once worked for the war
lord in that very palace.'

'Uh oh,' Dad shook his head. 'I bet he was wishing that he had gone on holidays another time.'

'Not Tashi,' said Jack. 'He slipped away to think, and when he returned he went to his grandfather's box of firecrackers and filled his pockets. Then he set off for the palace of the war lord. By evening, he reached the field where the soldiers were camped.

'He crept past the guards and found the uncles. They were miserable, sitting silent and cold, far from the cooking fires. Tashi whispered to them that they must get ready to leave at any moment, as he was on his way to the dungeon. One man clung to him, crying, "My little sister is only five years old, Tashi. She will be so frightened. You must find the children." Tashi promised to be back by morning.

'Then he went on alone. He remembered a
secret passage into the palace that he'd
discovered when he was living there before.
You entered in a cave nearby and came out
through a wardrobe in the war lord's very
own bedroom.'

'Ugh,' shuddered Mum. 'I'd rather be
anywhere in the world than *there*.'
'I know,' shivered Dad. 'A man like that,
you can imagine how his socks smell.'

'Well, anyway,' Jack went on, 'Tashi found
the cave and pulled aside the bushes
covering the entrance. He ran through the
damp tunnel and held his breath as he
pushed at the wardrobe door. It creaked.
What if the war lord had just come upstairs
to get a sharper sword?'

'Or change his socks?' put in Dad.

'Tashi held his breath. He peeped around
the door. The room was empty. He tiptoed
out into the hall and down the stairs. At the
last step he stopped. He felt the firecrackers
in his pockets, and quivered. A daring plan
had popped into his head. But, he
wondered, was he brave enough to do it?

'Instead of going further down the stairs into the dungeon, he found his way along to the kitchens. The cooks were busy preparing a grand dinner for the war lord and didn't notice Tashi as he crawled behind the oil jars and around the rice bins.'

'What was he doing?' asked Mum.
'Having a little snack, of course,' said Dad, taking a bite of Jack's scone.

'You'll find out if you pay attention,' said
Jack, and he moved his scone to the other
hand. 'When Tashi left the kitchen he could
hear the cries of the children, and the sound
of their sobbing led him down to the
dungeon. Two guards were talking outside
the dark, barred room where the children
were held. Tashi hopped into an empty barrel
close by and called out in a great loud
voice, *"The war lord is a beetle-brain!"'*

'NO!' cried Mum and Dad together.
'YES!' crowed Jack. 'The guards jumped as
if they'd just sat on a nest of soldier ants.
"One of those pesky children has managed to
get out!" the fat guard hissed. "Then we'd
better catch him," said the other, "before
the war lord boils us in spider sauce."

'As soon as they ran off, Tashi turned the
big key they had left in the lock and opened
the dungeon door.

'The children recognised Tashi and crowded around, telling him all that had happened. "Shush," whispered Tashi, "wait till we get outside. The danger isn't over yet."

'He led them quickly up the stairs and through the long hallways until at last they came to the great wooden front door of the palace. Tashi reached up and pulled on the big brass latch. The door swung open and the children whooped with joy. They streamed out, falling over each other in their hurry. Tashi picked up the littlest one and set him on his feet. "Home we go!" he cried.

'But no. Just then a huge hand reached
down and plucked Tashi up by the collar.
He was face to face with the furious war
lord. Their noses almost touched. The
war lord's skin was rough, like sandpaper.

"*RUN!*" Tashi called to the children. "Run
to your uncles down by the camp!"

'The war lord shook Tashi, as if he were a
scrap of dirty washing. His iron knuckles
bit into Tashi's neck. He breathed fish and
grease into Tashi's face. "So, you foolish
boy," he growled. "You have come back.
You won't escape again. Look well at the
daylight outside, for this is the last time
you'll see it. You'll work in the dungeons
from now on."

'Tashi thought of the mean black bars on the window of the dungeon. Only a cockroach could stay alive in there. His eyes began to water and he started to sniff.

'"Scared, are you?" the war lord jeered.
'"No, I can smell something," said Tashi, "can't you?"'
'Socks!' cried Dad.

'The war lord sniffed. The air *did* seem
rather smoky. Suddenly there was a loud
explosion and they heard feet pounding
over the stone floor. "Fire!" shouted the
war lord, and he dropped Tashi and ran
off towards the noise, calling for the
guards to follow him.

'Tashi sped down the steps and soon found the children and their uncles. They were waiting for him over the hill, beyond the camp. From there they had a good view of the palace.

'It was blazing fiercely—the windows were red with the glow of fire inside, and a great grey cloud of smoke climbed above it.

'"Weren't we lucky the fire started just then!" said the littlest boy. His brother laughed and looked at Tashi. "I don't think luck had anything to do with it," he said.

'"Well," said Tashi modestly, "as a matter of fact I did empty the gunpowder out of my firecrackers and laid a trail up to the kitchen stove. I hoped we would manage to get out before it reached the ovens. It blew up just in time."

'"What a clever Tashi!" the children yelled, and the uncles hoisted him up onto their shoulders and they sang and danced all the way home.

'Phew!' said Dad. 'That was a close shave. I suppose Tashi could relax after that, and enjoy the rest of his holiday. Did he have good weather?'

'Yes, at first,' said Jack, 'until the witch,
Baba Yaga, blew in on the winds of a
dreadful storm.'
'Baba Yaga?' said Dad nervously. 'Who is she?'
'Oh, just a witch whose favourite meal is
baked children. But Tashi will tell us all about
that. What's for dinner tonight, Mum?'

TASHI and the BABA YAGA

Jᴀᴄᴋ's ᴅᴀᴅ sᴀᴛ up in bed reading the newspaper. He had a cold, and his tissue box was nearly empty. '"Beach Houses For Sale",' Dad read aloud. 'How would you like to move to a house near the beach, Jack?' He blew his nose. 'Just imagine—an early morning swim, watching the sun rise over the sea. Look at this one—a nice little wooden house, with plenty of personality.'

'Looks as big as a beehive to me,' said Jack. 'Anyway, I like it *here*—near all my friends. Besides,' Jack narrowed his eyes and tapped the side of his nose slyly, 'you've got to be careful about exploring new houses. You never know what you may find inside.'

Dad put down his paper. 'Really?' He smoothed a place on the bed for Jack to come and sit down. He rubbed his hands together. Yes, he could definitely feel a story coming on—one of Jack's Tashi stories, no doubt. Since young Tashi had moved into the neighbourhood, and become best friends with Jack, they'd heard some amazing adventures.

'I suppose your friend Tashi knows all
about new houses?' said Dad.
'Yes, when he was back in the old country, a
new house did arrive in his village one day.'
'Arrive?' repeated Dad, puzzled. 'How
could a house *arrive*? No, wait a second.
MUM,' called Dad, 'MU-UM, come and
listen to a story!' He grinned at Jack. 'She'd
be so cross if she missed out.'
Mum came panting into the room, her arms
full of dirty washing. She plonked it on the
floor and curled up next to Dad.
'Wacko!' she cried. She glanced scornfully at
the washing. 'That can wait. So, what's it all
about?'

'Well, it was like this,' Jack began, and he shivered as he remembered Tashi's words of last night. 'Baba Yaga blew in to Tashi's village on the winds of a terrible storm.'

'Baba Yaga? Who is that?' coughed Dad. 'Someone looking for a new house?'

'Pay attention and you'll find out,' said Jack.

'And don't breathe on me,' said Mum.

'Well, one night, when Tashi was quite small, stinging rains lashed the village and wild winds blew washing off the lines and chickens out of their nests. Branches were torn from the trees and whole houses were whisked miles away.

'The next morning, when Tashi walked along the road, he saw people scurrying about trying to find lost belongings that had been scattered far and wide. He offered to help and, going further and further from the village, he found cooking pots and slippers high up in the trees.

'Because he was looking up, he almost stepped on a raven that was pinned under a fallen branch. Tashi gently lifted the bird from the leaves and twigs and placed it on a grassy mound. The bird was very weak and thirsty so Tashi gave it a drink of water from his bottle.

'"Thank you," said the raven. "You have been my friend. Maybe one day *I* will be able to help *you*."'

'Ho *ho*,' crowed Dad, and blew his nose like a trumpet.

'Well,' Jack went on, 'as Tashi walked on through the forest, he came upon a house in a clearing where there had been no house before. And what an extraordinary house it was! It stood on scaly yellow chicken legs, and the claws dug deep into the earth. Above, a thread of crooked smoke rose out of a crooked chimney.'

'Hmm!' Dad wrinkled his nose. 'Just like
the newspaper said—a nice little wooden
house with plenty of personality!'
'Ugh! Did Tashi dare to peep inside?' asked
Mum.

'Well,' said Jack, 'it was like this. He put down all his bundles and crept closer. He wanted to see more, but was a bit afraid. And then, suddenly, the door opened and an old woman stepped outside.

'"Aha, our first visitor has arrived, Alenka," she crowed to a young girl who came to the window. "Won't you come in and tell us all about yourself while you have a glass of tea?"

'Tashi hesitated for a moment, but he was
so eager to explore this weird house that he
thanked her and followed her inside.

'There was an enormous stove in one
corner of the room and nearby, on a stool,
lay a half-plucked goose. Sticky feathers and
smears of blood covered the young girl's
hands.

'As he sipped his tea, Tashi asked the old woman how it was that her house had appeared so suddenly in the forest. The old woman leaned towards Tashi and looked into his face. "My name is Baba Yaga," she rasped, "and I come from a land far, far away. The storm blew me right over the mountains, into this forest. But I don't think I'll stay here. It seems a dismal sort of place to me, not many children about." Her voice scraped like sandpaper on wood. Her black eyes pierced Tashi's own. Then she reached over and pinched his arm. "You look a nice juicy boy however, and if there's one thing I do enjoy, it's Boy-Baked-In-A-Pie."

'Tashi could hardly believe his ears; did she really mean it, or was she just teasing?'

'Probably just teasing,' Dad said heartily. Then he looked at Jack's face and gulped. 'Wasn't she?'

'Go on, Jack,' said Mum. 'What happened next?'

'Well,' said Jack, 'it was like this. Tashi was staring at her, half-smiling and hoping she was joking, when suddenly she smiled back. He gasped in horror. Her teeth were made of iron!

'He looked around wildly and saw, through the window, that the sun had vanished behind the clouds. The fence posts glowed white against the dark sky. Tashi peered closer. His heart thumped and he bit his lip, hard. On top of each post sat a small skull—a child's-size skull—with a candle lit inside it. "Wah!" he screamed.

'Baba Yaga leapt up. "Take the boy," she roared at her daughter, "and get him ready for baking. We'll have a fine meal tonight!" And she hobbled out into the forest to gather some herbs and mushrooms.

'Alenka dragged Tashi over to the oven. Her strong fingers bit down through his jacket like claws. With one hand she built up the fire, then dropped Tashi onto the oven spade, as if he were nothing but a loaf of bread.

'Quick, he thought, what can I do? He gazed longingly through the open door, and spied an old apple tree. *Aha!* His heart leapt with hope.

'"Don't you use apples and spice when you roast m-meat?" he asked. "Everyone in my village says that it makes a dish much tastier."

'"Does it now?" said Alenka. "I'll try it then."

'And she strode out of the room and down
the steps to gather some apples in her
apron, bolting the door behind her.

'Quick as lightning, Tashi pulled off his jacket and trousers and shoes and put them on the goose that was left lying on the stool in the corner. He stood back for a second to look. Wasn't something missing? Of course: the goose-boy needed some hair.

'*Hurry hurry*, yes, that would do. He snatched up a black sock that Alenka had been knitting and unravelled some wool. When he had arranged it with the curl over the goose's "face", it looked so real that Tashi felt a bit sick. He just had time to hide in the cupboard before Alenka came back.

'"That was a good idea of yours, Tashi," she said as she stuck some cloves in the apples. She pushed one apple up each leg and arm of the goose-boy's trousers and jacket, and then slid the oven spade right into the red heart of the oven.

'Inside his cupboard, Tashi trembled. He heard the oven door slam, and soon the smell of cooking crept in through the cracks of the wooden cupboard.

'When Baba Yaga came back, she scolded Alenka for not waiting for the mushrooms. '"Great greedy gizzards, why don't you do as I tell you? Boy-Baked-In-A-Pie needs mushrooms, and *you* need your brains boiled!"

'But the old woman stopped finding fault
when she sniffed the delicious smells coming
from the oven.

'"Apples and cloves," Alenka announced
proudly. "Tashi told me how to do it."

'They sat down at the table and began to
eat. Baba Yaga chewed on a small piece of
leg, and smacked her lips. "This dinner is
quite tasty," she said grudgingly. She paused
a moment.'

'For a burp, I bet,' said Dad. 'A woman like
that would have no manners.'

'Tashi didn't mention any burping,' replied
Jack. 'Anyway, *then* the old woman began
to look suspiciously at the meat. She poked
it with her fork. "This looks like goose."
She paused again. "It smells like goose.
It *is* goose!"

'The old woman stood up and pointed her craggy finger at Alenka. "You stupid, snail-witted lump! Can't you do anything right? Now where did that Tashi get to? You stay here and search the house while I see if he ran to the village."

'Alenka got down on her hands and knees and looked under the bed. She looked behind the screen and then she turned towards the cupboard. Through the crack in the door, Tashi could see her moving towards him. He began to shake. In the tight, dark space of the cupboard he could hardly breathe.

'But then he saw something else. There, across the room, sitting on the windowsill was his friend, the raven.

'"Are you looking for something?" the bird called.

'"Yes," said Alenka. "A juicy boy that was supposed to have been our dinner."

'"Ah," nodded the raven. "I saw such a boy hiding in the garden just now."

'"Good!" Alenka shouted, and she ran

'Quickly Tashi slipped out of the cupboard. He whispered, "Thank you!" to the raven as he clambered out the window. Then he ran through the forest, with the trees moaning in the wind and the storm clouds racing across the sky and a rusty old voice calling on the air like a crow at dusk.

'The next morning Tashi's mother was very cross that he had lost all his clothes. When Tashi told her that Baba Yaga had cooked them, thinking he was inside them, she didn't quite believe him.

'"Come, I'll show you," said Tashi, and he led her into the forest. The strange house was still there, standing on its bony old chicken feet. And the crooked smoke was still drifting out of the crooked chimney.

'Tashi's mother shivered, and drew him close to her. "What did I tell you?" said Tashi.

'But just then, while they were both still staring, the house rose up high on its legs and scurried out of the forest, flying over the mountains and away, never to be seen in Tashi's village again.'

Jack's parents were silent for a moment, thinking. Then Dad sneezed.

'Ugh!' he shivered. 'I hope that house doesn't blow anywhere near *here*. No one would want a place like that, even if they were selling it for chicken feed.'

Jack leapt off the bed with a grin. 'Funny you should mention *chickens*, Dad, because they were the cause of Tashi's next problem.'

'Well, the worst thing about chickens is chicken poo,' said Dad. 'That might be a smelly problem, but how could it be *dangerous*?'

'You'll see this afternoon,' Jack called over
his shoulder as he ran out of the room.
'Tashi's coming over and he'll tell you
himself!'
'Is it the afternoon yet?' asked Dad, who
didn't know what time it was since he'd
been in bed.
'No, not for hours,' Jack called back.
Dad groaned, and flopped back on the
pillow.

GONE!

At four o'clock Jack met Tashi at the
garden gate.

'Sorry I'm late,' panted Tashi, 'but three of
our chickens escaped through a hole in the
fence and we had to chase them to the creek
and back. Pesky things!'

Tashi wiped his feet on the mat. Jack looked
down curiously at Tashi's boots, and sniffed.

'Perhaps I'd better leave them outside,' said
Tashi.

'Perhaps,' agreed Jack.

'So,' said Jack, when they were sitting comfortably, 'did you get all three chickens back?'

'Oh yes,' said Tashi, 'but I remember a time when it wasn't so easy. Once, every hen in our village disappeared. Nothing was left behind—not even a feather floating in the air.'

'How dreadful,' said Mum, coming into the room. 'What did you do for eggs?'

'Well,' said Tashi, stretching out his legs, 'it was like this.'

'Wait,' cried Jack. 'Dad's still asleep. Fair's fair.' He scrambled upstairs, flung open his father's door, and shouted 'BABA YAGA!' Dad screamed and shot out of bed as if the witch was swooping through the window right behind him.

He was still breathing heavily when he was settled on the sofa with a rug over his knees. He stared at Tashi. 'I don't know how you could even look at chickens again after Baba Yaga,' he said, and sneezed.

'Hmm,' Tashi nodded, 'but a man has to eat. When all the hens disappeared, no one in the village had a clue where they could be. People were grizzling because they had to start work without their omelettes. They invented excuses to poke about in each other's houses, but they found nothing.

'One day my mother threw down her spoon
and said she was tired of trying to cook
without eggs. She sent me over to Third
Aunt, who worked as a cook for the wicked
Baron. Since he was the richest man in the
village, she thought that perhaps he might
have a few eggs left.'

'Oh I remember *him*!' cried Dad. 'He was that rascal who kept all his money on a mountain—'

'Guarded by a pack of white tigers,' shuddered Mum.

'Yes,' agreed Tashi. 'He had the heart of a robber, and the smile of a snake, and I didn't like going near him. But what else could I do? I set off at once and on the way I met Cousin Wu. He had just returned from a trip to the city, and he couldn't stop talking about the wonders he'd seen there. "The best thing of all," he said, "was the Flying Fireball Circus. You should have seen it, Tashi—the jugglers and the acrobats on the high trapeze—I couldn't believe my eyes."

'"You are lucky, Wu," I sighed. "I don't suppose we will ever see a circus here. The village would never have enough money to pay for one to visit."

'We walked along in silence for a while, and then I asked Cousin Wu if he wanted to come with me to the Baron's house. Suddenly he seemed to be in a great hurry to visit his sister, so we said goodbye and I went on my way.

'Unfortunately, just as I was opening the
gate to the Baron's house, the wicked man
himself leant out the window and saw me.
"Be off with you, you little worm," he
shouted. "I don't want to see you hanging
about my house!"'

'Worm—*he's* the worm,' said Dad crossly.
'Someone ought to squish him!'

'Well,' Tashi went on, 'I pretended to run
off home, but as soon as the Baron closed
his shutters, I ducked back into the kitchen
where Third Aunt had made some delicious
sticky sweet rice cakes, my favourite. When
I had wolfed down five or six, I remembered
the eggs.

'"Of course you can have some," said Third Aunt. "We have plenty. More than we know what to do with, in fact."

'"Have you?" I said. "That's very interesting." And I followed her outside to an enormous shed and waited while she unlocked the door. And do you know what? I found hundreds of hens—and some of them were my old friends! I recognised Gong Gong's Pullet and Second Cousin's big Peking Red.

'"Don't wait for me," I told Third Aunt.
"I'll fill this bowl and be out in a minute."
When she left, I walked amongst the birds
and made sure that all the village hens were
there in the Baron's chicken house. Then I
sniffed the smell of cigars. Strange, I
thought. Cigar smoke in a chicken house? I
sniffed again and the skin on my neck
tingled. Slowly I turned around. And there,
in the doorway blocking the light, stood the
wicked Baron.

'He marched inside and closed the door behind him. "So, little worms wriggle into peculiar places," he said with a nasty sneer. "But can they wriggle out again, I wonder?"

'"You have stolen all our chickens!" I cried. "Why? Whatever are you going to do with them?"

'"That is none of your business...but then, maybe I'll tell you since you won't be here long enough to do anything about it." And he grinned, showing all his glinting gold teeth. "I am going to sell half of them to the River Pirate, who'll be sailing past this house at midnight. Then tomorrow, I'll be able to charge whatever I like for my eggs because no one else will have any to sell. I'll make a fortune! Golden eggs, they'll be! What do you think of that, little worm?"

'I stared at him. It was hard to believe anyone could be so mean.'

'I know,' agreed Dad, nodding his head. 'The newspapers are full of crooks getting away with it. Makes your blood boil.'

'Well, I was determined *he* wouldn't get away with it. I edged toward the door. "You can't keep me here," I told him, thinking I could make a dash for it.

'The Baron laughed fiercely. It sounded like a growl. "Oh no, little fish bait, I have plans for you. I will lock you up in the storeroom until midnight, when the River Pirate will take *you* as well as the hens. A pirate's prisoner, that's what you'll be!" And he grabbed me and threw me over his shoulder like a bit of old rope, and dropped me into the cold, dark storeroom.

'At first, there was just darkness, and silence. But as my eyes grew used to the gloom, I saw the walls were thick stone, and a square of grey light shone in through one small high window. I felt all round the heavy iron door, but it was padlocked, as tight as a treasure chest. I bent down to study the floor, to see if there were any trapdoors, or loose stones. And it was then that I saw it. Lying in the corner, curled up like a wisp of smoke, was a white tiger.'

'The Baron's tiger!' screamed Jack. 'What did you do?'

'Well, it was like this. I just stayed where I was and made no sound. I could see that its eyes were closed. Its legs twitched now and then, as if it were chasing something in a dream. It was asleep, but for how long? I put my head in my hands. There was no way out. I felt like a fly in a web. Only *my* web was made of solid stone.

'If only I had my magic ghost cakes, I thought. I could walk through that wall, as easily as walking through air. I searched in my empty pockets. Wait! There was a small crumb. But would it be enough to get me all the way through those thick walls? Should I take the chance?'

'Yes, yes!' cried Jack.

Tashi nodded. 'I put the crumb on my tongue and as I swallowed I began to push through the stone. My right foot first—it was gliding through!—and then I stopped. The rest of my leg was stuck fast, deep inside the stone.

'I moaned aloud. Over my shoulder I saw the tiger stir. I saw one eye open. Then the other. I'd forgotten the colour of those eyes: red, like coals of fire. The tiger growled deep in its throat. It made me think of the Baron, and how he would laugh to see me trapped like this. Slowly, lazily, the tiger uncurled itself.

'I scrabbled through my top pockets. Nothing. I was frantic. The tiger was padding towards me. It leaned back on its haunches, ready to spring. It was hard to look away from its snarling mouth, but yes, there in the very last pocket of all, I felt something soft and squashy. Another cake crumb!

'I swallowed the crumb as the tiger sprang. Its jaws opened and a spiky whisker swiped my hand, but I was away, slipping through the stone as easily as a fish noodle slips down your throat.

'Outside it was cool and breezy, and I stretched my arms out wide and did a little dance of freedom. Then I saw Cousin Wu, coming back from his sister's. I ran to him and told him, in a great rush, what the Baron had done.

'"That thieving devil!" cried Cousin Wu. "I'd like to drop him down a great black hole, down to the burning centre of the earth! But first, let's go and tell the village."
'"You go," I said, "but just say to everyone that you've discovered who stole the hens—nothing more. There is something I have to do here first."'

'What?' cried Dad, hanging on to his blanket.

Tashi smiled. 'I had other plans for the Baron. You see, it was almost midnight. I hurried down to the Baron's jetty, to wait for the River Pirate. The moon was up, and soon I heard the soft *shush shush* of the motor. The boat came around the bend, riding the moon's path of silver. The Pirate tied up at the jetty, and stepped out.

'He was tall and looked as strong as ten
lions. I didn't fancy being taken as his
prisoner, but still I went to meet him. "I
have some news from the Baron," I began.
"He has changed his mind about selling
you the hens."

'The River Pirate frowned. It was a terrible

frown, and I noticed him stroke the handle
of his sword. Quickly I added, "But I have
something for you." I drew out of my
pocket a small bag of "gold" that a tricky
genie had given me some time ago. "The
Baron said that this is for your trouble."
'Well, the River Pirate stopped frowning,
and clapped me on the back.

'In the distance I could see a large crowd of people marching from the village. They were waving flaming torches high above their heads, shouting fiercely. And there was the Baron coming out of his house, on his way down to meet the River Pirate. He hurried over to see what all the smoke and noise was about, and when he saw me, he gasped with surprise.

'I walked up to him and said sternly, "Here come the villagers. Can you see how angry they are? How furious? You have two choices. Either I will tell them how you stole their hens—and who knows what they will do to you, with their flaming torches and fiery tempers." The Baron turned pale in the moonlight.

'"Or?" he asked. "What about the *or*?"

'"Or," I said slowly, stretching out the word like a rubbery noodle, "I can tell them you discovered that the River Pirate had stolen their hens, and, as an act of kindness, you bought the hens back for them."

'The Baron gave a great growl of relief.

"That's the one I like, Tashi, my boy!"

'But I hadn't finished. "And you will invite them all to see the wonderful Flying Fireball Circus, which you will bring here to the village next week."

'"The circus? Are you mad? You sneaky little worm, that would cost me a fortune!" roared the Baron.

'"Yes," I agreed. "Don't those flames look splendid against the black sky?"

'And when the Baron turned to see, the villagers were almost upon us. "WHERE IS THE THIEF! WHERE IS THE THIEF!" they chanted.'

'And did the villagers set upon him with
their fiery tempers?' Dad asked eagerly.

'No,' Tashi smiled. 'We all went to see the
acrobats and the jugglers and the daredevil
horsemen at the circus, and we had the best
night of our lives.'

'So,' Dad sighed, 'I suppose everyone had eggs for breakfast from then on and talked about the circus over tea, and Cousin Wu saw a lot of his sister.'

'Yes,' agreed Tashi, 'life was quite peaceful—for a while. Hey, Jack,' Tashi turned to his friend, 'let's go out into the garden and play Baba Yaga.'

'Okay,' said Jack. 'I'll be the witch and you can be the dinner,' and they raced outside to the peppercorn tree.

Dad went back to bed.

TASHI and the DEMONS

One fresh sunny morning, Jack and his
Mum were in the garden, watching Dad
plant a new gardenia bush.

'It's too *early* to be up on Sunday
morning,' Mum yawned.

But Dad couldn't wait to get his new
bush in the ground. 'Mmm,' he said,
putting his nose deep into a flower. 'That
perfume is fantastic!' He stood up, leaning
against his shovel, closing his eyes.

Jack saw an army of bull ants swarm over Dad's gumboots. Must be standing on a nest, he thought. Dad began to hop all over the pansy bed. He hit his shin with the shovel.

'Blasted things've got into my socks!'
he cried.

'Come over here,' said Mum. 'Rest a bit,
it's Sunday!'

Dad peeled off a sock while Mum lay
back in a warm patch of sun. She bunched
her dressing gown under her head.

'Ah, that's better,' she said. 'All we need
now is a story.'

'That gardenia should do well,' said
Dad, rubbing his foot. 'After all the rain
we've had, the soil is nice and moist.'

'Speaking of rain...' said Jack, settling
himself between them.

'A Tashi story, I bet!' cried Mum, sitting
up. 'What is it—floods, gushing rivers,
monster waves?'

Jack chewed a piece of grass. 'Well,
once, in Tashi's old village, it didn't rain for
months.'

'No good for *his* gardenias, eh?' said Dad.

'No,' replied Jack. 'It was no good for anything. It hadn't rained for so long that little children could hardly remember the sound of it, or the smell of wet earth. There was almost no rice left in the village, and the last of the chickens and pigs had been eaten ages ago. Every day Tashi's mother sent him a bit further to look for wild spinach or turnips or anything to add to the thin evening stew.'

'Erk!' Dad wrinkled his nose. 'Stew pew!'

'Ssh!' said Mum. 'And leave your foot alone. You'll just make it worse.'

'One day,' Jack went on, 'Tashi had been walking for hours when suddenly he came upon a gooseberry bush, covered with fat fruit. He happily filled his basket and was just cramming the last few berries into his mouth when he heard a cry. There, around the other side of the bush, was a girl.'

'Berry bushes have terrible thorns,' said Dad. 'I expect she'd scratched her hands.'

'I don't think so,' said Jack. 'Tashi just said she was very pretty—sort of shiny and special, like the first evening star.'

'Oh,' said Dad. 'Gosh.'

'Go on,' said Mum breathlessly.

'Well,' Jack continued, 'Tashi saw why the girl was sobbing. Her legs and arms were tied up with ropes. "Who did this? Who are you?" he asked.

'"Oh, please help me," the girl wept. "I am Princess Sarashina, and I'm the prisoner of two horrible demons. They frightened away my guards and dragged me from my travelling coach. They tied me up here two days ago and I've had nothing to eat or drink since then."

'Tashi began undoing the cords around her wrists. He noticed she was looking hungrily into his basket. But when he reluctantly offered her some berries, she said, "Oh no, not now, they might come back any minute. Where can we hide?"

'Tashi thought quickly…behind that
Dragon's Blood Tree? No, it was no use
hiding, he decided. He and the princess
would have to come out some time, and
then what?

'"You go back to my village," he said
finally, "and I'll come later, when I find
some vegetables. I'm very poor and no use
to demons. They won't hurt me."

'"You never know with demons."
Princess Sarashina shook her head. "My
Uncle Lee says demons are like muddy
water. You can never see to the heart of
them and they vanish through your fingers
leaving dirt on your hands. Besides, I don't
know the way to your village."

'"It's easy," said Tashi. "Just follow the
path between those tall trees, go past the
cemetery on your right and then the temple
on your left, over the bridge and there's the
village. Ask for Tashi's house and tell my
parents that I'll be along in a little while.
As for the demons—"

'"Have you ever met one?"

'"I've seen a few in my time," said Tashi. "But never up close."

'"I hope you never do." The Princess shivered. "Their eyes are red as blood, like two whirlpools trying to suck you in. Good luck, Tashi!" And she ran off towards the trees.

'Tashi wandered through the forest, looking out for wild herbs and demons. He found some sorrel and roots and when his hands were full he decided to make his way home. He passed the gooseberry bush and was just checking to see that he hadn't left any berries—he hadn't—when suddenly he was seized by two strong arms and thrown like a ball into the air.

'He looked down into a hideous face.
The eyes were red, just as Sarashina had
said, and inside their scarlet lids the
eyeballs were swirling like flaming mud.
Tashi felt himself being drawn into them,
like a stone into quicksand. With a huge
effort he looked away, staring instead at
teeth hooking over great fleshy lips.

'"Where is Princess Sarashina? What have you done with her?" the demon bellowed. Oh, how Tashi wished he hadn't come back to the gooseberry bush!

'"I haven't done anything to her," he said firmly, just as a second demon came bounding out of the forest. But both demons were now looking hard at Tashi's jacket. There, tucked into a buttonhole, were the cords that he had untied from Sarashina's hands and feet.

'"What are these then? Where is she?" roared the first demon.

'"I won't tell."

'The second demon knocked Tashi to the ground and sat on his chest. He stared deep into Tashi's eyes, but Tashi wouldn't look back. The demon shifted angrily. Then he smiled so all his dagger teeth glinted.

'"I think you *will* tell," he said slowly.

'Tashi didn't like that smile. He thought about demons and Uncle Lee's muddy water, and how you couldn't tell what was at the bottom of it. He knew the demon had a terrible plan, but no matter how hard he tried, Tashi couldn't imagine what it might be. He started to sweat under the demon's heavy legs.

'"I think this will persuade you," the demon said, and he clicked his fingers. A box popped into his hand. "If you don't talk, I am going to tip these spiders over you." He lifted the lid a little to show Tashi what was inside.

'Tashi caught a glimpse of hairy scampering legs and quickly shut his eyes. "I will never tell."

'He pressed his lips together as he felt spiders crawling over his face and up his nose. Taking a deep breath, he tried to still his mind. Yes, that helped. Then, with a great effort, he squeezed out a giggle. "They tickle!"

'The first demon roared with rage. "Give him to me!" He pushed the other demon aside and tied Tashi to a tree with his hands above his head. "Now we'll see how you like *snakes*!"

325

'He muttered a demon word and a barrel of snakes appeared under the tree. Tashi quivered as snakes slithered over his legs and under his jacket. But he managed to close his eyes, relaxing his muscles and making his mind still.

'"Oh good, snakes!" he cried, grinning. "I have three snakes at home, but they're much bigger than these. I let them sleep at the foot of my bed. Snakes like the warmth, you know."

'The second demon roared with rage.
"Give him back to me!" He poked the first
demon's chest with a steely finger. "We will
never find Princess Sarashina like this—or
get the ransom you said the Emperor would
pay!"

'Both demons glared at Tashi. Their eyes
glowed crimson. Then they turned to each
other and hissed one word: "*RATS!*"

'*Wah*, thought Tashi, I *can't* pretend with rats—sharp little yellow teeth, dripping with disease—*ugh!* He took a deep breath. "Rats don't worry me," he said loudly. "In fact, the more there are the better I like it. You can do tricks with rats, you know. Train them with a bit of cheese or meat...I do it all the time at home, with my pets Rattus and Ratz." Tashi smiled broadly at the demons. He was only able to smile, you see, because he'd just thought of a cunning demon trick.'

'That's my boy,' said Dad, looking relieved. 'I *hate* rats. We had one once in the kitchen, didn't we, Mum? It gave me nightmares and chewed my socks.'

'Well,' Jack went on, 'the demons stamped their feet and jumped about with fury.

'"Spiders and snakes and rats are really scary!" wailed the first demon. "Humans are supposed to be terrified by them." He grabbed Tashi by the jacket. "Why aren't you? What's wrong with you? What frightens *you*?"

'Tashi bit his lip and made his hands tremble. "The only thing that really scares me," he said, "is getting stuck in a Dragon's Blood Tree. Thank heavens there aren't any in these parts."

'"Ho, ho, that's where you're wrong!"
whooped the demons, and they untied him
in a flash and dragged him to a tree with
branches so thick and twisted together that
it was like a magic maze with no beginning
nor end.

'"One, two, three, up!" they boomed
and the demons tossed Tashi up into the
tree.

' "Goodbye, Tashi!" they gloated.
"You're trapped now. No one has ever
found their way out of a Dragon's Blood
Tree, hee hee!"

'But Tashi disappeared.

'The demons waited. "Where did he go?" asked the first demon uneasily. They gazed up into the net of branches. Not even a rat could wiggle out through those. They bounded back to the gooseberry bush for a better view of the treetop. Nothing.

'"He's gone!" the demons screamed, and they jumped into the tree to find him. They peered and poked about, crawling over each others' faces as they searched for Tashi.

'Meanwhile, Tashi wriggled deeper and

deeper into the darkness of the tree. When he came to the centre of the tangled branches, he wound his way down to a hollow in the trunk. With a shiver he slipped inside. It was so black in that tunnel, and tiny soft things flitted past his cheek. The air grew musty and thick. But Tashi kept climbing down, his fingers finding rough holds. His eyes were stinging as he stared into the dark, until at last he spied a faint ray of light. Squeezing through the opening, he crawled on his belly over the roots and ran off home.

'The demons never did find their way out of the Dragon's Blood Tree, and as far as Tashi knows, they are still writhing about in the dark, roaring at each other.'

'And so what happened to the Princess, the one like the evening star?' asked Dad.

'I was just getting to that,' Jack replied. 'Princess Sarashina and Tashi's parents were almost finished their stew of dandelion roots when Tashi burst in the door. His family bombarded him with questions and the Princess was particularly interested in his demon-tricking method.

'"How did you find a way out of the Dragon's Blood Tree?" she asked him admiringly.

'"Wise-as-an-Owl told me," said Tashi. "He's taught me a million things about herbs and plants. Look for the dragon's tunnel at the centre of the trunk, he said, and follow it down till you see the light."

'Princess Sarashina was excited to hear this, and asked if Tashi could introduce her to Wise-as-an-Owl some time. Tashi agreed, and then he walked her down to the river where they found a boat to take her home.

'The next day the boat returned, laden deep in the water with bags of rice and fruit and chickens, enough food to feed the village for the summer. And with the food there was a note saying "Thank you, Tashi" from the Emperor, and an invitation from the Princess for him to visit the palace.

'That night, the villagers decorated Tashi with coloured streamers and carried him around the village on their shoulders. The feasting and laughter grew even louder as clouds blotted out the moon and the rains began to fall.'

Mum and Dad lay on the grass with their eyes closed. They didn't move. Jack looked at their faces. He prodded them.

'We're practising,' said Mum.

'We're trying to still our minds,' said Dad.

'Look, there's a bull ant!' cried Jack, and Dad leapt up as if a bee had stung him.

'Well, better be getting back to my gardenia,' said Dad. 'So when's Tashi coming over, Jack? Maybe he could give me some advice about my plants. What do you think?'

'Sure,' said Jack. 'I'll go and ring him up.'

'And I'll make him some sticky rice cakes,' said Mum. 'In just a minute,' she added, closing her eyes.

The MAGIC BELL

'Look out, Tashi! Hide behind this tree,
quick!' Jack pulled Tashi down beside him.

'What is it?'

'Look, *there*.' Jack pointed to the veranda of number 42. An old man leant over the balcony. He had wild curly hair and a cockatoo on his shoulder. He didn't look very dangerous to Tashi. But then Tashi had seen a lot of evil and calamitous things in his time, it was true.

'That's Mr B. J. Curdle. He's always pestering me,' hissed Jack. 'I'm just walking home from school, right—like now, minding my own business—and out dashes old Curdle, stopping me and asking *how I am*.'

Tashi frowned. 'What's so terrible about that?'

'Well, he makes these dreadful
homemade medicines from plants in his
garden, and he wants to try them out on *me*!
Once, I felt sorry for him—his cockatoo had
a limp—so I went in. Instead of lemonade
he gave me this thick yellow stuff to drink.
He said it was strengthening medicine. Yuk!'

'And did it make you strong?'

'You've got to be kidding! That mixture
made me weak as a baby—it tasted like
mashed cockroaches. I felt like throwing up
all the way home. The man's a menace!'

When the old man had gone back inside, and the two boys were walking home, Tashi said, 'What you need is a Magic Warning Bell, like the one we had in my village. It rang whenever danger was near.'

'Ooh, that *would* be handy. What did it look like?'

'Well, it was very old and beautiful, the most precious thing we had in the village. When dragons came over the mountain it would ring out, and once, when a giant wandered near, its clanging was so deafening that even people working in the fields had time to escape. Lucky for me, it rang the day the River Pirate arrived.'

Jack stopped on the path. 'Oh, I remember *him*—he was that really fierce pirate you tricked with a bag of fake gold.'

Tashi nodded. 'I had to, or I'd have been carved up like a turkey. But I always knew when he discovered it he would come back to get me.'

Jack shivered. 'So what did he do?'

'Well, it was like this,' said Tashi. 'I was in the village square getting some water from the well when the bell tolled softly. It seemed to be ringing just for me.

'I stood there, frozen, trying to think.
But all I could see in my mind was that
Pirate, stroking the end of his sword.
I sipped some water. That helped. I decided
that the first place he'd look for me would
be my house, so I dropped my bucket and
ran to my cousin Wu, who lived high up on
a hill overlooking the village.

'From Wu's front window I could see the River Pirate tying up his boat. Just the sight of him gave me the shivers. He was *huge*— the muscles in his arms were like boulders. I watched him stride along the jetty, turning into the road...he was heading straight for my house! My mother told him she didn't know where I was, but he banged about inside anyway, frightening her and my grandparents. He knocked a pot of soup off the fire and kicked over a table, then went charging about the village asking for me.'

Jack kicked a stone ferociously. 'They'd better not tell him where you were!'

'Well, a few villagers had seen me running up to Wu's house, but they all said they had no idea where I'd gone. Still, there was one little boy who didn't understand the danger I was in. He skipped up to the River Pirate calling, "Do you want to know where Tashi is? Well—" but at that moment three large women sat on him.

'"Well *what*?" growled the River Pirate.

'"Well so do we," the women replied, and the Pirate scowled and hurried on. He searched all day, growing more and more angry. People ran into their houses and locked the doors, but he threw rocks at their windows and tore up their gardens. That night, on his way back to the boat, the River Pirate stole the Magic Bell.'

'Oh no!' cried Jack.

'Oh yes!' said Tashi. 'The next morning, when they noticed that the bell was gone, the people were very upset. The Baron told everyone that it was my fault because I had tricked the River Pirate in the first place. People began to give me hard looks. They said that the bell had hung over the well since Time began and now, because of me, the village had lost its special warning. Some little children threw stones at me and their parents looked the other way. I felt so miserable I could have just sat down in a field and never got up.

'So I went to see Wise-as-an-Owl, to ask his advice. He was busy at his workbench when I walked in, filling jars with herbs and plants.

'"Ah, Tashi," he smiled as I came in. He looked at me for a moment. "You'd better help yourself to some willowbark juice over there."'

Jack shuddered. 'What's that? Does it taste like mashed cockroaches?'

'No,' said Tashi. 'But it can cure head-aches. I've learnt everything I know about plants and potions from Wise-as-an-Owl—he's an expert on the medicine plants of the mountain and forest. So I told him yes, I would have a dose, because I *did* have a pounding headache and a terrible problem.

'Of course Wise-as-an-Owl knew all about the River Pirate. He'd watched him stamping all over his herb garden out the front. "Go and face the villain, Tashi," he told me. "It will go better if *you* find *him* first."

'He gave me two packets of special herbs to keep in my pocket. "Wolf's breath and jindaberry," he said. "Remember what I've taught you and mind how you use them."

'I thanked him and looked around for the last time at the plants and jars and pots of dandelion and juniper boiling on the stove. Then I set out for the city at the mouth of the river. There I would find the River Pirate.

'I walked for two days, and as I trudged through forests and waded through streams, I thought about what I should say to him. On the last night, lying under the stars, I decided that I'd try to make a bargain with him. What I'd offer him would be fair, and would mean a big sacrifice for me!

'I had no trouble finding the River Pirate down in the harbour. He was sitting at the end of the jetty with his black-hearted crew.

You could hear them from miles away.
They were dangling their legs over the side,
passing a bucket of beer to each other and
shouting and singing rude pirate songs at
the tops of their voices. Every now and
then they would tear great hunks of meat
from a freshly roasted pig—stolen, you
could be sure.'

'"There you are, you treacherous young devil!" the River Pirate spluttered when he saw me, leaping up and showering my face with greasy gobbets of pig. He grabbed my arm and yanked me toward him. His hand flew to his sword.

'"Wait!" I cried. "Listen!" I took a deep breath to stop my voice from trembling. Suddenly I had terrible doubts that a River Pirate could care about people being fair or making sacrifices, but it was the only idea I'd had. "If I work for you for a year and a day," I said boldly, "will you give back the bell?"

'The River Pirate just laughed. He threw back his great bony head and roared, "I will keep you for *ten* years and a day—and the bell as well!" Then the crew grabbed me and tossed me into the boat.

'By sunset we'd set sail. When the first star glittered in the sky, the cook told me to go down into the galley and start chopping mountains of fish and vegetables. And every day after that I had to do the same arm-aching jobs. The cook was spiteful and the work was hard and boring—except when it was frightening. Like the time another pirate ship attacked us.'

'*Enemy* pirates?' cried Jack. 'What did you use as a weapon—your kitchen knife?'

'Well,' said Tashi, 'it was like this. One moonless night, a swarm of bawling, yelling-for-blood pirates sprang onto our boat. They took us completely by surprise. Where could I hide? I glanced frantically around the boat and spied a big coil of rope. I scuttled over and buried myself in the rope just as the enemy Captain bounded up. He was barking orders and threats like a mad dog when he suddenly caught sight of the River Pirate. Swiping at the air with his sword, he gave a vicious battle cry—and tripped over me! *Wah!* I shivered when I looked up into his face, but he didn't hesitate for a moment. He picked me up as if I were just a weevilly old crust and flicked me overboard.

'Lucky for me there was a rope ladder hanging from the side of the boat. I grabbed it and swung down, clinging onto the last rung as I dangled in the black and icy water.

'My fingers were stiffening with cold and it was hard to hang onto the fraying strands of rope. Something slithery kept twining around my legs! I kicked hard and looked down into the dark waves. A giant octopus was staring up at me, its tentacles groping for my ankle. Then, to my horror, I felt my shoe being sucked from my foot!

'At that very moment, just when it seemed that my mother would never see her precious boy again, I heard the River Pirate and his men bellowing out their song of victory. I could hear the dreadful splash as enemy pirates were thrown over the side.

'Oh, how wet and wretched I was when I climbed back into the boat. But all I got was the River Pirate's ranting fury. "Why didn't that mangy magic bell ring to warn us?" he shouted, as he wiped the blood of an enemy pirate from his eye.

'"It only rings for the place where it belongs," I told him, and he scowled so deeply that his eyebrows met in the middle.

'The next morning, I saw three pirates racing up to the deck to be sick over the side. By afternoon two more men and the cook looked quite green. They wobbled around as if their legs were made of noodles. As our village came into sight, I said to the River Pirate, "If I can cure your men of their sickness, will you let me go?"

'"No!" snarled the Pirate, but just then he bent over and clutched his stomach.

"Aaargh, I'm dying... Go on then, but be quick," he gasped.

'I slipped down to the galley where I had hidden my packets of medicine plants. Quickly I threw some into a pot and boiled them up.

'The men only needed a few mouthfuls each before they stopped rolling about on the deck and sat up. One even smiled. The River Pirate was hanging over the side of the boat like a piece of limp seaweed, but he turned his head and begged for me to hurry.

'"And will you give me back the bell as well?" I asked him. The River Pirate ground his teeth. I tilted the pot a little. "I hope I don't spill these last few spoonfuls," I worried.

'"Ah, take the bell, take it. It doesn't work anyway," the River Pirate hissed.

'And so that's how I came back to the village with the magic bell.'

Tashi looked at Jack and laughed. 'Do you realise we've walked right past your house and mine?'

'Well,' said Jack, grinning, 'come back to my place and have a glass of lemonade. Or we could always call in on Mr Curdle if you'd prefer... But tell me, what happened when you got home?'

'The villagers all crowded around, welcoming me and saying they were sorry for their harsh words. But when I took the bell out of the sack, there was a great shout and people threw their hats in the air. We hung the bell back on its hook over the well. And then—something that had never happened before—it gave a joyful peal!'

'Gee,' said Jack, 'wasn't it lucky that the pirates got sick so that they needed your medicine!'

Tashi smiled. 'I think Wise-as-an-Owl would tell you that luck had nothing to do with it. Sometimes medicines that make you sick are almost as useful as those that make you well.'

'Aha!' said Jack, giving Tashi a knowing look, and they leapt up the steps of Jack's house, two at a time.

TASHI and the BIG STINKER

'What kind of sandwiches have you got today, Tashi?' asked Jack.

'Egg,' said Tashi.

'Oh.' Jack pulled at some weeds growing under the bench. There were only ten minutes until the bell.

It was a dull kind of day, thought Jack.
The sky was grey all over. There wasn't a
single dragon or battleship or wicked face
in the clouds. And then Tashi had been
busy taking a boy to the sick bay – Angus
Figment had been bitten by a strange
green spider which made Angus's finger
go all black and dead-looking. Tashi said
it needed urgent treatment, so they hadn't
even had time to play.

'Dragon Egg.'

'What?'

'My sandwich.'

'Ooh, let me see.'

Tashi licked the last crumb from the corner of his mouth. 'Sorry, I just finished – boy, was I hungry! I could have eaten ten thousand and six of them!'

'What do dragon eggs taste like?'

'Salty, and a bit hot, like chilli – your tongue tingles as if it's on fire.'

'Gosh,' said Jack. 'I just had cheese.' He stood up gloomily.

'Once somebody really did swallow ten thousand and six of those eggs. It was terrible. Everyone said that's why there are so few dragons around any more. We were lucky – Third Aunt had already salted away piles of them, just in case.'

Jack sat down. 'In one gulp? Swallowed them, I mean.'

'Oh, sure,' said Tashi, stretching out his legs.

'Who was he? Come on, tell me, we've still got nine minutes before the bell.'

'Well,' said Tashi, throwing his lunch scraps into the bin, 'it was like this. On a grey, still afternoon, remarkably like this one in fact, I was sitting with my friends in the schoolhouse when suddenly the Magic Warning Bell began to ring. We all ran straight home, I can tell you! Our mothers came in from the fields and our fathers gathered up the animals and bolted the doors of their shops. What danger could there be? I wondered. Was it the war lord, stung by wasps and gone mad? Was it blood-thirsty pirates? Ravenous witches?

'The ground began to tremble and the dishes clattered on the shelves. Peeping through a crack in the shutters, I saw a giant striding down the street.'

'Chintu!' yelled Jack. 'Remember how you were prisoner in his house once and Mrs Chintu –'

'It wasn't Chintu, Jack. This giant was almost as wide as he was tall. He swelled out in the middle as if he had a hill under his jumper. Well, he passed our house, thank goodness, but he stopped next door and do you know what? He just lifted the roof off, as easily as you please. He scooped up a whole pig that was roasting on a spit and gobbled it down as he went on his way to the end of the village.

'As soon as the earth stopped shuddering under our feet, everyone ran into the street. They were shouting with fright, telling of their wild escapes from death. "He missed me by a hair," Wu was gasping. "That great foot of his came down like a brick wall, and squashed my poor hens flat."

'"Just as well you were roasting a pig at the time, Mrs Wang," said Wise-as-an-Owl, "otherwise he might have taken you instead." A fearful groan ran through the crowd.

'"My word, yes," said Mrs Wang. "I
just heard this morning that two people have
disappeared from the village over the river."

'People were still muttering and moaning
when the village gossip ran up. Wah! That
one practically knows what you're going
to say and who you're going to visit before
you do!'

'Oh, we used to have a neighbour like
that – Mr Bigmouth. He was like the local
newspaper.'

'Well, anyway, Mrs Fo – the gossip – shouted over everyone. "My second son's wife's cousin works for Chintu the Giant, and he has just told me that Chintu's Only Brother has come to live with him. My cousin says Only Brother is a hundred times worse than Chintu. He says Only Brother eats from morning to night!" Another moan rippled through the crowd and Wise-as-an-Owl turned to me, just as I knew he would.

'"Tashi," he said, "you are the only one of us who has been to Chintu's castle and managed to leave alive. Do you think that you could go again and find out if this is true?"'

'Oh no,' said Jack. 'You didn't have to go, did you?'

'Well,' said Tashi, 'it was like this. I didn't want to, but then I thought it could be my roof that was lifted next time, and no pig in the courtyard! "All right," I said, "I'll get ready straight away."

'My mother packed some food and a warm scarf in a basket. "Be careful, Tashi," she said, "and give these plums to Mrs Chintu with my best wishes."

'I gave her a hug, and set off. It was a night and a day's hard walking ahead of me but I remembered the way well. When I arrived at Chintu's castle I stopped and listened. There was a great muttering and clanging of spoons and forks coming from the kitchen. I made my way towards it and pushed open the door. (That took a while – giants' doors are heavy!)

'There, in the kitchen, was Mrs Chintu.
She was rolling some dough, her face creased
with bad temper. I ran over and tugged at
her skirt.

'"Well, hello, Tashi," she said, most
surprised. "What are you doing here?"

'I told her about Only Brother's visit to the village and how frightened the people all were that he would come again. But when I asked if there was anything she could do to help us, Mrs Chintu threw down her chopper and cried, "I wish there was, Tashi. Only Brother is driving *me* crazy as well. He eats all day long, I never stop cooking, so fussy he is with his food. And he keeps Chintu up drinking till dawn, the both of them singing at the tops of their voices. But whenever I ask Chintu to tell him to go, he says, 'He is my Only Brother, I could never ask him to leave.'"

'Just then Chintu stamped into the kitchen roaring, "Fee fi fo – "

'"Now don't start that all over again," Mrs Chintu snapped. "Here's Tashi come to see us. You remember him, don't you? He's the boy who – "

'"Didn't we eat him?"

'"No," said Mrs Chintu hastily, "that was another boy altogether. Is something the matter?"

'Chintu flopped down like a mountain crumbling. "You know how I've been waiting for the pomegranates to ripen on my tree down by the pond? Well, I just went there to pick some and I found that Only Brother has stripped the tree bare and eaten the lot."

'"I told you he should go," said Mrs Chintu.

'"Now don't *you* start that all over again," Chintu roared and he stamped out.

'"You see," sighed Mrs Chintu, "Only Brother will be here forever."

'"Unless we come up with a cunning scheme," I said. "Now let me think…"

'Mrs Chintu sat me on the table. "You'll think better if you're comfortable," she said.

'I closed my eyes and swung my legs and then an idea came. "Did you say Only Brother was a fussy eater?"

'"Yes, I did. Everything has to be just so, even if he does guzzle it all down in a trice."

'"Well then," I said, "for Step One, when you give him his dinner tonight, make sure that his helpings have four times as much pepper as he likes."

'At dinner time, Only Brother gulped down three or four spoonfuls of stew before he realised how hot and spicy it was. "UGH!" he bellowed. "This stew would burn the tonsils off a warthog! No giant could eat it!"

'Chintu, who had no extra pepper in his dinner, took a spoonful. "What's wrong with it?" he growled. "You probably aren't hungry because you are full of *my* pomegranates."

'The two brothers went to bed, scowling. There was no drinking or singing that night. Good, I thought, now for tomorrow – and Step Two.

'The next morning was Chintu's birthday. Mrs Chintu spent all morning making a magnificent birthday cake. When he saw it, Chintu licked the icing on the top and said, "Now, wife, we must be sure Only Brother doesn't see this before dinnertime! I'll hide it in the cellar."

'I waited until Chintu was out of sight and then went to find Only Brother. I described the beauty of the cake and Only Brother's eyes glistened. "Would you like to see it?" I asked. "Just to look at, not to touch, of course." Only Brother would.

'We went downstairs to the cellar and Only Brother stood before the cake, mouth watering. I quietly slipped away.

'That night, after dinner and presents, Chintu went away to fetch his cake. There was a tremendous, ear-splitting roar. He came upstairs with an empty plate and a frightening scowl.

'"Oh, that," said Only Brother, shrugging his shoulders like boulders. "I meant to have just one little slice, but before I knew it, I had finished every sweet-as-heaven crumb. Mmm, delicious, delectable…ah!"

'"I've been looking forward to that cake all day!" Chintu kicked Only Brother out of the way and stomped upstairs to bed. "Only *Bother* should be his name," he hissed under his breath. Another early night.

'Good, I thought, now for tomorrow and Step Three.

'The next morning Chintu went down to the river early and stopped a fishing boat laden with lobsters, octopus and fish. He bought the whole catch and went home to tell his wife. "We will have a wonderful meal tonight – shark fin soup and seafood stew. I have left it all in a net in the river to stay cool – just tell me when you want it."

'But when Mrs Chintu sent him down to get the fish, he found Only Brother had eaten the lot – and one or two fishermen as well. Chintu shook his fist and growled.

'"Oh that," said Only Brother, shrugging his shoulders like boulders. "When Tashi told me about the fish I meant to have just one or two, but before I knew it, I had finished them all. Delicious, delectable...ah!"

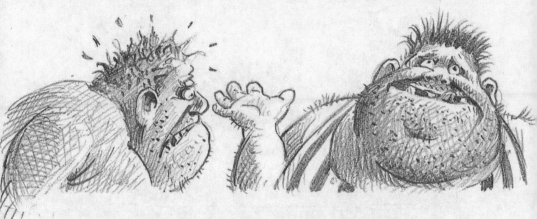

'Chintu ground his teeth (it sounded like rocks crashing against each other!) and told his wife she would have to find something else for dinner. But Mrs Chintu and I were already making our preparations. I told her to tip two big sacks of beans into the cooking pot. "We'll have bean stew," I said, "and into Only Brother's bowl we'll put a few handfuls of these special berries and spices that Wise-as-an-Owl gave me."

'Only Brother liked the stew so much he had six big bowls of it. And sure enough, after a while, when he and Chintu were sitting drinking their tea, the beans did their work. "BLATT, BANG, PARF!"

'Great gusts of wind exploded from Only Brother's bottom. They were like bombs going off. And the spices we'd added to his stew made the explosions terribly, horribly smelly.

'Chintu threw open the windows and door, beetles curled over on their backs, their legs waving weakly in the air, and the canary dropped off its perch.

'Mrs Chintu ran outside, her apron over her nose. Even I was growing dizzy from trying to hold my breath, and I followed her outside.

'The smell came after us. I wiped my eyes. "How can it be so strong, Mrs Chintu?"

'"Well, Tashi, Only Brother is a giant after all, with a giant-sized bottom that makes a giant-sized smell!"

'Inside the castle Chintu was bellowing,
"What a stink! What a pong! This is too
much – off you go!" and he pushed his
brother out the door. He galloped upstairs
and gathered Only Brother's clothes and
bag and threw them out the window. "Go
and find someone else to keep that great
stomach of yours full, why don't you!"

'"I'm glad to go," sneered Only Brother. "The food here doesn't suit me at all. Your wife uses too much pepper and her stew gives me wind. Besides," he added as he picked up his slippers, "there's a dreadful smell in your castle. You should do something about it." And he burped like a volcano erupting.

'Mrs Chintu and I did a little victory dance and then she said, "I think you had better slip away home now, Tashi. I saw Chintu giving you hard looks when Only Brother mentioned that you told him where to find the fish."

'I was only too happy to obey. But when I reached the village and tried to tell the news of Only Brother's going, no one would come out into the street.

'"We can't talk now, Tashi, there is this revolting stink. Can't you smell it? Look, even the trees are wilting!"

'"Oh, that," I said, grinning. "That's Only Brother – and it's the very reason for his leaving!"'

The bell rang out over the playground, and Jack stopped laughing. 'There's our warning to get to class,' he said. 'So, quickly, did the villagers give you a reward?'

Tashi grinned. 'No – do you know what happened? Instead of saying how brave I was to get rid of the fearsome giant, people still moan about the time I caused the terrible smell!'

Just then Angus Figment ran past. He waved, and Tashi saw that his black, dead-looking finger looked healthy again. 'It was texta,' Angus cried. 'Mrs Fitzpatrick washed it.'

Tashi laughed, and Jack blew loud exploding raspberries on his arm all the way back to class.

The MAGIC FLUTE

'Dad,' said Jack, 'can I ask you something?'

'Sure,' said Dad. 'What's it about – turbo engines, shooting stars, hermit crabs – I'm good at all those subjects!'

'No,' Jack said, 'it's like this. Say your friend is in trouble, but when you go to save him, you hurt the person who got him into trouble. Does that mean you did the wrong thing?'

'Which friend is that, Jack?' said Dad. 'Would it be my mate Charlie over the road, or is it Henry, the one I play cards with?'

'Oh, Dad, it doesn't matter,' sighed Jack. 'It's the idea, see – a question of right or wrong. Or say you owe someone a hundred dollars and...'

'Who owes a hundred dollars?' Mum came in with three bowls and spoons.

Jack rolled his eyes. 'It doesn't matter who, Mum! Maybe I'd better tell you the whole story – just the way Tashi told me.'

'Oh boy, icecream, peaches and a Tashi story for dessert!' Dad cried gleefully.

'Yes,' said Jack sternly. 'But listen carefully, because I'll ask you some questions at the end.'

Dad leant forward, frowning thoughtfully, to show how serious he could be.

'Well,' began Jack, 'back in the old
country, it had been a good summer and
the rice had grown well. People were
looking forward to a big harvest, when a
traveller arrived with dreadful news. The
locusts were coming! In the next valley he'd
seen a great swarm of grasshoppers settle
on the fields in the morning, leaving not
one blade of grass at the end of the day.'

Dad shook his head. 'Awful damage they do, locusts. You can ask me anything about them, son. Anything. They're one of my best subjects.'

'Later,' Jack said. 'Well, the Baron called a meeting in the village square.'

'That sneaky snake!' exploded Dad. 'He diddles everyone out of their money, doesn't he!'

'That's the one,' agreed Jack. 'But now the Baron was very worried because he owned most of the fields, although everyone in the town worked a little vegetable patch or had a share in the village rice fields.

'At the meeting, Tashi's grandfather suggested hosing the crops with poison but there wasn't time to buy it. Someone else said they should cover the fields with sheets, but of course there weren't enough sheets in the whole province to do that. Tashi racked his brains for an idea but nothing came.

'Just when everyone was in despair, a stranger stepped into the middle of the square. He was a very odd-looking fellow, dressed in a rainbow coloured shirt and silk trousers. On his head was a red cap with a bell. The people had to blink as they stared at him – he glowed like a flame.

'"I can save your fields from the
locusts," he said. Tashi looked up
into his eyes. They were pale
and hooded.

'"Can you really? How?" the people shouted as they crowded around. They wanted to believe him, and there was

something about him, this man. You could feel a kind of power that made you think he would deliver whatever he promised to do. But his eyes were full of shadows.

'"What will you need?" asked the Baron.

'"Nothing except my payment," replied the stranger. "You must give me a bag of gold when the locusts have gone."

'The people quickly agreed, and it was just as well they did. Only a moment later the sky began to grow dark and a deep thrumming like a million fingers drumming could be heard.

'Clouds of locusts appeared overhead, clouds so big and black that the sun was blocked completely, and then wah! just like that, the noise stopped and they settled on the village rice fields and gardens.

'But before the locusts could eat a blade
of grass, the stranger brought out his flute
and played a single piercing note. It echoed
in the silence and the locusts quivered.
Six shrill notes followed, and as the last
note sounded, the locusts rose as one, and
flew away to the south. In three minutes the
air was clear.

'There was a stunned silence. People looked at each other, hardly able to believe what they had just seen. Tashi's grandfather ran up to the stranger and shook his hand, thanking him, but the Baron stepped in and cut him off. He gathered the Elders around him, saying, "Let's not be too hasty in our thanks. We can't be sure it was the stranger's flute that drove off the locusts. Maybe they would have gone of their own accord. And, in any case, a bag of gold is far too much to pay for one moment's work."

'When Tashi's father and the Elders disagreed, the Baron went on, "I know none of you has more than a few silver pieces between you, so who do you suppose would have to pay the most of it? Me, of course. Well, I won't do it, and you must all stand by me."

'Tashi felt a shiver of dread. This was the wrong thing to do. He could see that many of the others were unhappy too, and some of them started to argue with the Baron but he brushed them aside. He walked over to the stranger and tossed him a single gold coin, saying, "Here you are, fellow, you earned that coin easily enough."

'The stranger let the coin fall to the ground and slowly looked around at the people. "Do you all agree with him?"

'The people shuffled and looked away.

'"You will be sorry – oh, how very sorry," the stranger said quietly, and he drifted away, the bright flame of him shimmering in the distance.

'On the way home Tashi's grandfather took his hand and sighed.

'"We did a bad thing today, Tashi. We robbed that man of his reward."

'"Yes," said Tashi, "and I have a horrible cold feeling in my tummy telling me this is not the end of it. There was something about the way the stranger looked at us when he left. He's not an ordinary man, that's for sure."

'Tashi's family said that there was nothing they could do tonight but that in the morning they would speak with the Elders. They would find the stranger and promise to pay him, a little at a time.

'Tashi was too restless and worried to sleep. Finally he jumped out of bed and went off to see if Wise-as-an-Owl had returned yet. He had been visiting his Younger Sister who lived in the next village. Surely he would have some good advice.

'And that is why Tashi, alone of all the children in the village, never heard those first beautiful, magical notes from the stranger's flute. The children sat up in bed and listened. They ached to hear more. And soon it seemed that their veins ran with golden music, not blood, and they had to follow those notes to stay alive. Quietly they slipped from their houses and followed the music, out of the town, across the fields and into the forest.

'Next morning there were screams and cries as parents discovered that their children were missing.

'"I knew it! I knew it!" Tashi cried as he ran back into the village. Just then he spied some pumpkin seeds on the road. Hai Ping! Tashi's friend Hai Ping nibbled them all the time, and what's more he'd had a hole in his pocket lately so that he left a trail of seeds wherever he went. Without a word Tashi set off, out of the town, across the fields and into the forest.

'As the darkness of the trees closed around him, Tashi heard the faint notes of the sweetest, most lovely melody. It was like Second Cousin's finest dark chocolate dissolved into air. It made his mouth water, his ears ache, his heart pump quickly. And his fears of the stranger came flooding back. Now he knew why he'd been so uneasy about the piper. There was a story his grandmother once told him about a piper and a plague of rats. Tashi bent down and scooped up some clay to stuff into his ears. It was the hardest thing he'd ever done. He closed his eyes as the sounds of the music and forest died away.

'The pumpkin seeds had been getting harder to find and now they stopped altogether. But Tashi continued along the path, following clues he'd learned to read – a broken twig, a thread caught on a thorn bush. At last, through the trees, he saw two little boys. They were the smallest of the village children and were straggling behind. They mouthed something which Tashi couldn't hear, and pointed up ahead.

'Tashi saw the other children nearing the top of the hill. Suddenly he realised where they were all heading and his blood froze. The path ended in a sheer drop, down, down, a hundred metres down to the rushing waters of a mountain gorge. The piper was playing the flute while the children streamed past him – towards the cliff. He was playing them to their deaths! Wah!

'Tashi raced up and burst out of the bushes. He butted the piper over, knocking the flute out of his hands. The children stopped, their eyes no longer blank, their minds no longer bewitched. Slowly they gathered around as Tashi and the stranger struggled towards the edge of the drop.

'"The piper was leading you over this cliff!" Tashi gasped. The children formed a wall and closed in on the piper.

'With a desperate pull, Tashi broke free
from the stranger and rolled away towards
the flute, which was lying half-hidden in the
grass. He picked it up and hurled it with all
his strength out over the cliff edge.

'The stranger gave a groan of rage but Tashi cried, "It wasn't the children's fault that you weren't paid. You had better go quickly before our parents come."

'The stranger looked up at the stony faces of the children and he shrugged. They moved aside to let him pass and all watched silently as he disappeared into the forest.

'The children met the search party of parents on the way back to the village and they told them what had happened. Some parents wept, and they looked at each other with shame.

'"Just think," they said, "but for Tashi, we would have been too late."

'The Baron kept very busy away from the village for the next few weeks and when he did finally return, he looked rather guilty and was so polite that people thought he must be sickening for something. But he was soon back to tricking people out of their wages and charging too much for his watermelons again, so life went on as before.'

'Blasted Baron!' cried Dad. 'He's got the morals of a dung beetle!'

'Worse. Dung beetles
do some very good
work,' put in Mum.

'But don't you see,'
said Jack. 'It wasn't right
that the piper never got paid – '

'But he was about to do a very dreadful
thing!'

'But if he hadn't been treated badly in
the first place – '

'Well,' said Mum, clearing away the
dishes, 'people have been discussing what's
right and wrong for centuries – and we've
only got half an hour before *The Magic
Pudding*'s on.'

'Yeah,' agreed Dad. 'Why don't you ask me about turbo engines – they don't take so long, and they take you far!'

Jack grinned. 'The day Tashi found a pair of magic shoes, he travelled 100 kilometres in one leap!'

'No, really?' cried Dad. Then his face dropped. 'But I bet that's another story, right?'

'Right,' laughed Jack. 'And now, Dad, the clock's ticking. What would you have done if *you* were the piper?'

TASHI and the
DANCING SHOES

One Saturday, Jack invited Tashi for lunch
to meet his Uncle Joe.

'He's my father's brother,' Jack told him
proudly. 'He's been travelling all over the
world.'

'That's interesting,' said Tashi. 'I wonder
if he's ever been to *my* village.'

'We'll ask him,' Jack said excitedly.
'You can swap stories about snake-infested
forests and wild escapes from war lords.
It'll be great!'

Tashi and Joe did have a lot to talk about. They talked all through the soup, well into the beef with noodles, pausing only when the apple cake was served.

'It's very good to meet an uncle of yours, Jack,' said Tashi, taking a bite of his cake. 'Have you got any more?'

'There's some in the kitchen,' said Mum, hopping up.

'He meant *uncles*, Mum,' laughed Jack. 'You know, if we asked all *yours* to lunch, Tashi, we'd have to hire the town hall!'

Tashi nodded. 'It's true. But I'll tell you something. No matter if you have forty uncles and fifty-six aunts and nine hundred and two cousins, all of them are precious.' He sighed. 'Take Lotus Blossom, for example.'

'Who's that?' asked Dad, scratching his head. 'An uncle?'

Tashi scooped up the last of his cake. 'No, Lotus Blossom is my cousin. We used to play chasings near the river in summer. *Wah*, was she a fast runner! Nearly quicker than *me!* She'd go streaking off on her own then hide in the tiniest, most impossible places. I'd take ages to find her.'

Tashi finished up his cake and pushed back his chair. 'So when they told me Lotus Blossom had disappeared, I wasn't too worried. At first, that is.'

Uncle Joe leaned forward. 'Disappeared, eh?' He nodded knowingly. 'What was it? Bandits, war lords, *kid*nappers?'

Dad winked at Jack. 'Here we go!' he whispered, bouncing on his chair.

'Well, it was like this,' began Tashi. 'One afternoon, my mother and I had just come back from a visit to Wise-as-an-Owl, when there was a furious knocking at the door and Lotus Blossom's grandmother, Wang Mah, stumbled in. Her face was wet with tears and strands of hair from her bun were plastered across her cheeks.

'"I've lost her!" Wang Mah burst out. "One minute my dear little Lotus Blossom was playing in the courtyard right next to me – the *next*, she was gone!" She wrung her hands. "Oh, what will happen when night falls?"

'My mother sat her down on a chair.

'"I was just painting my screen," Wang Mah went on. "You know, the one with the Red Whiskered Dragon? Well, I couldn't get the green right on the scales – "

'"Where did you look for her?" I interrupted.

'Wang Mah threw up her hands. "Oh, everywhere! The fields, the cemetery – I've told the whole village, practically. Everyone's out looking, but no one can find her. Oh, my little one, where could she be?"

'Well, I knew we wouldn't find her sitting there in the house worrying, so I told my mother that I was going to join the search party and that I would be back later.

'"Oh, thank you, Tashi," cried Wang Mah. "If anyone can find her, you will, I know."

'I wasn't so sure, but I crossed my fingers and gave her the sign of the dragon for luck. But as I walked towards the village square, a cold fear was settling in my stomach. Whenever Grandmother was painting one of her screens, she didn't hear or see anything else for hours. Lotus Blossom might have been missing since dawn. So I decided to go at once to the village fortune teller.'

Uncle Joe nodded wisely. 'I went to one last year, when I was back in the tropics. Did I ever tell you about the time – '

'Yes,' said Dad quickly.

'So, Tashi,' said Mum, 'did the fortune teller have any news?'

'Well, it was like this. Luk Ahed had done horoscope charts for everyone in our village, so I thought he might give us a clue about Lotus Blossom. Luk Ahed is very good at telling the future, but not so brilliant at keeping things tidy. He rummaged through great piles of sacred books and maps of the stars and bamboo sticks. But he couldn't find her horoscope anywhere.

'"I'll start on a new one right away,"
he promised. Then he grunted with
surprise. He had *my* chart in his hand.

'"Just look at this," he marvelled. "I see
a great adventure awaiting you, Tashi,
just as soon as you find a very special pair
of red shoes with green glass peacocks
embroidered on them."

'I walked out of there very thoughtfully, I can tell you. I could almost remember seeing such a pair of shoes, but where? As I turned the corner into the village I heard the familiar rat-a-tat-tat coming from the shoemaker's shop.

'"Hello, Tashi," Not Yet called from his open door. Our cobbler was called Not Yet because no matter how long people left their shoes with him, when they returned to see if they were ready, he always said, "Not yet. Come back later."

'Well, I stopped right there on the doorstep. Of course, *that's* where I'd seen those strange shoes. I ran into the shop and asked Not Yet if he still had them.

'"I think so," said Not Yet. "I know the ones you mean. They were here when I took over this shop from my father years ago." He poked around at the back of the shelves and finally fished out a dusty pair of shoes. He wiped them clean with his sleeve.

'The shoes were just as I remembered. They were red satin and glowed in the dingy room. I took some coins from my pocket and asked, "Could I take them now?"

'Not Yet look at the worn soles and heels and clicked his tongue. "Not yet," he said. "Come back later."

'So I went down to the river for a while and looked along the banks and in our usual hiding places for any sign of Lotus Blossom. After an hour, without a speck of dragon luck, I returned to the shop.

'"Be careful with them, Tashi," Not Yet said as he handed the shoes to me. "Be *very* careful." And he looked at me in a worrried way.

'Clutching them tightly to my chest,
I ran as fast as I could to the edge of the
village. The shoes glowed like small twin
sunsets in my hand. When I stopped and
put them on, my feet began to grow hot
and tingle. I gave a little hop. At least
I meant to give a little hop, but instead
it was a great whopping *leap*, followed by
another and another, even higher. I couldn't
help laughing, it felt so strange. I ran a few
steps, but each step was a huge bound. In
a few seconds I had crossed the fields and
was down by the river again.

'Well, even though I was so worried about Lotus Blossom, I have to tell you I couldn't help being excited about the shoes.'

'Who could?' cried Dad. 'No one would blame you for that!'

'So I decided to run home – just for a minute, you know – and show my family. But those shoes had other ideas! They went on running in quite the opposite direction: over the bridge and into the forest. I tried to stop, but the shoes wouldn't let me. I tried to kick them off, but they were stuck fast to my feet. I was getting very tired, and a little bit scared.'

'Who wouldn't be?' said Dad.

'Even I, with my vast experience, would be alarmed by the situation,' put in Uncle Joe.

'Yes, and then I saw the long shadows of the trees and the deepening dusk. Soon it would be dark, and I didn't know where on earth the shoes were taking me.

'Just then I heard a shout. The shoes bounded on and stopped suddenly near the edge of a deep pit. A tiger pit! I shivered deep inside. I'd had quite enough of tigers, remember, when I was trapped with one in that wicked Baron's storeroom.'

'Old Baron *bogey*,' muttered Dad.

'A voice yelped again, "Is anyone there?" And do you know, it was Lotus Blossom!

'"Yes, it's me, Tashi!" I called, and the shoes moved forward. I leaned over the side of the pit. "Hello, Lotus Blossom. How did you come to fall down there? You weren't *hid*ing, were you?"

'"No!" yelled Lotus Blossom, stamping her foot. "It's no joke being down here. I got lost, and I was running, and there were branches over the pit so you couldn't see it. Oh, Tashi, I've been here all day, so frightened that a tiger might come and fall in on top of me."

'I jerked back and shot a look over my shoulder. But what could I do? I had no rope or any means of getting her up. Then my toes tingled inside the shoes, reminding me. Yes! My splendid magic shoes could take me home in no time and I would be back with a good long rope as quick as two winks of an eye.

'But at that moment Lotus Blossom began to scream. My heart thumped as I saw a large black snake slithering down into the hole, gliding towards her.

'I didn't have time to think. The shoes picked me up and jumped me down into the pit. *Wah!*

'Maybe I'll land on the snake and squash him, I thought. But no, the snake heard me coming and slid to one side.

I landed with a crash.

'"Hide behind me, Lotus Blossom," I said, facing the serpent. Lotus Blossom did as I told her, but doesn't she always have to have the last word? She picked up rocks and threw them at the snake, shouting "*WAH! PCHAAA!*"

'"Leave him, Lotus Blossom!" I whispered, but it was too late. The snake was enraged. It drove us back into the corner, lunging fiercely.

'"Put your arms around my waist and hold on," I told Lotus Blossom.

'No sooner had she done so than my feet began to tingle. The magic shoes jumped me straight up the steep side of the pit and out into the clean, fresh air.

'I hoisted Lotus Blossom onto my shoulders and with a few exciting bounds we were back in the village square. The bell was rung to call back the searchers, and you should have seen them racing joyfully towards us! They swept Lotus Blossom up into their arms, clapping and cheering like thunder. Wang Mah grabbed her, and scolded and wept, her long white hair tangling them both together. But when the crowd saw me doing one of my playful little leaps – well, *flying* right over their heads! – they gasped in amazement.

'"Look at those shoes! Where did he get them? Look at him fly!" they cried.

'I was just taking my bow when I spied a face in the crowd that I had hoped never to see again: my greedy Uncle Tiki Pu.'

'Oh, *him!*' Jack turned to Uncle Joe. 'He's the worst uncle ever. When he came to stay with Tashi, he threw all the toys out the window to make way for his things!'

'I just brought my pyjamas and a change of underpants for the weekend,' said Uncle Joe quickly. 'Is that all right?'

'When the crowd drifted away,' Tashi went on, 'I walked home. I was feeling very gloomy, muttering to myself, when suddenly Tiki Pu's shadow loomed over me. He was rubbing his hands together with glee, and my heart sank. But I needn't have worried about him coming to *stay* – that was going to be the least of my problems.

'"You must come to the city with me, Tashi," he said, gripping my shoulder hard. "I know the Emperor well. Er, not the Emperor himself, perhaps, but certainly his Master of Revels. He could arrange for you to dance at the Palace. We will make our fortunes!"

'*We* will! *Our* fortunes? I thought.

'Tiki Pu was very insistent, never letting me have any peace with all his jawing on – "imagine, the *Em*peror, the *Em*peror!" – so in the end I agreed to go.

'The next morning, Tiki Pu stood on my toes (yes, it hurt, but at least it was quick) and off we bounded. It was amazing – a journey that took days of normal walking was over in half an hour. Suddenly, there we were at the front door of the Emperor's Master of Revels.

'The Master didn't look too pleased to see Uncle Tiki Pu. But after he had watched me do six somersaults from one leap, and dance up one wall, across the ceiling and down the other side, he clapped Tiki Pu on the shoulder.

'"The Emperor is giving a grand dinner tonight," he said. "The boy will dance for him at the Palace."

'"Will the Princess Sarashina be there?" I asked.

'"No, she is away visiting her aunt," the Master of Revels called over his shoulder as he hurried away to make the arrangements. Then he stopped. I saw him look back at me, and a sly expression came over his face. His eyes narrowed into a mean smile.

'We had only gone a little way when the Master came after us. He had two huge evil-looking guards with him.

'"Take those shoes from the boy," the Master ordered. "They should fit my son perfectly. He will be much more graceful. Why should *this* clumsy oaf have the honour of dancing before the Emperor!"

'"The Master's honourable son will bring him glory and gold!" said the first guard.

'"Praise and presents!" said the second guard.

'"The shoes won't come off," I said loudly. "I've *tried*."

'The guards rushed at me and pushed and pulled, but they couldn't remove the shoes.

'"Oh, well – chop off his feet!" ordered the Master. "We can dig his toes out of the shoes later."

'I looked desperately at my uncle. Tiki Pu took a very small step forward. "Ah," he stammered. "You shouldn't really, I mean to say, that's not very – "

'"Be quiet," snapped the Master, "or we will chop off his head, and yours as well."

'Tiki Pu stepped back quickly. "Oh, in that case…"

'Some uncle, I thought bitterly.

'The guard drew out his mighty sword and swung it up above his head…But before he could bring it down, the door flew open and Princess Sarashina burst into the room.

'"What are you doing?" she cried. "Put that sword down at once. This is Tashi, the boy who rescued me from the demons and saved my life! Just as well I came back early, Tashi. What a way to repay your kindness." She scolded the Master of Revels and his guards out of the room.

'Well, I was never so glad to see anyone in my whole life. So when the Princess invited me to take tea with her, I followed her into a beautiful room all hung about with silks and tapestries, and we talked and laughed until nightfall.

'That evening I danced for the Emperor and the Court. I twirled high over people's heads and swooped and ducked and glided like a bird.

'"Miraculous!" they cried, throwing
coins at me, which Uncle Tiki Pu hastily
gathered up. The Emperor gave me a nice
little bag of gold for my trouble, but Tiki
Pu was at my side at once. He whisked the
bag from my hand.

'"I'll keep this safe for you, Tashi my
boy," he beamed,
as he slipped it into
his pocket.

'"Is there anything else I can do for you,
Tashi?" the Emperor asked.

'"Not for me, your Highness, but there
is something my uncle would dearly like."

'Tiki Pu pricked up his ears and gave me
a toothy grin.

'"And what is that, my boy?" the Emperor smiled.

'"My uncle has always had a great desire to travel." Out of the corner of my eye I saw that Tiki Pu looked very surprised. I whispered something in the Emperor's ear.'

'What? What?' cried Dad.

'I know, I know!' cried Uncle Joe.

'Well, the next day I returned home alone and went straight at once to see Luk Ahed, the fortune teller. "You were right about the shoes," I said, "but I've had enough adventures for the time being, and I'm so tired. Can you tell me how to take them off?"

'"Nothing could be easier," said Luk Ahed. "All you have to do is twirl around three times, clap your hands and say, Off shoes!"

'I followed his instruction and oh, the relief to wiggle my toes in the cool dust. I carried the shoes home and carefully put them in the bottom of my playbox.

'"And Tiki Pu hasn't come back with you?" my mother asked when I told her about the grand dinner and the Emperor and Princess Sarashina.

'"No, he couldn't. A ship was leaving the next morning for Africa and the Emperor thought that it was too good an opportunity for Tiki Pu to miss, seeing he likes travel so much."

'My mother gave me one of her searching looks. "What a clever Tashi," she said at last, and smiled.'

There was a little silence at the table. Then Dad snorted loudly. 'Some uncle, all right, that Tiki Pu. Of all the lily-livered, cowardly…You wouldn't say *he* was a precious relative, would you, Tashi?'

'About as precious as a crocodile hanging off your leg!' put in Uncle Joe.

'He may have met a few by now,' grinned Tashi. 'Crocodiles are quite common in Africa, aren't they?'

'So I believe,' said Joe. 'In fact once, when I was in a typical African forest,

I saw a crocodile grab the muzzle of a zebra. Pulled him into the river, easy as blinking. Dreadful sight. A Nile crocodile, it was. Notorious man-killers. Did I tell you about the time...?'

And so Tashi stayed till dusk crept in all over the table and Dad had to put the lights on and Tashi's mother called him home for dinner.

'Come back tomorrow, young fellow!' urged Uncle Joe. 'I'm cooking *crocodile!*'

The FORTUNE TELLER

'Funny how crocodile tastes almost exactly like chicken,' remarked Dad.

'Yes, same chewy white meat,' said Mum.

Uncle Joe stared very hard at his plate. 'Actually,' he said, after a long pause, 'they were out of crocodile at the supermarket. Fancy! In Tiabulo, where I've just come from, you can buy it everywhere: canned, baked, boiled…Great for late night suppers when the fish aren't jumping.'

'Thank the stars we don't live in Tiabulo,' Dad whispered to Jack, behind his hand.

It was Sunday, and the family were sitting down to lunch. It was a late lunch because Uncle Joe had taken ages to cook it, but Tashi had only just arrived. He'd been making the dessert.

'Have you ever tried ghost pie?' asked Tashi. 'It's a secret recipe learned from ghosts I once knew.'

'No,' said Uncle Joe, 'but I remember a fortune teller once said – '

'Luk Ahed?' asked Jack.

'No, another one, in the Carribean Islands. Anyway, this man told me that when I was forty-three I would visit my brother and meet a wise young lad who would offer me a most mysterious dessert.'

'Aha!' Dad smacked his forehead. 'Ghost pie! Eat a slice and walk through walls. What's more mysterious than that? Your fortune came true then, didn't it?'

'Sometimes it does,' Tashi said slowly, 'and sometimes it doesn't.'

Jack looked hard at Tashi. 'Did you go back and see *your* fortune teller?'

Tashi nodded. 'Yes, and it wasn't long before I wished I'd never stepped foot in the place.' He put his fork down. 'Luk Ahed had been so clever telling me about the magic shoes, I decided to visit him again. I thought maybe he'd find some more surprises in my horoscope.'

'And *did* he?' asked Dad eagerly.

'You can *bet* on it,' said Uncle Joe, playing hard with his peas. 'They always do.'

'More than I'd ever bargained for,' agreed Tashi. 'See, it was like this. Luk Ahed was just finishing his breakfast when I arrived, but he put down his pancake and licked his fingers. He was like that – always happy to see you, always eager to help. It was only a few days since my last visit to him, so my chart hadn't been completely buried under his books and papers.

'"Here it is!" he cried, pulling it out. He was so surprised and pleased with himself at finding it quickly that he did a little jig and almost upset his breakfast over the table. "Come and sit beside me on the bench while I read, Tashi," he invited.

'"Anyone who has already had such an exciting life as yours would be sure to have a very interesting future ahead of him."

'Well, I watched him read for a minute, and then suddenly he stopped smiling and covered his eyes with his hands.

'"Oh, Tashi," he said in a sorrowful voice.

'"What? What is it?"

'"Oh, Tashi, on the morning of your 10th birthday you are going to die!"

'"But that will be the day after tomorrow! Are you sure, Luk Ahed? I'm so healthy – look!" I jumped up and down and did one-arm push ups to show him I wasn't even breathing hard.

'Luk Ahed shook his head sadly. "I'm sorry, Tashi, but we can't argue with destiny."

'"There must be something we can do. Couldn't *you* put in a good word for me?"

'Luk Ahed laughed unhappily. "*I'm* not important enough for that, Tashi. No, once your name has been written in the Great Book of Fate, there is nothing..."
He paused. "Except your name hasn't been entered in the Book yet, has it? And it won't be written in until New Year's Eve... in two days' time. And if on that evening you were to..."

'I was beginning to notice that Luk Ahed had a very annoying habit of not finishing his sentences. "If I were to *what*, Luk Ahed?"

'The fortune teller was feverishly looking through his sacred books. "The Gods like to enjoy a particular meal on New Year's Eve," he said. "Very simple, but special. Each God has his own favourite dishes. Now, if we were to serve our God of Long Life his own personal special meal, cooked to perfection…"

'"He might put me back in the Book of Life!" I finished his sentence.

'"Exactly."'

'So what are the special dishes?' asked Uncle Joe. 'Not crocodile, by any chance? Braised perhaps, with noodles?'

'No,' Tashi shook his head. 'Wild mushroom omelette with nightingale eggs. Speckled trout with wine and ginger. And a bowl of golden raspberries.'

471

'Gosh!' said Dad. 'Where would you get a nightingale egg? *Are* there any in your part of the world, Tashi?'

'Not that I knew of – I'd never seen any nests in our forests. For a moment I did feel low, I can tell you. It all seemed impossible. But then I thought of my friend, the raven. He *had* said, "Just whistle if you ever need my help." Remember when he was hurt after that terrible storm, Jack? The night Baba Yaga blew in? And I knew the children I had rescued from the war lord would gladly gather the mushrooms for me. And Lotus Blossom's mother had a pond at the bottom of her house where I was almost *sure* I'd seen speckled trout swimming. Maybe it wasn't impossible after all.

'So I hastily said goodbye to Luk Ahed and ran home to the mulberry tree where the raven sometimes perched. He flew down at my second whistle and when I told him about the dinner and the nightingale eggs, he said, "Give me your straw basket and I will be back with them tomorrow."

'The village children were very excited when I explained about the mushrooms.

'"We'll find enough for twenty Gods, Tashi," they shouted. Off they ran with their bags, clattering over the bridge into the fields and forest.

'Meanwhile, I hurried to Lotus Blossom's house. Her mother wasn't so happy to lose the beautiful speckled trout – they were her last three – but she gave a good-hearted smile as she scooped them out of her pond and handed them to me in a bowl of water.

'I raced back to the square where Luk Ahed stood, waving his hands. There was a great argument going on in the village about who would be the best people to cook the dishes. No one was listening to Luk Ahed, who was calling for order. Finally everyone agreed that Sixth Aunt Chow made the most delicious omelettes, but that Big Wu and his Younger Brother, Little Wu, should cook the fish.

'Next morning, cooking fires were set
up in the square so everyone could watch
and advise. The children were back before
noon with beautiful baskets overflowing
with four different kinds of mushrooms.
In the early afternoon the raven returned.
He looked quite bedraggled and tired,
but in the basket were a dozen perfect
nightingale eggs.

'Mrs Li brought out a bottle of her
prized wine to add to the fish and I left
them all busily chopping ginger roots and
celery and bamboo shoots.

'Now the hardest task lay ahead. In all
our province I had only ever seen one bush
of golden raspberries. And it belonged to
my enemy, the wicked Baron.'

'Oh, no!' cried Jack.

'Oh, yes!' said Tashi. 'I had brought my magic shoes with me but I decided not to put them on. As I walked slowly to his house I went over in my mind exactly *how* I would go about asking the Baron for a bowl of his berries.

'But I didn't have to ask. He had already heard the news and he was waiting for me with a fat smile on his face.

'"Well, Tashi," he gloated, "I hear that you are in need of some of my berries."

'"Yes, please."

'"Oh, you'll have to do much better than that." He shook a playful finger at me. "Something like this. Now, Tashi, say after me: Please, please most kindly, honourable and worthy Baron, could you give some berries to this miserable little worm Tashi, who stands before you?"

'I gritted my teeth and managed to force out the words, but the Baron pretended he couldn't hear and made me say it all over again. When I had finished, he thumped his fist on the table and shouted, "No, I couldn't! After all the trouble you have caused me, I'll be glad to be rid of you. Not a berry will you have."

'I was just leaving his house when Third Aunt called after me. She worked in the Baron's kitchen, remember, Jack? Well, she came close and whispered, "There *is* another bush of golden raspberries, Tashi. It belongs to the Old Witch who lives in the forest. But don't take any without asking her. The berries scream if anyone except the witch picks them."

'Oh dear, I didn't like the sound of that but what was I to do? It was the Old Witch's berries or none.

'This time I slipped my magic shoes on and I was in the forest in a few bounds. I found the Witch's cottage and there in the garden at the back of the house was a small raspberry bush. There were only a few golden berries on it but they looked round and juicy. I touched one gently and it gave a little scream.

'A door opened at once and a bony old figure in a dusty black cloak came hobbling down the path.

'"Who is meddling with my raspberry bush?" she shrieked.

'She looked like a bunch of old broom sticks strung together. She was even more hideous than people had said. Her blackened teeth were bared in a fierce growl and her bristly chin was thrust out so far in rage that her beak almost touched it. I turned to run. I expected my magic shoes would take me to safety in one bound, but something in the way she stood there, alone on the garden path, made me stop. Her mouth puckered around her gums and her eyes were sad. Come to think of it, I had never heard of her harming anyone.

'I took a deep breath and said, "I was just looking at them, Granny, because I have a great need of golden raspberries at the moment."

'She cackled. "Oh, you have, have you?"
And she sat herself down on a bench. "Tell
me about it then."

'When I had finished, she pulled herself
up on my arm. She grinned at me, and with
her mouth no longer set in a growl and her
eyes sparkling with interest, she didn't look
nearly so scary. "Come on then," she said,
"we'll make a nice pot of tea and then you
can pick your berries. There aren't many
left but you'll find enough to fill a bowl,
I'm sure."

'You can imagine how joyfully I ran back with my basket of fruit. But when I reached the bridge by the Baron's house, he was standing there, blocking my way. His eyes bulged when he saw my berries and with a roar of rage he charged towards me and knocked the basket up in the air and into the river. I hung over the railing and watched in despair as the berries bobbed away downstream.

'"How are you going to prepare your wonderful meal now, eh, clever Tashi?" the Baron sneered.

'I struggled to hold in my bitter feelings and faced him calmly. "We'll prepare the rest of the meal and I will take it to the mountain top, to the *Gods*, together with a note explaining that the delicious golden raspberries are missing because the wicked Baron, *YOU*, knocked them into the river."

'The Baron's jaw dropped and his mouth opened and closed. "That won't be necessary, my boy. Couldn't you see that I was just having a joke with you?"

'I folded my arms and said nothing while the Baron pleaded with me to take all the golden raspberries I needed.

'Finally, I shook my finger at him. "Oh, you will have to do much better than that. Now, Baron, say after me: Please, please most kindly, honourable and worthy Tashi, could you take the berries of this miserable worm of a Baron, who stands before you?"

'The Baron gritted his teeth and forced out the words. He even tried to smile as I picked his fruit. I thanked him politely for holding the basket for me.

'It was late afternoon by the time I got back to the village and everything was ready. A wonderful omelette filled with delicate flavoursome mushrooms lay on some vine leaves upon my mother's best platter. My mouth watered as I lifted the lid from the dish of speckled trout in wine and ginger and pickled vegetables that only Big Wu and Little Wu knew how to prepare. We washed the raspberries in fresh spring water, dried them and placed them gently in a moss-lined basket.

'Luk Ahed and I carried two baskets each and when we reached the mountain top, we spread out a gleaming white linen tablecloth and set out the meal. It was perfect.

'When it was nearly midnight we hid behind a tree and waited. On the stroke of twelve we were dazzled by a blinding silver light. We blinked against the light, closing our eyes for just a moment, but when we could see again the cloth was bare.

'Luk Ahed and I ran all the way back down the mountain and hurried to his house to see if my horoscope had changed. Luk Ahed peered at the chart, his brow wrinkling deeper with every second. I was holding my breath, and began to feel faint. If he didn't answer soon, I thought I might fall over and die right where I stood.

'"Tashi, the bad news is that all our work preparing that magnificent meal was for nothing."

'"!!!???!!!??"

'Then he smiled guiltily, bowing his head. "The *good* news is that you didn't need to do any of it. Look, here where I read *10th* birthday, it was really your *100th* birthday. You see, a little bit of breakfast pancake was covering the last zero."

'We stared at each other for a moment and began to laugh.

'"Let's not tell the village," said Luk Ahed. "They might be a little bit cross with me."'

The family looked at Tashi with their

mouths open. Uncle Joe's was still full of ghost pie, and a dollop fell out onto the table.

Jack cleared his throat. 'So how do you think you'll feel when you are nearly one hundred and you know you're going to die?'

'Oh,' Tashi waved airily, 'if I'm not quite ready, I'll just prepare another perfect meal for the God of Long Life.'

'Here's to a l-o-n-g friendship then,' said Uncle Joe, raising his glass of wine. They all clinked glasses and wished each other well. Then Uncle Joe added, 'You know, Tashi, that ghost pie really was excellent. It's given me a lot of energy. I think I'll go and stretch my legs after that long meal.' And he rubbed his hands together with excitement.

'It only lasts for three days!' Tashi called out, but Uncle Joe had already walked through the kitchen wall, and was gone.

'Great way to travel,' he yelled from the garden. 'See you soon!' And they heard him humming the old song, '*No walls can keep me in, no woman can tie me down, no jail can hold me now, da dum da dum da dum...*'

TASHI and the
HAUNTED HOUSE

'Well, look who's here!' cried Uncle Joe,
as he spied Tashi strolling up the garden
path. He leapt from his chair and sprinted
across the lawn.

'I was just thinking about you, my boy!
There's someone *special* I want you to meet.'
Uncle Joe's eyes were dancing and he kept
fidgeting in his pockets and sucking at his
moustache while he shot quick, shy glances
around the garden.

The rest of the family were busy digging
and planting for Spring. Tashi saw a new
herb patch near the steps and Jack was
potting a tomato plant. Suddenly, a dark-
haired lady stepped out from behind the
box hedge.

'Primrose! There you are!' Joe cried
proudly.

Primrose smiled and put out her hand
for Tashi to shake.

Uncle Joe looked from one to the other, beaming. 'I met Primrose up north, you see, when I was camping by a river *jumping* with barramundi.'

'Oh, so that's where you went after you walked through the kitchen wall?' Tashi asked with interest.

'Yes, yes, and I told dear Primrose all about your ghostly adventures, Tashi, as she and I fished by the river in the moonlight and fell hopelessly in love. Do you know, Primrose is not only the best angler I've met in my time but she's also an amazing musician. A percussionist!'

'I just tap on things,' Primrose said mildly. She picked up a teaspoon lying on the table and tapped lightly on the glasses and jugs, making a tinkling little tune.

'What I like best, though,' Primrose said confidingly to Tashi, 'is to make sounds with things from the natural world. I'm always searching for different, curious things to tap.'

Just then Jack came over, his hands black with dirt. 'Do you know, Tashi, Primrose can make scary, ghostly noises, just with bottles and wood and things? If you close your eyes and listen, you'd swear a million ghosts were breathing down your neck!'

Tashi nodded as Mum began pouring lemonade for everyone.

'You remind me of my cousin, Lotus Blossom,' Tashi said to Primrose.

'What, the one who keeps disappearing?' Joe asked in alarm.

'Yes,' said Tashi. 'But not because of that. No, once Lotus Blossom and I were in a situation of terrible danger and we needed to summon up the sound of ghostly voices. She did it very well.'

'Ghosts, eh Tashi?' put in Dad, as he peeled off his gardening gloves. He nudged Joe happily.

'So, tell us about Lotus Blossom,' said
Primrose. 'Was she a percussionist like me?'

'No,' grinned Tashi. 'She was a pest. But
she did have some good ideas. Especially
when it came to the haunted house.'

Everyone watched as Tashi took a sip
of lemonade.

'Go on,' urged Mum.

'Well, it was like this. Ever since I can
remember, the ghost house has been there,

crouching in the gloomiest part of the forest. No one from our village had set foot in that place, ever. Well, not for thirty years, anyway. Not since something dreadful happened to the old couple who used to live there. We children could never find out exactly *what* happened. The grown-ups would look frightened when we asked and say, "We don't want to talk about it."'

Jack snorted. 'That'd be right.'

'Sometimes we'd scare ourselves sick by running past the house or dare each other to go right up the path. So far only Ah Chu and I had actually dared to creep up and knock on the door.

'Then one winter's evening, Ah Chu's father caught up with us on the way home. He'd been in the forest burning charcoal and his hands were black with soot. They looked a bit like yours, Jack! But I still remember how they trembled when he shook my shoulder.

'Don't go near the ghost house,' he
warned. 'I've just seen a light flickering in
the window. Who knows *what* is prowling
around in there!'

'Wah! He hurried on his way and we
went on making our dam in the creek.
Neither of us said a word, but you can be
sure we were both thinking about the ghost
house, and the strange light burning there.
We knew that the next day we would just
have to go and see for ourselves.

'Darkness comes early in those winter afternoons so we hurried through the forest, our hearts thumping at every bird calling, or branch snapping.'

Cra-ack! Primrose broke a stick over her knee and Dad nearly fell off his chair.

'Sorry,' she whispered. 'I was just adding sound effects.'

'Well, Lotus Blossom came with us that afternoon because she hates to miss out on anything and, besides, she said she would tell Ah Chu's father if we didn't let her come. Off she went running as fast as she could through the trees, far ahead of us, until we lost sight of her. But when we drew near the house, wasn't she leaning against a tree, panting, with a stitch in her side?

'I couldn't help laughing, but then Ah Chu said he had to stop too, because he had a pebble in his shoe and a sore foot. So I had to go up the path alone.

'I crept along slowly, over patches of damp green moss and through vines as thick as your fist. The house rose up before me, dark and full of shadows – it was like an animal in its lair, half hidden by the webbed shade of the trees.

'The latch lifted stiffly in my clammy hand and the door creaked open. "Come *on*!" I called over my shoulder and waited while Ah Chu and Lotus Blossom pushed each other up the path.

'I went first. It was black as a bat's cave inside, and smelled of mould. The further in we crept, the colder it grew. It was like walking into a grave. Something sticky and soft brushed against my face – *ugh!* – spiderwebs! When my eyes grew used to the dark I saw dust hanging in long strands from the rafters like ghostly grey ribbons.

'Then Lotus Blossom yelped suddenly as her foot went through a rotten floorboard. Wah! She nearly fell through the hole!

'"I thought something grabbed my ankle," she whispered.

'We clung together, listening to the silence. Even our breathing was loud. And then came the sound of a careful footstep from the room above our head. Ah Chu moaned.

'I stepped forward. "Is anybody there?"
I called.

'We heard a creak and a flurry of steps
and then *crash*! A great beam that had
been holding up the ceiling came hurtling
down, landing in a huge cloud of dust just
millimetres from my nose.

'We all reached the door at once, so for
a moment no one could get out. Ah Chu is
quite plump and almost filled the doorway
by himself but he and Lotus Blossom finally
pushed through and were down the path
like pellets out of a peashooter.

'I was about to follow, I can tell you – '

'Quick, quick, didn't you get out of there?' cried Jack.

'Well, I looked back, just for a second, and there, sprawled among the rubble of the fallen ceiling was a young woman. She lifted her head and groaned, so I raced back to her.

'"Are you hurt? Have you broken something?"

'She tried to stand up. "My ankle aches terribly," she whispered. "Oh, I knew the floor was rotten but I was so frightened. I thought you were someone sent by my cousin to take me back." She looked at me closely. "You're not, are you?"

'"No, I'm Tashi. I don't even know your cousin. Why are you so scared of him?"

'"When my mother and father died, my cousin Bu Li moved in. I always hated him – he's so much older than me and strong as an ox. He kept me locked in the house from morning till night, dyeing his silk. "You'll stay here and be my slave," he bellowed at me everyday, "until you tell me where you've hidden that emerald ring your mother left you." But I *wouldn't*! She told me before she died that I could use it to start a new life, and that is what I'm going to do."

'Ning Jing, for that was her name, pulled out a little bag hanging on a string around

512

her neck. I looked at the ring respectfully. It was the first emerald I'd ever seen; it was green like the moss outside, green like a cat's eyes in the dark.

'I noticed that Ning Jing was rubbing her ankle, so I said, "If your leg is hurting, why don't you stay here tonight and rest it?"

'Ning Jing nodded. "But I would need some food, Tashi. I have only this one fish cake left."

'"Tomorrow, straight after school, I'll bring you some more food from home. And then you can go on your way to the city."

'I had gone down the path only a little
way when Ah Chu and Lotus Blossom
popped out of some bushes to join me. We
stopped and sat for a while in the gathering
dusk as they peppered me with questions.
I told them all about Ning Jing and her
horrible cousin, and the emerald winking
like a cat's eye.

'"Thank the Gods of Long Life," sighed
Lotus Blossom. "I'm so glad that the ghost
was instead a Ning Jing!"

'They both promised that they would
come with me the next day with the food.

'Never was a day so long. As soon as school was over we raced home to collect the food. Ah Chu, who always took a great interest in eating, raided his mother's kitchen so well that he took an age to arrive, laden down with heavy baskets. And that is why, of course, he needed to sit down for a little rest on the way to the house while we went on ahead. And that's how he came to hear three men blundering about in the forest. He pricked up his ears like a fox when he heard the name Ning Jing.

'"Demon of a woman!" hissed the
man with the long thin beard. "That
Ning Jing – her mother was just like her.
Stubborn as a mule, tricky as a weasel.
Now which way did she go?"

'"There's no track here, no sign of her
at all."

'"Well if you'd been keeping your eyes
peeled instead of picking berries and stuffing
yourself, we wouldn't have lost her!"

'When Ah Chu had heard enough, he
stood up quietly and trickled off through
the trees.

'Bursting into the ghost house, he cried, "Three men are looking for Ning Jing in the forest."

'"Does one man have a long straggly beard?" asked Ning Jing. When Ah Chu told her, she buried her face in her hands. "I can't fight my cousin any more," she murmured through her fingers. "Oh what will I do, Tashi?"

'She looked straight at me then, and so did the others. I was just beginning to feel a little bit annoyed about people always asking me that question, when I had an idea.

'"Don't worry," I said to Ning Jing. "I've just thought of a plan. Ah Chu, you hurry back to where you saw the men. Tell them you've seen a young woman – a stranger in the forest – and that she's staying the night in an old empty house close by. Don't forget to mention that the house is haunted, and something dreadful once happened there."

'Then I told Lotus Blossom that her job was to follow Ah Chu, but to stay hidden from the men. "You've got to make sure that they're all thinking about ghosts by the time they reach this house."

'"How?" she asked.'

'By making ghostly noises!' cried Primrose suddenly. And she blew into the empty lemonade bottle on the garden table, making a low wheezy moan.

'That's it, my clever one!' cried Uncle Joe, squeezing her arm.

'You've got it!' agreed Tashi. 'I told Lotus Blossom I didn't know quite how she'd do it, but I knew she'd think of something.

'Well, Ah Chu quickly found the men in the forest as they were still standing there arguing.

'"Take us to the girl then, young fellow,"
said Cousin Bu Li, "and you'll have a little
something for your trouble." Turning to his
men he laughed, "And he'll get a fist in the
belly if he doesn't!"

'"Ooh, sir, I don't know if I can, sir,"
shuddered Ah Chu, making his hands
tremble. "That old house is haunted, ever
since two people were murdered there...
hung by their necks from the rafters!"

'"Haunted eh?" cousin Bu Li crowed.
"A fine place she's chosen to hide. Why,
she'll be glad to see us!"

'But Ah Chu noticed how pale he'd suddenly become.

'As they moved through the forest, the men grew quiet and jumpy. Suddenly they heard a low wailing and whistling like a whipping autumn wind. They stopped and peered around. But not a leaf moved in the stillness. Cousin Bu Li shivered. "Just a bird," he muttered, and moved on.

'A minute passed and now there came thin whooshing sounds like a hundred Samurai swords swiping at the air. Then a tremendous rattling noise of thunder made the men hold their hands to their ears, but the sky above them was clear and still as a piece of blue silk. A blood-curdling shriek – like a man having his throat cut from ear to ear – rushed the men through the forest, clutching onto each other's coats as they went.

'When they arrived at the path leading
to the house, Cousin Bu Li needed all his
promises of gold to urge the men on.

'"Ning Jing!" he shouted. "Come out at
once or you'll be sorry for the rest of your
short and miserable life!"

'There was no sound.

'The men edged into the house. They tasted the damp and the dust. They peered through the dark and the cobwebs. Then a deep shuddery wailing started and the men looked up to see a gaping black hole in the ceiling. The wail poured out of the darkness, filling the room like a river rushing into the sea.

'The two men turned and fled. Only cousin Bu Li stood his ground. Then the hairs on his neck stiffened.

'A light appeared, shining up into the
hole in the ceiling. It lit up a ghastly sight:
Ning Jing's headless body (he knew it was
Ning Jing because that was her dress with
the blue peacock on the front) and it was
swinging from an iron hook. A sob drew
his horrified gaze to an old chest in the
corner. Resting on the top of the chest was
... her head. The eyes in the head wept and

the mouth sobbed, "Oh, cousin, why did you drive me to my death?"

'Cousin Bu Li screamed and raced for the door. He bolted out of the house and ran so fast through the forest that he caught up with his men, passed them in a flash and left them far behind. He never went near that forest again for as long as he lived.

'Meanwhile, I wriggled out of Ning Jing's dress. You see, she was taller than me so the collar of her dress had covered my head. Ah Chu and Lotus Blossom, who had arrived back a few minutes before, helped me down and Ning Jing came out from behind the chest. She and her head skipped over to join us.

'"Oh, Tashi, that was wonderful. I'll never forget Cousin Bu Li's face when he looked up and saw – what he thought he saw!"

'Lotus Blossom was really cross. She said it was all very well for us, but she and Ah Chu hadn't heard about the plan and they'd had a nasty shock when they saw that swinging body and talking head. She shivered, saying the next time I had a clever idea I needn't bother to invite her along.

'"Well, who invited *you*?" I said, and she gave me a good pinch on the arm!

'Later, as we were enjoying a little snack of Ah Chu's food, I said to Ning Jing, "It was strange that you happened to be in the haunted house the very day we came."

'"Not so strange," said Ning Jing. "This house once belonged to my grandparents."

'"It did?" we cried. "What happened to them?"

'"What? What?"

'Ning Jing looked thoughtful. "I think that is something you should ask your parents."

Tashi sat back in his chair and grinned at Jack. 'And that was all we were ever able to find out.'

Jack said disgustedly, 'All grown-ups are the same, even the young ones. They never tell you anything.'

'Some do. Percussionists do,' argued Primrose. 'For example, I could tell you what Lotus Blossom used to make that whistling wind sound, the whipping Samuari swords, or the rattle like thunder.'

'Lotus Blossom probably told Tashi everything already,' protested Jack.

Tashi leaned forward and tapped his glass. 'No, she didn't, Jack. We had quite an argument, actually. I suppose she was still mad with me about the fright she got.' Tashi grinned into his lemonade. 'So, Primrose, how did she do it?'

'Well, come down into the garden and I'll show you. Now, let's see, what'll we need? Some small branches for whipping swords, I think, and pebbles to turn in a basin...'

But Jack and Tashi had already leapt up and dashed off across the lawn. Blood-curdling shrieks were heard as they disappeared amongst the trees.

The BIG RACE

Jack burst into the kitchen on Monday afternoon. 'Guess what happened at school today!'

'What?' cried Mum and Uncle Joe and Primrose, who stopped playing the conga drums to listen.

'Our class was in the assembly hall and we were doing a stomping dance when suddenly the stage floor fell in beneath us – '

'Batter the barramundi, was anyone hurt?' asked Uncle Joe.

'No,' replied Jack. 'Mrs Fitzpatrick leapt across the stage and saved Angus Figment who was right on the edge of this great ginormous hole. All the teachers gathered around and asked why wasn't there *ever* enough money for public schools and now they'd have to come up with *another* amazing idea for fund-raising to fix the floor, when Tashi stepped in – '

'Ho ho!' cried Dad, who'd just come in the door.

'Yes, and Tashi said, really quietly, you know how he is, that back in the old country he'd raised enough money to build a whole new school! When all the teachers asked "How?" Tashi said, "Well, it was like this – "'

Suddenly the kitchen was filled with a drum roll from the congas.

'Thank you, Primrose,' Mum said, holding her head. 'Perhaps we can leave that for the end of the story, dear.'

'Yes, let's,' agreed Primrose enthusiastically, 'or better, what about one super duper roll for the climax, and a soft, furry one for the finish?'

Mum nodded weakly. 'So, how did he do it, Jack?'

'Well, Tashi said everybody had known for ages that something would have to be done about their village school-house. The walls were all wrinkled and powdery with dry rot. Sometimes, the children could hear rustling sounds of white ants chewing at the wood.

'But it was an awful shock when suddenly one morning – luckily while everyone was outside – the large roof beam cracked and sagged. Just a minute later the whole building slowly collapsed, and the walls quietly fell in like buckling knees.'

'BOOF! BANG! BOOM!' went the drums.

'That's not the climax!' Mum protested. 'And didn't Jack say *quietly*?'

'Sorry,' grinned Primrose. 'I couldn't resist. That was an exclamation mark.'

'Well, anyway,' Jack went on, 'teacher Pang and the children stood open-mouthed at the sight of their school-house turned in one moment into a pile of dust and rubble.

'"What luck!" cried Ah Chu (who hated spelling tests). "No more school! Who's coming fishing?"

'"Not me," said Tashi. "Fishing is one thing, holidays are fun, but just think, to have no school at all, ever! It would be so boring."

'A meeting was called in the village to try to find a way of building a new school. A few people brought along some timber and roof tiles and put them in the middle of the square, but there was not nearly enough. No one had any money to spare, as usual.

'And then, two strangers wandered into the square. They were a mysterious-looking pair. Their clothes didn't quite fit and although their large hats hid most of their faces, Tashi thought he saw a pair of yellow tusks as one smiled. And there, as one stranger turned to point Tashi out to the other, Tashi saw a a tail poking out from under his coat! *Demons!*'

'Oh, *those* thick-headed thugs!' cried
Dad. 'Remember when they poured spiders
and snakes onto Tashi and he tricked them,
jumping into that old Dragon's Blood tree?'

'That's right,' said Jack. 'And that's why
Tashi was especially nervous now. Because
demons are always dangerous, but angry
demons with revenge in their hearts are
diabolical. And now what on earth were
they doing in his village square?

'The demons stood still as stones,
listening to all the talk and wild
suggestions. But finally one of them
boomed over all the voices.

"'No, no, what you must do is give us a race around the village! We'll race one of these children." He pointed a claw-finger at Tashi. "This little dillblot here, for instance. If he wins, we'll give you all the bricks and timber for a new school."

"'And if he loses?'"

"'If he loses, he'll be ours to do with as we will." And behind his hand he gave a laugh that cracked with demon spite.

'Oh NO!" cried the villagers and Tashi's family. Especially Tashi's family.

'But the Baron pushed through the crowd. "I think that's an excellent idea. Who would like to wager that Tashi wins?"

'The villagers were so eager to show their faith in Tashi that they all put their hands up before they realised they had been tricked into agreeing.

'"That's settled then," the Baron smiled nastily. The demons poked each other in the ribs and sniggered.

'*He's* the dillblot!' exploded Dad. 'That Baron could buy ten new school-houses for the village and not even dent his mountain of money. But would he? Never!'

'"First I'll go home and get my running shoes," Tashi told the villagers. "I'll be back here in one hour," he called over his shoulder.

'"Yes, so will we," hissed the demons and Tashi spied fat drops of drool sliding out from beneath their tusks.

'"Now where are they off to?" Tashi wondered as the family hurried home with him, begging him not to take part in the race.

'"Don't worry," Tashi comforted his mother. "I'll be quite safe with these on." And he pulled his magic dancing shoes out of the playbox in his room. "In just a few seconds I can leap across fields and forests with these."

'While he was putting on his shoes, he told the family that they were right to be suspicious about the strangers; they were the two demons who had tortured him with spiders and snakes once before. The family was horrified.

'"I thought there was something odd when they called you a dillblot," said Tashi's father. "What does that mean? I said to myself. Now I know – *demons* eh? They're famous for their poor vocabulary.

'Now Tashi, my boy, if you must do this, please test your shoes one last time to be sure that the magic is still working."

'Tashi agreed, and when they returned to the square all the villagers were waiting.

'The Wicked Baron raised his silk handkerchief. "Let the race begin!"

'The demons bared their tusks and their terrible eyes spun and blazed but at the

word "GO!" they shot off towards the
forest. Tashi had never seen anyone run
so fast.

'He waited until he felt his feet tingle and then he was away. In two minutes he had flashed past the astonished demons. He'd just reached the half-way mark when, as his foot touched the ground for the next step, a loop of tough vine closed around it and he was jerked upside down – he found himself swinging from a tall tree. Hadn't he stepped right into a Tashi-trap the demons had prepared for him? *Wah!*

'In the distance he could see the demons coming nearer. He struggled and rocked himself in anguish. He knew what they would do to him once they found him dangling helplessly from a tree. He jerked and twisted but the vine held him fast.

'And then he noticed that he *was* swinging a little. He arched his back and drew up his knees. His swings grew wider and higher. Just a little more and he was able to grab at a branch of a tree and pull himself up.

'There were crashing sounds down in the
bushes below and two hot and dripping
demons went panting past. Tashi sat astride
the branch and slipped the vine over his
ankle. Then he scrambled down to the
ground and set off again.

'He was just catching up with the
demons when he noticed that a mist was
rolling in through the trees. In an instant
it had thickened so much that the demons
ahead disappeared from sight. Tashi crept
on slowly, feeling his way, bumping into
trees. The fog was cold like a rain cloud,
and tasted stale and wet on his lips. He
kept blinking against the grey light but it
was as if a bandage had been pulled tight
over his eyes. He jumped when he heard
demon voices right beside him.

'"I can't believe you let the misty stuff out of the bottle in *front* of us instead of behind us! How did you reckon we'd find our way through this fog-thing?" shouted the first demon.

'"I didn't think," whined the second. "Couldn't you get it back in again?"

'"You can't put the fog-thing back into a bottle once it's out, you dillblot. Don't you know anything? At least Tashi won't be able to see either. We'll just have to sit here until it blows away. *Dill*blot."

'Tashi moved on carefully until his outstretched hands met a fence. He followed the fence around until he came to a familiar gatepost. "I know this gate!" he thought joyfully. "It belongs to Granny White Eyes."

'Granny White Eyes was so called because she could not see. Tashi and the other children of the village loved going to her house because she always had an interesting story to tell. Her brother had been a sailor and she'd accompanied him on many trips to exotic parts of the world.

'Tashi crawled up the garden path and knocked on the door. Lotus Blossom opened it.

'"Hello, Tashi. Oh, Granny White Eyes," she called into the darkness behind her, "it's Tashi come to see you!"

'An old woman came slowly to the door. "Tashi! Come in, what a lovely surprise. I wasn't expecting you today."

'"Well, this isn't exactly a visit," said Tashi. "It's like this," and he told her about the school-house and the demons and the race. "So," he finished, "I was wondering if you could lead me back to the village, Granny White Eyes."

"Of course I can," she laughed. "Mist or no mist, it makes no difference to me. I know every twist and turn in the path as well as my own kitchen. Come on."

'Tashi held on tight to her coat and they set off at a brisk pace through the blinding mist. Just before they reached the village, the fog cleared and Tashi stopped.

'"I can see now. Granny White Eyes, would you like to run like the wind with me on my magic shoes?"

'Her face creased into a wide smile. "Tashi, I would."

'Tashi knelt down and she climbed onto his shoulders. Granny screamed with delight as they sped over the ground.

'"Oh Tashi, I never thought I would fly through the air like this. It's wonderful."

'And didn't the village cheer as they zipped into the square? The people crowded around to hear what happened, nudging each other, trying to get close to Tashi. All except the Baron, of course. He went home.

'A bedraggled pair of demons finally found their way back to the village. They cursed and spat and "dillblotted" every-where, but by late afternoon they had unloaded a cartful of bricks and tiles in the village square.

'And that is why the new school-house has Tashi's name over the door, and why sometimes, on cold Monday mornings, (especially when there's a spelling test) his friend Ah Chu mutters, "What a clever Tashi!"

Mum sighed happily, then jumped as if she'd been shot.

'BOOF! BANG! BOOM!' went the drums.

'You were a bit late weren't you, Primrose?' said Mum crossly.

'A little,' admitted Primrose. 'I got caught up in the story and forgot.'

'Well, I haven't forgotten about that stage floor at your school, Jack,' said Dad, shaking his head. 'Has Tashi spotted any helpful demons in this suburb?'

'Not yet,' said Jack. 'But he's keeping his eye out.'

TASHI and the
ROYAL TOMB

When Jack and Tashi raced to the classroom one Monday morning, they screeched to a halt at the door. Was this the right room? The walls were splashed with paintings of pyramids, mummies lying in tombs, strange writing made up of little pictures. From the ceiling hung masks of jackals and fierce-looking kings, and the heavy air smelled sweet, musty like Jack's jumper drawer where Mum kept a bag of dried flowers.

'Look!' cried Jack, pointing to gold pots of incense burning on the windowsill. The smoke hung in a curtain above their heads, mysterious, exotic.

'In ancient Egypt,' Mrs Hall, the teacher, said grandly as she swept into the room, 'pharaohs were buried in mansions of eternity –'

'Pyramids!' called out Angus Figment.

'Magnificent tombs,' agreed Mrs Hall, 'with burial chambers inside, filled with everything the king might need for the afterlife –'

'And the pharaohs were made into mummies before they were buried,' put in Angus Figment. 'All their livers and stomachs and whatnot were pulled out first, and then the bodies were washed with palm wine and covered with salt, and the priests used to burn incense to take away the pong because all the gasses in the bodies must have stunk like crazy –'

'Thank you, Angus,' said Mrs Hall.

Angus looked around the room happily. He'd been mad on ancient Egypt since kindergarten, and knew all sorts of interesting details about burial methods and coffins. His mother had grown worried about him in Year 1 when he'd talked about embalming the cat, but the school counsellor told her Angus just had a terrific imagination, and soon he'd move on to other things. His mother (and the cat) were still waiting.

'The Viking kings used to have their slaves and warriors buried with them,' Jack put in.

'Back in my country,' Tashi said quietly, 'we had tombs, too.'

Mrs Hall looked at him. Her eyes were round with interest. 'Did you ever see any?' she asked. 'Were there any ancient burial sites near your village?'

'Oh yes,' said Tashi. 'A royal tomb was discovered, and I was nearly buried alive in it!'

'Like a Viking slave!' cried Jack. 'Tell us what happened!'

'Yes,' said Mrs Hall, eagerly pulling up her chair near Tashi. 'Please do.'

'Well,' said Tashi, 'it was like this. Big Uncle had decided he needed a new well. You see, he lived quite far from the village and his wife was tired of having to trudge all that way for their water. So he asked our family to help him dig a new well on his land. Of course, when I told the teacher that I had to miss a day at school, Ah Chu and Lotus Blossom wanted to come too and help.'

'And did they?' asked Jack enviously.

'Oh yes,' said Tashi. 'You know how
Lotus Blossom always gets her way. It was
fun at first. We poked about in the soil, the
men carried away buckets of stones and we
built castles with them – that is until Ah
Chu sat on them to eat his lunch.

'But the really thrilling part came when the men dug deeper and began to scoop out marvellous treasures, one after the other.

'Ah Chu found a bowl decorated with a golden dragon and then, right next to me, Lotus Blossom gently brushed the soil away from a beautiful bronze tiger.

'When Big Uncle himself uncovered a full-sized terracotta warrior, he told everybody to stop work.

"'This looks like an important find," he said. "We'll have to send word to the museum in the city and let the archaeologists come out and see it."

'Well, I was disappointed – I'd been hoping to find some exciting thing, too. I stepped over to look more closely at the warrior's battle robe and touch the scarf around his neck. I examined the warrior's face, and looked into his eyes. And then, it was spooky, everything around me went still for a moment, like when the wind stops in the middle of a storm. I could have sworn the warrior was holding my gaze. There was a circle of silence around us, with just our eyes speaking.

'"What?" I whispered, and perhaps I heard a faint sound. But now Big Uncle and my father bustled up to move everyone away from the digging and to fence it off with a rope.

'Just then, too late, the Baron came charging up the hill. "What's this I hear?" he shouted. "I don't believe it! A burial site found here on your land?"'

'Typical,' groaned Jack. 'That selfish money-bags ruins everything!'

'Yes,' agreed Tashi. 'He's got snake oil running in his veins instead of blood, I bet. Well, he blustered "Why wasn't I told?" and "This will be worth a fortune! To think, the number of times I've crossed this very field, never suspecting what was lying under my feet."'

'"Well, if it is a King's tomb," my father said gravely, "the government will claim it, you know. It won't be *our* fortune."

'The Baron looked at us with contempt. "These people simply have no idea," I heard him mutter to himself. No one was supposed to go near the dig until the experts from the city arrived, but the Baron jumped the rope fence and went in to take a good look around.

'Big Uncle gloomily went searching for another spot for his well and I *tried* to be patient. But I kept picturing the warrior's eyes and how he seemed to be speaking to me.

'On the fifth day, the team of archaeologists from the city arrived, and they were very excited. "This is a small tomb," Director Han explained, "but very important."

'Teacher Pang had brought the whole school up to hear the verdict and nearly everyone else in the village had followed. They crowded closer to listen.

'"We'll dig out this fallen soil and restore the walls and the brick floor of the tomb, and then we'll put all the warriors and their swords and things back just as they were," Director Han told them. "Unfortunately, as often happens, it seems the King's burial chamber itself has been robbed and destroyed, but there are still many precious things here in the outer tomb. I'm sure we will find more."

'Teacher Pang was excited. "Imagine, children, we'll be able to step into the tomb and go back two thousand years in time!"'

'How *marvellous*!' Mrs Hall couldn't help exclaiming, knocking Tashi's pencils off the desk. 'Do you know, when the Great Pyramid was opened up, hot air rushed out and an Egyptian archaeologist said, "I smelt incense...I smelt time... I smelt centuries...I smelt history itself!" *Imagine*, children, what that would be like!'

'I'm going to be an archaeologist when I grow up,' said Angus Figment.

'Well,' Tashi went on, 'several people from the village were given jobs digging, and I begged so hard that Director Han said I could be in charge of the teapot for the men's refreshments. This meant I often passed by my particular warrior, and always I felt the soldier's eyes were following me. But there was so much to see and do, with amazing finds each day: strange coins, weapons, buckles of gold, and even a terracotta chariot and horses.

'So it wasn't until the dig was almost finished that I felt the pull of the warrior's gaze. Glancing around to make sure no one was near, I knelt down and whispered to him, "What is it?"

'To my amazement, I heard a faint voice: "*Help me.*"

'"How? How can I help?"

'"My wife has just been unearthed over there by the chariot. I will never be able to rest until we are standing side by side."

'"That can't be," I told him, "there aren't any women in the tomb."

'"My wife dressed as a warrior. No one suspected she was a girl. We were part of the King's guard, and after I discovered her secret I fell in love with her and we married. Could you bring her over to my side so that we will have at least this short time together?"

'I thought for a moment. It was fine in the day when all the workers were talking and singing around me, but I must say I didn't like the idea of coming to the tomb at night. Still, I heard myself saying, "All right, I'll come back after dark when everyone has gone home."

'I was really glad there weren't any ghosts about when I arrived at the dig that night. I had great trouble finding the warrior-wife, even with the lantern I'd brought, and still more trouble lifting her into a wheelbarrow that luckily was lying about.

'I saw the warrior's eyes glow with joy.
I was just unloading her beside him when
I heard voices. So I ducked down behind
a rock and waited.

'The light of the lanterns lit the faces
of three men as they drew near. I gave a
little snort of disgust. Of course! Who else
would it be, to come robbing the tomb?
The beastly Baron. He and two of his men
were arguing. The men were saying that it
was unlucky and dangerous to steal from
a tomb.

'"Nonsense!" snapped the Baron. "No one has even seen these golden drinking vessels yet, so they won't even know they're missing."

'The men very reluctantly agreed to do what he wanted and they moved closer to where I was hiding. I jumped back and stumbled on a stone. Wah!

'In the blink of an eye the men seized me, and just as I'd said a moment before about *him*, the Baron growled, "Who else would it be? Why is this boy always under my feet plaguing me?"

'"What do you want us to do with him?" asked the fiercer of the two men.

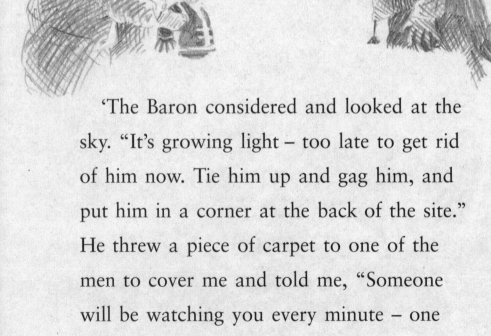

'The Baron considered and looked at the sky. "It's growing light – too late to get rid of him now. Tie him up and gag him, and put him in a corner at the back of the site." He threw a piece of carpet to one of the men to cover me and told me, "Someone will be watching you every minute – one movement and it will be your last."

'Then the men bundled me up and stashed me away as if I were nothing but a bag of old rags.

'"We'll have to leave the sack of golden goblets here for now," I heard one of them say. "Put them back under the warrior's feet. Now let's go. That Han always arrives at first light, and the diggers from the village won't be far behind."

'The morning crept on. The sun rose high in the sky, glaring down on me. My throat was so dry it felt as if it had been scraped with sandpaper. My tongue grew huge in my mouth. I could hardly breathe under the heavy dusty carpet and although I sneezed several times, no one heard because of the tight gag over my mouth. The cords around my wrist cut into my skin. And all the time, when I wasn't dreaming of water, oh beautiful water, I was thinking, just how were they going to "get rid of me"?

'My brain was hurting with trying to think of a way to raise help. And how could I think properly when there was this strange voice in my head telling me to "Push back, push back . . ." What did it mean? The voice was inside me, but it wasn't my own. It was as if someone else had got hold of my head and was telling me what to think.

'I could hear Lotus Blossom and Ah Chu, sometimes passing so close, calling my name, asking if anyone had seen Tashi.

'"It's not like Tashi to just disappear, leaving us with no tea," Big Uncle grumbled.

'By late afternoon, only the last two warriors needed to be moved back into place. The Baron's men made sure they were there on the spot. "It will be dark in a moment," they pointed out to Director Han. "Perhaps it would be better to start throwing the rubbish over the cliff and leave the two warriors till morning? We don't want to drop them because we can't see what we're doing."

'"Yes, I agree," Director Han nodded, "and we'll cover the rubbish up with soil before we go."

'"*Waaah!*" I screamed silently under my carpet. "They'll dump me over the cliff with the rubbish. If I don't die from the fall, I'll be buried alive under the soil." And all the time the strange voice in my head was growing stronger – it was shouting now, "Push *back*!" I could no longer ignore it. I focussed my mind on the voice. And as I listened, a picture came into my mind. I saw the eyes of my warrior – they were wide and staring at a small ledge jutting out of the wall behind me. "*Push back*," he said to me urgently.

'I pushed back into the wall of the tomb.
Something moved behind me. A door was
opening in the thick stone wall. There was
nothing to hang onto and I fell backwards
down a flight of steps into the darkness
of a small room.

'By the dim light coming from the open door above, I could see that I had fallen down into the King's secret burial chamber. I saw an open coffin, and inside lay a skeleton in a magnificent jade burial suit. My heart leapt, but there was no time to look further. I glanced around quickly. There were two crossed swords at the foot of the coffin. I rolled myself over to one, and pushed it up against the edge of the coffin with my shoulder. Then I began to saw at the cords around my wrists. The sword was as sharp as it must have been two thousand years ago.

'In a moment my arms were free. Quickly I released my ankles and pulled away my gag. The relief! But there was no time to waste. I could hear footsteps running towards me.

'The Baron's men were at the doorway. I saw in horror that they were starting to close the door on me – they wanted to seal me in the tomb with the dead King! A bolt of fear sent me hurtling up the stairs like lightning, yelling and screaming, "Ai-eee! Help! Down here!"

'"That's Tashi calling!" I heard Lotus Blossom shouting, "Over here, everyone!"

'They came bursting through the doorway, ducking around the Baron's men, who suddenly remembered their wives wanted them somewhere else. The Baron was close behind them but when he heard Big Uncle and Director Han hurrying down after him, he called out, "So this is where you have been, Tashi. We were looking everywhere for you."

'I gave the Baron a long hard stare.'

'I would have given him a great hard kick!' exploded Jack.

'I would have cut out his organs and put them in a canopic jar!' cried Angus Figment.

'What's a canopic jar?' asked Jack.

'The thing was,' Tashi went on, 'I had no real proof that the Baron had been stealing from the tomb and meant to kill me. There was nothing concrete, really, so when I finally answered him, I said, "Yes, this is where I've been," and raising my voice so that everyone could hear, "and before I found the King's tomb, I came across a big sack of golden goblets. You'll find it over there, buried by the last two warriors."

'The Baron's jaw dropped. "What a clever Tashi," he said quietly.

'But Director Han paid no attention to them. He was skipping about the secret tomb, crooning with delight over the richly decorated burial chamber and the jade suit.'

'So it was you, Tashi, who made the most important find,' crowed Jack. 'Just think, the *King's* tomb.'

'Well,' said Tashi modestly, 'the inner tomb did make the find complete. Director Han was given a promotion and he presented our family with jobs and free passes to the tomb for the rest of our lives. My two warriors still stand side by side and every time I visit them, their eyes seem to glow with happiness.'

There was silence in the classroom for a moment as everyone tried to imagine the tomb, and the treasures, and warrior love beyond the grave.

'Did they used to mummify kings in your country, Tashi?' asked Angus Figment.

'No,' replied Tashi. 'They buried them in these splendid tombs.'

'Oh,' said Angus thoughtfully. 'Because in Egypt, well, they used to mummify all sorts of things. Even cats. Of course when the cats were dug up in my great-grandfather's time, most of them were made into garden fertiliser.'

'Thank you, Angus,' said Mrs Hall, 'and now, if you can manage not to turn our stomachs any further, perhaps you would like to share with us some more of your interesting facts about the ancient people of Egypt.'

Angus did like, and his information about Egyptian medicines and the hooks used for removing brains from mummies was enjoyed by all – well, everyone except Alex Pickle, who was sick into the potplant in the corner.

The BOOK of SPELLS

'What are you going to do for your
project on ancient Egypt?' Dad asked Jack
one afternoon.

'I don't know yet,' said Jack, scratching
his head. 'Angus Figment is writing a Book
of the Dead.'

'Good heavens,' said Mum, coming into
the room. 'What does his mother say
about that?'

'She thinks it's fascinating, actually,'
said Jack. 'See, the Egyptians used to write
magic spells on sheets of papyrus, and put
them inside the tombs with the mummies.
That way, people's afterlife was sure to
be happy and safe.'

'How can you be safe when you're dead?' asked Dad.

Jack sighed. 'The Egyptians believed in the *afterlife*, Dad. It's, like, you go on existing somewhere else.'

'Hmm,' frowned Dad. 'I don't know whether the newsagency sells papyrus.'

Mum groaned. 'So what's Tashi doing, Jack?'

Jack leaned forward on his chair. 'Well, he hasn't decided yet either, but when Angus told him about his Book, Tashi went all serious and silent.'

'Oh ho,' said Dad, drawing up his chair. 'I bet Tashi knows a thing or two about magic spells. Are you going to tell us a story by any chance?'

'I might,' said Jack. 'You see, in Tashi's village the most precious possession of all was the Book of Spells. But you might say it was a book of *life*, because it was filled with the most marvellous cures for all kinds of diseases and problems. The Book had to be guarded day and night. But one dreadful day, it disappeared.'

'Who would take it?' asked Dad. 'A bandit? A *demon*?'

'Well, it was like this. One morning
Tashi's mother gave him a pot of soup
to take up to Wise-as-an-Owl, who hadn't
been very well lately. Tashi knocked at
the door, and waited.

'"Come in, Tashi," called Wise-as-an-
Owl from behind the door. He somehow
always knew when Tashi was there.

'When Tashi stepped into the room,
he saw someone else sitting with his
old friend.

'"Ah, Tashi," Wise-as-an-Owl beamed, "see who has come from the city to visit me! My son and I have decided that it's high time he began his study of plants and medicines if he is to take up the work of the Keeper of the Book after me." The old man's eyes twinkled. "My Son with Much-to-Learn will stay with me until he finds a house where he and his family can live."

'Tashi bowed and put his pot on the table. He politely asked Much-to-Learn about his home in the city, and his children, but all the while he couldn't help looking at the Book that lay on the desk before him. It was richly bound in red leather, with ancient glowing letters on the cover. Tashi fingered the fine brass clasp and lock that could only be opened by the golden key Wise-as-an-Owl wore around his neck.

'Tashi couldn't remember a time when the Book was not part of his life. Over the years, he'd watched while his friend had consulted it for cures of illness, pestilence and heartache. Tashi knew whole passages by heart. But later, on the way home, he felt glad that, now Wise-as-an-Owl was growing frail, his son should have come to study and work with him.

'Tashi was curious to see how Much-to-Learn was getting on with his study, but the next week, when he called, a terrible sight met his eyes.

'Wise-as-an-Owl was sitting rocking backwards and forwards in his chair, tearing his thin white hair while his son tried to calm him.

'"What is it? What has happened?" cried Tashi.

'"Someone has stolen the Book," groaned Wise-as-an-Owl. "We have

searched the house a dozen times. It's just
disappeared. Yesterday we were studying
the cure for warts and wax-in-the-ear
when there was a shuffling noise outside.
We went to investigate and when we came
back, the Book – which I had left right
here on the desk – was gone!"

'He slumped down on his stool. "I have
spent a lifetime studying it, Tashi, but
there are always new cures to find in the

Book, new spells to help poor souls –
whatever will we do?"

'Tashi came close and put his hand
on the old man's shoulder. "I will find
the Book for you, Wise-as-an-Owl,"
he promised.

'As Tashi was walking home, he was
so deep in thought he didn't hear Lotus
Blossom and Ah Chu running up behind
him until they were almost on top of him.
He shoved them off, saying gruffly, "I can't
come and play now!"

'Lotus Blossom shoved him back so hard that Tashi stumbled. "Why so high and mighty, Lord Tashi?"

'"Leave him alone," said Ah Chu. "You can see there's something wrong with Tashi if you'd just bother to look. He probably hasn't had his lunch yet and his stomach is growling. Mine is."

'Tashi couldn't help smiling then, and he quickly told them the trouble.

'"Oh that's the worst thing I ever heard!" cried Lotus Blossom. "We'll help you."

'"Good," said Tashi. He was relieved. "We can split up and ask all through the village if anyone has seen a stranger wandering about. Meet me back at my place after lunch."

'As Lotus Blossom turned to go, she whispered, "Sorry."

'"You can't help having sharp elbows," said Tashi.

'Lotus Blossom grinned and ran off.

'Neither Tashi nor Ah Chu could find word of anyone strange about the village, but Lotus Blossom did learn something. She had been out to see Granny White Eyes, who always knew what was going on in the village. And sure enough, Granny told Lotus Blossom the bad news.

603

'"Tashi's Uncle Tiki Pu is back. The cobbler, Not Yet, saw him on the road passing Wise-as-an-Owl's house."

'"Oh, no!" moaned Tashi. "That Tiki Pu would sell his own grandmother for a jar of honey."

'But Lotus Blossom was looking at him steadily. "Will you be going after him, Tashi?"

'When Tashi nodded, she nudged Ah Chu. "Then we'll be coming with you. After all, the Book is precious to the whole valley."

'"Thank you," said Tashi, a bit
awkwardly. "We'd better start out right
away. He'll be heading back to the city
I should think."

'Ah Chu cleared his throat. "Um, I'll just
hurry home and get some food together.
It's going to be a long afternoon and I
smelt something really good being cooked
this morning. Be back in ten minutes."

'Tashi couldn't carry both Lotus Blossom
and Ah Chu on his magic shoes, so the
three friends shared out Ah Chu's baskets
and set off on foot.

'They walked quickly but it was almost
dinner time before they came across Tiki
Pu standing on the river bank. He was
deep in conversation with one of the river
pirates, and he seemed very busy winking
and grinning.

'Tashi sprang forward but, to his surprise, it was the pirate who handed Tiki Pu a bulky parcel and pocketed a bag of coins in return. Whatever he was up to, Tiki Pu wasn't selling the Book of Spells.

'They waited until Tiki Pu was alone and then Tashi ran after him and told him about the missing Book.

'"Did you see anything suspicious as you passed Wise-as-an-Owl's house this morning, Uncle?"

'Tiki Pu looked thoughtful and stroked his nose. "What will you give me if I tell you?"

'"Poor Tashi," Lotus Blossom whispered loudly to Ah Chu, "having an uncle like Tiki Pu."

'Tiki Pu coughed and said loudly, "Ha ha, can't you take a joke, Tashi? Where's the fun if we can't have a joke amongst friends? Yes, well, the only person I saw on the road was...the Baron."

'"Thank you, Uncle." Tashi swung round to his friends. "Let's go. I should have guessed. If something precious is missing, who needs suspicious strangers when we have our very own Baron at home?"

'"You thought *I'd* taken it, didn't you?" Tiki Pu said as they turned to go.

'Tashi smiled guiltily as he waved goodbye, but Tiki Pu just shrugged.

'"He's probably annoyed he didn't think of stealing it himself," Lotus Blossom sniffed.

'They were lucky enough to get a lift back to the village with a passing boat, sharing Ah Chu's delicious sticky-rice cakes and lychees with the boatman.

'"It will be quite dark before we get back to the Baron's house," Lotus Blossom said presently. They thought about this for a moment.

'Tashi nodded. "Yes, and I just hope there won't be any white tigers in his cellar this time."

'Ah Chu choked on his rice cake.

'They crept cautiously through the Baron's gardens, flinching at shadows. Ah Chu held Lotus Blossom's hand – so that she wouldn't be frightened.

'They reached the Baron's window and peered in.

'There he was, sitting at his great carved table. And what do you think he had before him? The red leather Book of Spells. The brass clasp had been broken with a poker, which lay on the table beside him, and now the Baron took a deep breath and opened the Book.

'The three friends watched his face.
His jaw dropped. He turned the page.
A vein began to swell on his forehead.
The Baron's thick finger flipped page after
page and his rage mounted, until at last he
flung the Book on the floor and jumped
on it. Tashi slid over the windowsill and
stepped into the room.

'"Good evening, Baron. You look
upset."

'"The pages are all blank!" spluttered
the Baron. "There isn't a single word in
the whole Book."

'"No," said Tashi. "That's because you didn't open it with the golden key that Wise-as-an-Owl wears around his neck. If the Book is opened without it, the words fade right off the pages."

'The Baron gaped at Tashi and sank down heavily onto his chair.

'"How could you?" Tashi burst out angrily. "How could you steal such a precious thing that is used to help all the village?"

613

'"Why shouldn't I?" shouted the Baron. "Why should Wise-as-an-Owl have it, just because his father had it before him? He never made a penny out of it; he doesn't deserve it."

'Tashi looked at him in wonder. It was no use talking to such a man. He picked up the Book but the Baron grabbed it out of his hands.

'"If I can't use it," shouted the Baron, "nobody will. It can burn!" And he ran to the fire.

'Tashi jumped after him, grabbing his arms, trying to reach the Book, but the Baron held it above his head.

'"You'd better let me take it back quickly, Baron," said Tashi, trying to stop the quiver in his voice. "My friends have gone up to the village to tell everyone that the Book has been found."

'Lotus Blossom and Ah Chu, who'd been peeping over the windowsill, quickly ducked their heads down.

'"We don't want a lot of people hearing that you had *stolen* it," Tashi said softly.

'The Baron lowered his arms. He thought about that. "What about the clasp? It's broken."

'"I'll take it to Not Yet. He mends locks as well as shoes these days and, if you pay him well, he might break the habit of a lifetime and do it straightaway."

'In no time at all, the Baron had agreed, Not Yet had set to work, and the Book was back in Wise-as-an-Owl's trembling hands.

'Tashi and his friends watched anxiously as he slipped his key into the brass lock and turned it. The Book fell open. White, blank pages . . . at first. Then slowly, as they watched, faint markings appeared; a moment more and clear black letters marched boldly up and down the pages.

'The knowledge was back where it belonged.'

'Ah,' sighed Mum with satisfaction.

'What beats me though,' said Dad, pounding his knee, 'is how that crook of a Baron stays out of jail!'

Jack smiled. 'Don't worry, Dad. I'm sure there'll be justice in the *afterlife*.'

Dad snorted and went to find a pillow to punch.

TASHI, LOST
in the CITY

'This lift is stuck,' said Jack. He pushed
the ground floor button again. Nothing
happened. Sweat prickled his forehead.

Tashi put his hand on Jack's shoulder.
'Don't worry, we're in a big mall.
Someone will find us soon. All we have to
do is sit and wait.'

Jack could hear his heart thumping. 'I don't like being shut in small places. Especially when no one knows where we are,' he added quietly.

Tashi sat on the floor and pulled Jack after him.

'And I'm *busting*,' whispered Jack.

'Take five deep breaths,' said Tashi, 'and think about something else.'

Jack looked at the great steel doors. 'I wish I'd gone to the toilet *before* we went to see the skateboards. If only we had a piece of ghost cake we could pass right through those doors, easy peasy –'

'You know,' said Tashi, stretching out his legs, 'this reminds me of a time I was trapped in a dark cellar by a man with a glass eye and a dagger in his belt.'

Jack sat up straight. 'Did the eye look real?'

'No,' Tashi shook his head. 'It was more like a marble, with a black pupil painted on like a bullseye. But it was the other eye that scared me. Cold and mean and deadly, like a shark's.'

'Gosh,' said Jack. 'How did you escape?'
'Well, it was like this,' Tashi began. 'It was the year our village had a really good harvest. To celebrate, Grandma decided to take me to the city with her to help buy the family's New Year presents. Little Aunt said we could borrow her cart and horse, Plodalong.'

'Was the city a long way from your
village?'

'Oh yes,' nodded Tashi. 'We had to
set out at first light. By late morning we
were in the teeming cobbled streets of the
city. Oh Jack, I'd never seen anything so

wonderful. My head swivelled from side
to side. I didn't know where to look first.
There were stalls of candied apples and
roasted ears of corn and silvery fish in
tanks.'

'I hardly had time to glimpse the curio shops and the bookstalls before we had to duck our heads under silk banners announcing family weddings and births. And the *noise* – everything was so much louder than in my village.'

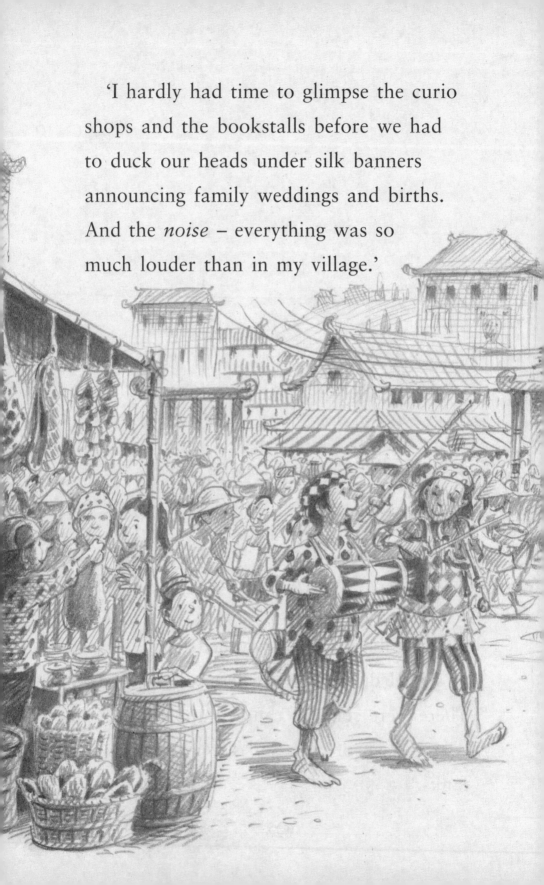

'Street hawkers were calling out their medicines, and stallholders beckoned us to see their toys. And all the time the air thrummed with violins and the drums of street musicians.'

'Is this where you met the man with the glass eye?'

'Not yet,' said Tashi. 'First we had to leave the horse and cart with an old friend of Grandfather's, and then we dived into the crowd.

'"We'll have to be careful, Tashi," said Grandma, "or our money will drip from our hands like water."

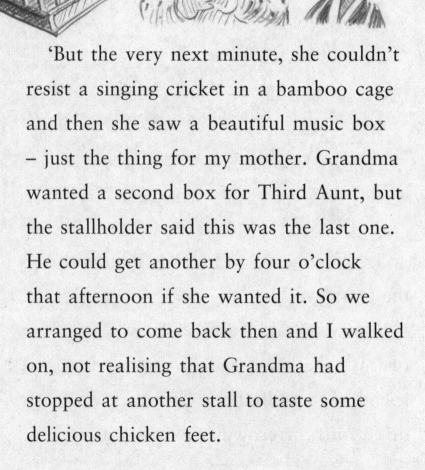

'But the very next minute, she couldn't resist a singing cricket in a bamboo cage and then she saw a beautiful music box – just the thing for my mother. Grandma wanted a second box for Third Aunt, but the stallholder said this was the last one. He could get another by four o'clock that afternoon if she wanted it. So we arranged to come back then and I walked on, not realising that Grandma had stopped at another stall to taste some delicious chicken feet.

'I was looking at the hills above the city – the sun was striking the white walls of the palace at the top – and the light was almost blinding. I turned to ask Grandma if this was the famous Palace of Expanding Joyfulness, or was it the Pavilion of Perfect Harmony? But she was no longer beside me.

'"Grandma!" I called. "GRANDMA!"

'Acrobats moved on to the road, and strangers rushed past, pushing and shouting. But there was no Grandma. I hurried back to the place I'd last seen her. Still no sign of her. I raced up and down the street looking in doorways and behind stalls. I couldn't breathe properly. How quickly everything changed from excitement one minute to being lost and alone the next.'

'Yes!' murmured Jack. 'I know what you mean.'

'Well, as I made my way through the press of people, I heard a commotion and cries of "Mad dog! Mad dog!" Suddenly, as the crowd parted, I saw a big brown dog, foam frothing from its mouth. People were running in all directions like beads scattered on a path, but the dog was chasing a little girl, attracted by her piercing screams. Quick! What to do?

'Through the open gate of a courtyard nearby I spied a sheet hanging on a rail. I ran in and whipped it off.

630

'The dog was nearly upon the girl,
but it stopped when I drew near with
my arms wide open, hidden by the sheet.
I flung the sheet over the dog, bundled it
up and popped a clothes basket over it.

'The girl's mother was thanking me
when the stalls around us began to shake.
The road shuddered beneath our feet
like something alive. The house with the
clothesline collapsed, and the one next
to it. People were screaming again. And
then, as quickly as it had started, the
trembling stopped. The world was still,
as if holding its breath. There was
complete silence – until we were all
startled by cries coming from the collapsed
houses. People were buried alive in there!
Some folk rushed over and pulled beams
and bricks away. Just when everyone
thought it was safe, I heard a faint cry
from the back of the second house. I lifted
a broken screen and saw the head of a
man poking out from a mound of rubble.
A large rat was investigating his nose.

'A wall beside him looked as if it might fall, but I threw a brick at the rat and called for help. As I worked at the wood and bricks, I looked into the man's baleful eyes –'

'Aha!' cried Jack. 'Bullseye!'

'Yes. One eye was darting angrily all around but the other was fixed straight ahead. A shiver ran through me. Not a word passed between us but I thought, "This is a bad man."

'A few people heard my cries and
came to help. When the man was able
to scramble out of the rubble, he dusted
himself off and said curtly, "I suppose
you want a reward."

'I stiffened. "I don't need one."

'"Just as well," the man snapped, and
without another word, he strode off
through the crowds.

'My legs were trembling. "Wah!" I thought, "I've had enough of this city. If only I could find Grandma and go home."

'Just then a kindly looking stranger stopped beside me and I asked if he had noticed a little old lady carrying a bamboo cage. The gentleman clapped his hands. "Yes, I have. She just went around the corner here." And he led me into an alley.

'The alley was empty and dark. A smell of old garbage and sour wine seeped from the shadows between the buildings. "Tch," said the man, "she must have gone into Beggars Lane. We'll soon find her."

'He took me by the arm and pulled me along to a dilapidated house. *Lucky Chance Hotel* was painted over the door in peeling letters. I was really feeling uneasy about this man and was trying to think of a polite way to leave when he tightened his grip on me. His long sharp fingernails dug into my wrist. He hustled me into the house and shoved me downstairs into a cellar. I scrambled back to the door, too late. The lock clicked. "Why do I ever leave home without a ghost cake?" I groaned.

'I closed my eyes for a moment to get used to the dark. When I opened them, I saw some straw matting, a broken chair and a boy cowering in the corner. "Who is that man?" I asked the tearful boy. "What does he want with us?"

"'He's going to sell us to work in the salt mines," sniffed the boy, "and that'll be the end of us. My father worked there once, before he escaped. He said children were lucky to last a year."

'I shuddered. We told each other our
names, and we wandered over to the
barred window. Standing on tiptoe, we
could see a bit of footpath. I broke the
glass with my shoe and together we
called, "Help! Help!" but the alley was
deserted. No one came by and our throats
grew hoarse. Wang slumped to the floor
and began to cry again in disappointment.
I put my hands over my ears. "Be quiet
now, Wang. I'm thinking."

'Wang bit his lip. "Are you thinking of
a way to escape? Look around, you can
see – there isn't any way."

'"There's always a way if you stay calm and think hard enough," I told him firmly.

'Wang kept up a hopeful silence for another few minutes before he confided, "I'm glad you are here, Tashi. It's better with two, isn't it?"

'I smiled and nodded but I couldn't agree. I thought it was better being alone and lost in the streets than here, waiting to work in the salt mines.

'I stood holding the window bars in the comforting warmth of the sun and noticed how it sparkled on the pieces of broken glass. Yes! Maybe that would work. I tore off a piece of peeling wallpaper and held a shard of glass over it.

'Wang looked on curiously. "What are you doing?"

'"Come and see."

'I held the glass still and let the sun concentrate on one small spot. Sure enough, after a minute, the paper began to brown and smoke. A tiny flame appeared and we blew gently as I dropped bits of matting on it. Gradually I added splinters, then pieces of broken chair until there was a good blaze going and the walls were smouldering.

'Using Wang's jacket, I fanned the smoke out through the broken window. The house remained silent. My heart began to thud. Smoke was thickening all around us. I told Wang to pull his shirt up over his nose and mouth. My eyes were streaming and every time I breathed, my throat stung. Oh, maybe I'd done the worst thing – maybe we'd finish up being smoked like pieces of pork! Then we heard shouts and the sound of running footsteps.

'"Quick!" I grabbed Wang's arm. "Come over here against the wall."

'We were just in time. The door burst open and two men ran in and began to beat the flames with their coats. They didn't see us behind the door. Wang and I slipped out while their backs were turned.

'We raced up the stairs to the open
front door – to freedom. But as we were
about to leap out into the blue daylight,
the doorway darkened. It was blocked
by an enormous man standing there with
folded arms.

'As I gazed up into the man's cold hard face, I saw only one eye looking back at me.'

'The man you dug out of the rubble!' cried Jack.

Tashi nodded. 'The muscles in his arms were hard as steel. His hand reached down to his belt and pulled out a silver dagger. I forced my gaze away from the dagger and stared straight up into his fierce snapping eye. I clenched my jaw and said quietly, "Now, sir, I *do* need my reward."

'We glared at each other for a long moment. Wang was whimpering behind me. I saw the man's eye glitter. And then he stepped aside and motioned for us to pass.

'"My debt is paid," he said.

'We raced past him and out into the cool fresh air, never stopping until we were back amongst the bustling crowds.

'Wang thanked me again and again and
wanted me to come home with him, but
I heard the clock striking the hours. Four
o'clock. I looked about. Yes, there was
the clock tower, and now I remembered –
the music box stall was close by it.
I quickly told Wang that my grandmother
would be waiting for me, and ran off.

'Keeping the tall tower in sight, I wove my way through the streets, and sure enough, I found Grandma beside the stall, peering anxiously at the passing people.

'"Oh, there you are at last, Tashi! Fancy leaving me to carry these heavy parcels by myself."

'"Sorry, Grandma," I said. I took her bags and hugged her. "I was held up."'

The boys sat in the quiet of the lift and then Jack said, 'I know how Wang felt, though.'

'What do you mean?'

'Well, what he said about being together. When you're stuck in a tight spot, it seems much less scary with two of you.'

Tashi nodded and together they looked at the great steel doors.

'But I'm still busting,' Jack confided. 'Do you need to go?'

'No,' Tashi shook his head. 'My mother says I'm like a camel. I can hold on practically forever. But see, there's a trick to it – you just have to train your mind and imagine you are somewhere completely different. For instance, I was still far away, thinking of what happened after our trip to the city.'

'You and Grandma went home and
had a big delicious dinner I suppose,'
said Jack. 'And before you went to bed,'
he added, a bit desperately, 'you went
to the toilet in peace.'

'Not exactly,' said Tashi. 'See it was
like this…'

ON the WAY HOME

'Just a minute, did you hear something?'
Jack asked. 'Hold your breath.'

The two boys sat in the lift, listening.

'Nothing,' sighed Jack, cracking his
knuckles. 'We'll be trapped here forever.'

'No, it won't be long now,' said Tashi.
'I can feel it in my bones.'

'Which ones?'

'My left leg. It sort of tingles, deep in
my kneebone, when something's about
to happen.'

'Did it tingle like that on the way home
from the city?'

'Oh yes,' said Tashi, 'but not until dark fell. You see, while I was being kidnapped, Grandma had been very busy shopping. "Oh Tashi," she cried. "This city is such a treasure chest!" She was tired – there was city dust caked into her frown lines – but her eyes were gleaming with happiness.

'"We should be starting for home now, Grandma," I said, noticing how low the sun sat in the sky. "You know the road through the forest is lonely and famous for brigands."

'"Yes, yes," she agreed, "but just look at these presents, quick, before we go."

'You should have seen the things Grandma had bought. She'd found a wonderful shop with musical instruments and, with the money she had been saving just for me, she'd bought a silver flute. We kept opening and reopening our parcels,

forgetting about the time, listening to the
music boxes and trying out the flute, and
the ivory combs in Grandma's hair.

'At last, seeing our shadows long on
the ground, we loaded our shopping into
the cart and climbed in after it. Grandma
passed me a flaky bun and clicked her
tongue at Plodalong who snorted and
slowly moved off.

'The smells and sounds of the city faded, and soon there was only the noise of our wheels creaking over the dirt. We went quite a way in silence, and I watched the trees turning inky-black against the sky. Grandma flicked for Plodalong to quicken his pace, and he did, for a few steps.

'"He's not as frisky as he used to be," said Grandma, and I smiled at the thought of Plodalong ever being frisky. It seemed the effort was too much for him because he stumbled and slowed down even more.

'"We'll never get home before dark," Grandma fretted. "Perhaps we should stay the night at the inn up ahead."

'The inn didn't look very inviting. An unkempt fellow with his shirt buttoned up the wrong way opened the door, and I was even less happy to go in. The man looked like a brigand, but Grandma was already asking for two beds for the night. The brigand (I was quite right) waved us into a large room with some bare tables and a few hard chairs.

'"Make yourselves comfortable, please do," he grinned. "Some tea for our guests, Fearless," he growled to one of his companions.

'"Right away, Ferocious," the other replied.

'"Those are unusual names, sir," remarked Grandma mildly.

'"They are well-earned, madam," smirked Ferocious.

'"And you, sir, what is your name?" Grandma turned to the third man who slouched in the doorway, drinking something dark from a bottle.

'"He hasn't earned his name yet," growled Fearless. "We call him No Name."

'"I see." Grandma introduced herself as she sat down on one of the hard chairs. But the two brigands weren't paying any attention. They were discussing the ransom money they were going to ask for us, their guests!

'"Excuse me," said Grandma, "we couldn't help overhearing. I can't believe you would be so cruel to us. We have never done you any harm."

'The brigands looked surprised and shuffled their feet.

'"In any case," Grandma went on, "I'm afraid you'll not find anyone in our village with the money to pay a ransom for Tashi and me." And when we told them the name of our village, they agreed that no one there ever had two coins to rub together.

'But Ferocious had pricked up his ears at my name. He stared at me, nodding slightly, and as he stroked his hairy chin I saw mushed bits of noodle and prawn fall from his whiskers. I tried not to breathe in his smell of old swamp water. "There's one person in your village with money," he said, his eyes sharpening. "And from what I hear, he would pay a tidy sum to be rid of you, young Tashi."

'I breathed out in such a burst of annoyance that I nearly choked. The Baron! How I hated that man. He was so greedy and rich, of course his fame

would have spread amongst villains like
Ferocious: cruel, heartless men, with only
money on their minds. I closed my eyes
for a moment and thought. "Ah, so,"
I said, yawning a bit, giving myself time,
"it seems you have not also heard that
I have magic powers? It's well known that
if anyone tries to hurt me, my touch can
turn them to stone."

'The men jeered uneasily.

'"Very well," I said, "try me."

'Ferocious and Fearless began to mutter
together in a huddle. Still clutching his
wine bottle, No Name made his way
across the room towards them. He swayed
on his feet, stopping now and then to get
his balance.

'As I peered into the smoky candlelight,
I noticed how different he seemed from
the other two – with his old silk waistcoat
and his beard braided into two dusty
plaits. He caught my eye and gave a
nervous shiver, like an animal whose fur
has been stroked the wrong way.

'"Come here and pay *attention*,"
Ferocious spat at him. There was a
little more muttering and then Ferocious
clapped Fearless on the back. "*I* know,"
he said in a loud whisper. "There's more
than one way to skin a cat," and with
a quick glance at me, "or a boy." He
pulled Fearless aside. "We'll wait till he's
asleep and then No Name can creep into
his room and finish him off in the usual
way."

'*The usual way?* I didn't like the sound
of that. "Why me?" complained No Name,
pulling frantically at his plaited beard.

'So I was ready when the door opened
quietly that night. I was hiding behind
a cupboard and watched grimly while
No Name tip-toed (*he* didn't want to be
turned to stone) into the room. He wasn't
swaying on his feet now, but I saw his
hands tremble as he pulled a pistol from

his belt and pointed it at the bump in the
bed clothes. "The Gods forgive me,"
he moaned as he pulled the trigger.

'BANG! Had he missed? No Name
edged further into the room. No he hadn't:
a red stain was seeping through the sheets.
Mumbling to himself he staggered out of
the room, leaving me to clean up the ripe
tomatoes I had thoughtfully settled on the
pillow and under the bedclothes.

'The next morning I bounced into the kitchen. "Mmn, that smells good."

'The brigands dropped their chopsticks and stared. They hurried to fill my bowl with rice porridge before they dragged No Name away into the far corner. "I did, I *did*," I heard him protesting.

'"Well, we'll have to do something quickly," Ferocious hissed. "Blackheart is coming tomorrow and he won't want to find unfinished business here." Ferocious was twisting his shirt buttons. No Name grew so pale he looked as if he might pass out.

'In the early evening when the robbers were preparing dinner, Fearless whispered to No Name, "Have you got it?" No Name nodded and slipped a paper cone into his hand. I was on my guard at once.

'Fearless poured the soup into the bowls and sure enough, I saw that some powder was tipped into mine. I jumped up and made a fuss about helping Grandma to her chair and collecting her soup, and in the confusion I swapped Ferocious's bowl with mine.

'That night I smiled to myself as I heard groans and curses ("You could have killed me!") from the brigands' room. I wasn't surprised when, just after dawn, I learned that Ferocious was feeling poorly and didn't want breakfast.

'All morning Fearless and No Name grew more and more agitated as they waited for Blackheart to arrive. There were three wine bottles lined up on the great table and they were nearly empty. No Name paced up and down, tapping the bottles with his chopsticks, making a tune.

'"If you don't stop that," Fearless finally shouted, "I'll cut off your piddling plaits and stuff them up your noseholes!"

'No Name sank onto a chair. He rocked himself and stared at the floor. When Ferocious came in, holding his stomach, I moved closer to hear snatches of their conversation.

'"Everything hurts," Ferocious groaned, and closed his eyes.

'"But what will Blackheart say about the boy?" whined Fearless. "You know what he does to people who…"

'"How were *we* to know?"

'"A boy who turns people to *stone*…"

'A feeling of dread stole over me, too. It was cold and clammy, like the hand of a ghost, and it reached inside and twisted my stomach. Blackheart, I was sure, would not be so easy to trick.

'By the time we heard a horse approaching the inn, No Name was rocking wildly, wringing his hands. Grandma got up from the chair. "If you're quick," she whispered to him, "you could just let us go. Blackheart need never know we were here."

'"That's right," I agreed. "We'll slip out. There's still time."

'"It's no use," wailed No Name. "He would find out. He always does. Here, boy," he turned to me, "hide under the table while I think."

'The door flew open.

'"Why was no one ready to take my horse?" thundered Blackheart.

'Grandma's hands flew to her face. Striding through the doorway was a giant of a man. He had the cruellest snarl of a mouth I had ever seen. This was a face that knew no pity. Blackheart didn't notice Grandma standing against the wall. He was dragging No Name outside to gather up his boxes of loot and plunder.

'While they were gone I came out from under the table. "Oh dear, now I have seen your master, I am really very sorry for you all."

'Ferocious and Fearless gaped at me. "You're sorry for *us*?"

'"Yes, he reminds me exactly of a pirate who once captured me. He was pitiless too, and when he was told that I could turn his enemies to stone at a touch, he didn't know whether to believe it or not. So do you know what he did?"

'Ferocious and Fearless looked at me uneasily. "Well, what did he do then?"

'"He made his men touch me, one by one. Slowly their limbs turned to marble, then their bodies. They cried for mercy but it was too late; their lips froze and their poor despairing eyes looked to me for help. But once touched, there was nothing I could do. You can see their marble figures to this day by the well in our village."

'Ferocious shuddered. "Quick," he said, "out you go, out the back door. Your horse and cart are down the track under the trees. We'll keep Blackheart busy until you're out of sight."

'Grandma and I slipped out and scrambled into the cart. Almost as if he knew, Plodalong set off at a smart trot, happy as we were to leave the inn behind.

'Grandma flicked the reins. "It was lucky you had that good idea, Tashi. I hope Ferocious doesn't ever come to our village looking for the marble statues."

'I laughed. "I don't think he will. In any case, I've already made up a good reason for them being gone."

'Grandma tweaked my ear. "What a clever Tashi!"

Jack grinned at his friend. '*Did* you ever see the brigands again?'

'Only No Name. But he wasn't a brigand anymore when I spotted him.'

'What was he doing?'

'Juggling firesticks on a high wire.'

Jack's mouth fell open in surprise. 'Didn't he fall off?'

Tashi shook his head. 'No, he'd given up the drink. Said he didn't need it now that he was doing what he'd always loved best.'

'What, balancing on a high wire?'

'That's right. He was once a travelling acrobat, you see, and he'd left home very young to see the world. But it wasn't long before he got lost in the city, just like I did, and he fell in with thieves and brigands.'

In the thoughtful silence, the two boys gazed at the lift doors.

'Of course, as Grandma says, *some*

people never climb out of the dark pit of greed and selfishness.'

'No,' agreed Jack. 'Like that Blackheart.'

'Or Bluebeard,' Tashi said grimly.

Jack swung around to face Tashi. 'Who?'

Tashi shivered. 'When I met Bluebeard, all the other evil men I'd ever met seemed *gentle* in comparison.'

Just then the floor underneath the two boys shuddered. Their stomachs lurched as the lift began to drop like a stone.

'What's happening?' cried Jack.

The lift stopped suddenly, with a loud jarring thump. The boys clutched each other, breathing fast.

Then a voice came from the other side.

'Hullo? Anyone in there?'

'YES, *YES*, we're here!'

'Just a jiffy and we'll get you out,' called the cheerful voice. 'Only a few more minutes…'

Jack and Tashi looked at each other.

Jack squirmed. He squeezed his legs together hard. 'So, tell me, how did you meet Bluebeard?'

But Tashi sprang up and began hopping about. 'It was too terrible to talk about now. To tell you the truth, Jack, I'm really busting, too. I'll…I'll tell you on the way home.'

And at that moment the great steel doors opened and a ginger-haired man stepped through with a big smile. But the boys flew past him like streamers in the wind and headed straight for the sign…

TASHI and the
FORBIDDEN ROOM

Jack hung up his bag in the hatroom and raced into class. 'Sorry I'm late but –'

'You were kidnapped by bandits,' said Mrs Hall.

'Strangled by mummies!' called out Angus Figment.

'Held up by Uncle Joe,' sighed Jack.

Mrs Hall's eyes lit up. 'Uncle Joe? The brave traveller with many tales to tell of secret jungles and famous fishing spots around the world?'

'Yes,' said Jack. 'He's just come back from the Limpopo River in Africa.'

'Ooh!' Mrs Hall bounced on her seat with excitement. 'I've only ever *read* about Africa. How I would like to *go* there! Well, class, today we will have a chance to be explorers ourselves. We're going to choose a pen friend – someone who lives far away. You will write telling them about your life and they'll write back about theirs. Now let's look at this marvellous world of ours and think where we would most like to explore.'

Jack put up his hand. 'Can we choose our own person to write to?'

'Well, yes. And would this be someone your Uncle Joe has met?'

'No.'

Mrs Hall waited. She waggled her eyebrows wildly at Jack. But Jack said nothing more.

At morning tea, Jack sat down next to
Tashi. 'I'd like to write to someone from
your village. I bet your grandfather has
seen a lot in his time.'

'Yes, but his English is tricky.'

'I just want to ask him one question:
which one of your adventures he thinks is
the scariest.'

'Hmm,' said Tashi, unwrapping his rice
cake.

'Do you think it would be the same
one you'd pick?'

'No. The one I'd pick stays in a small dark corner of my mind. I try not to think of it, but a certain monster of a man will always haunt me.'

Jack was silent for a moment. 'Is this the man you started to tell me about in the lift? Bluebeard?'

Tashi nodded. 'He was so full of venom, he could kill a snake.'

'Gosh,' said Jack. 'What was so bad about him?'

'Well, it all began with the castle on the hill,' said Tashi. He took a deep breath. 'The castle had stood empty for many years. It had twenty-three bedrooms, upstairs and downstairs, and they were dark and dusty with cobwebs. But one day Second Aunt called to tell us that she had just met the new owner. He was a wealthy merchant, she said, tall and

handsome, with hair as blue-black as a
raven's wing.'

'Bluebeard!'

Tashi shuddered. 'The colour of his
beard gave him his name. After this story
is told, Jack, let's not talk about him
again. I am only telling you because you
are my best friend.'

Jack nodded gravely.

'Well, at first we were excited about the new owner of the castle – you know, a mysterious stranger from outside the village – and we couldn't wait to see him for ourselves. We were even more excited when Lotus Blossom burst in with news.

'"Guess what!" she yelled. "You'll never guess, no you won't in a million moons – "

'Grandma told her it was rude to interrupt people's dinner, and that if she didn't watch out she'd give her a dose of witch's warts to improve her manners. But then I saw that look in Grandma's eye.

'"Well, now that you're here," she said, "you'd better tell us."

'"It's about the handsome stranger," crowed Lotus Blossom. "I know something *you* don't know!" and she danced around the table.

'Oh, Jack, that girl might be my cousin but sometimes she's more annoying than a wasp in summer!'

'I know what you mean,' nodded Jack. 'I wish I'd had a dose of witch's warts for Uncle Joe this morning.'

'Well, finally Lotus Blossom told us the news. The wealthy new owner had asked her Elder Sister Ho Hum to marry him!

Their father was very pleased, because although Ho Hum was pretty she was such a languid sleepy sort of girl he'd been worried she would never do anything with her life but sit in her comfortable chair and doze.

'Everyone was busy in the next few weeks, helping to clean up and decorate the castle. We had big parties to welcome the stranger. All the villagers said how well Ho Hum had done to find such a husband – everyone except me, that is. On the day I met Bluebeard I saw something that showed me a glimpse of his evil heart.'

'What?'

'Well, it was like this. At one of the parties I noticed Granny White Eyes asking for a cup of water.'

'Oh, I remember her,' said Jack. 'She's the old blind lady who helped you beat the demons.'

'Yes, and I saw Bluebeard fill a cup from the dog's water bowl to give to her! He had a nasty smile. I dashed over and, pretending to be clumsy, knocked it out of her hand. I gave her fresh water, but my heart was heavy.

'It was even heavier the next day when
I visited Not Yet at his shop. He was
trembling. "Oh, Tashi," he moaned, "that
monster Bluebeard was here this morning
to collect the shoes he'd left for me to
mend. Just because I said they weren't
quite ready, he threatened to –" Not Yet's
face crumpled. "Tashi, if anything happens
to me, I want you to have my hammer
with the ebony handle." Not Yet wouldn't
say any more. He just bundled me out
and locked his door and windows.

'I hurried off to tell Ho Hum what had happened. But she didn't believe me.

'"You've got it wrong, Tashi," she said. "Anyway, everyone gets angry with Not Yet when their shoes aren't ready."

'The next day Ho Hum and Lotus Blossom came to take me on a trip up to the castle. Bluebeard was away on some business in the city and he'd given the castle keys to his bride so she could make sure that the new bed had arrived.

'While Ho Hum had a little rest, Lotus Blossom and I explored the gardens, ran up and down the stairs and shouted along the corridors. We came back for Ho Hum, and looked into each of the twenty-three rooms until we arrived at the tower at the top of the castle. The door was locked.

'"We can't go into that room," said Ho Hum. "Not ever."

'"Why not?" asked Lotus Blossom. "What can be in there? Don't you want to know?" She knelt down to look through the keyhole. "I can't see anything; it's blocked. Oh please, Ho Hum, let's have one little peek inside."

'I think Ho Hum had been just waiting for someone to persuade her. She had the right key ready in her hand! When she opened the door, we all gasped. There were hundreds of wooden chests stacked with treasure, cloths of gold and peacock fans.

'"Look," cried Lotus Blossom, "over there! That's the cabinet of jade figures that was stolen from the Baron last week. Ho Hum, it seems that you are marrying a robber!"

'At that very moment I heard faint cries coming from behind some carved screens. Lotus Blossom and I pushed them aside and stood frozen with horror.

'Five young women were hanging by their wrists, tied to iron rings set in the wall behind them!

'My heart started racing and a chill like iced water spread down my back. Not Yet was right – only a monster would do such a thing. Quickly we went to the girls and gently tried to undo their straps. Their faces and arms were white as ghosts, and when the cruel leather straps came off the girls cried in agony.

'They knelt on the floor and slowly told us their stories. One by one they had married Bluebeard, only to find they displeased him in some way.

'"My mistake was to sing while I cleaned the house," sobbed the first girl. "Bluebeard said singing was for birds, and birds should be in cages."

"'I served his tea too hot," said the second girl. "My father always liked the way I made tea, but Bluebeard said it burnt his mouth."

"'I talked to a neighbour –" sighed the third girl.

"'I dropped a plate –" whispered the fourth.

'"And I fed a stray cat," said the fifth wife. "Bluebeard punished us all by locking us up. Then one night, when all the village was sleeping, he brought us to this castle. I don't know how many days we have been here, but I am sure he means us to starve to death!"

'"Let's get out of here," Ho Hum said
urgently. But we heard a creak on the
stairs. Bluebeard's deep, harsh voice
floated up to us. Quickly, Ho Hum
ducked down behind the cabinet.

'"We'll come back for you," I whispered
to the girls, pulling the screen back in
place. Lotus Blossom grabbed my hand
and we slipped in behind the curtains just
as Bluebeard strode into the room.

'He was followed by two men with faces sharp as knives. "Take these boxes down to the cart – oh, that cabinet too – " he snapped. The men lifted the Baron's cabinet and Ho Hum was left staring into the furious eyes of her husband-to-be.

'His face grew dark as a storm. "I knew it!" he hissed. "You have disobeyed me in the one thing I asked of you, just like all the others. Take her away," he growled to one of the men behind him.

'Of course, wouldn't you know it, Lotus Blossom couldn't keep still on hearing that. She sprang out from behind the curtain, yelling at Bluebeard. "What do you mean, *take her away*?" she bellowed. "What are you going to do with Ho Hum? You can't lock her up forever for disobeying you!"

Bluebeard looked at Lotus Blossom
as if she was just a bug on his shoe.
He took his time, considering whether to
squash her or not. "Take them both below
to the room with the barred windows,"
he finally told the men, "then finish
loading the cart." And he marched off,
out the door.

'I waited as the men took the sisters
and the boxes, and when they were gone
I tiptoed out from behind the curtain.
There was only one thing to do and
luckily I had come prepared.

'*Wah*, you should have seen Ho Hum
jump as I stepped through the wall.

'"Where did you come from, Tashi?"
she gasped.

'"I never did trust that Bluebeard, so I
brought my magic shoes and these ghost
cakes, in case," I told her.

'We explained to Ho Hum how easy it
is to walk through walls once you've eaten
a piece of ghost cake. But then we had to
decide: which wall to go through now?

'"It's no use going through the door," I whispered, "there's sure to be a guard in the hallway." I listened carefully at the wall of the next room. "We don't want to walk into a roomful of Bluebeard's robbers." I took a deep breath. "I'll go first."

'"No, we'll go together," said Lotus Blossom. So they swallowed their ghost cakes and we all stepped through the wall. INTO A ROOMFUL OF ROBBERS!

'They were sitting around a table with
their feet up and for a moment they were
stuck to their seats in surprise. I seized a
sword from the nearest robber, and I ran
up the wall in my magic shoes. I skimmed
across the ceiling, swishing the sword
round and round my head. I moved so
quickly I was just a blur of red coat and
whistling sword, bouncing off the walls
and floor and ceiling like a demon,

shouting, "Out, out, OUT! Before you
lose your EARS!" The stupefied robbers
fought each other to be first out the door,
and out of the castle.

"'Well done, Tashi," said Ho Hum.
For once she looked quite lively. "That
was...very interesting."

"'We still have to get out of the castle,"
I panted, trying to get my breath. "And
Blubeard won't be so easy to frighten."

'We crept down the hall towards the
stairs and we could see the open front
door – so inviting! My foot was on the
first step when I saw Bluebeard stride
into the entry hall from the cellar. He was
carrying two more iron rings. Quickly we
shrank against the wall and crept back
into the shadows.

'A tall vase stood outside the room with
the barred windows. I silently pointed to
Lotus Blossom and Ho Hum to hide
behind it and I squeezed in behind a suit
of armour on the other side of the door.

'Bluebeard's face was set and his mouth was grim as he unlocked the door of the room. He stepped inside. We heard a sound of surprise as he looked around and found the sisters missing. Quick as a thunderclap I slammed the door shut. Ho Hum turned the key in the lock just as Bluebeard hurled himself against the door. Too late.

'We raced like the wind down to the village square and straight over to the Warning Bell. People came streaming out of their houses and shops, wanting to know what had happened. As soon as we told them about Bluebeard, they grabbed their shovels and pitchforks and carving knives and we all hurried back to the castle. The cart loaded with treasure was still outside where the robbers had left it. Lotus Blossom ran ahead, climbing the tower to free the poor wives, while I led the way to the room where Bluebeard was held.

'He put up a tremendous fight when
we burst in on him. I'll never forget the
look on his face. He bared his teeth like
a wild dog, and he leapt on the nearest
man, cursing and hurling punches. "Get
out of my way, you miserable wretches,"
he snarled. "My men will be here any
moment to tear you apart!"

'He thrashed his way through the villagers like an army until four men linked arms and surrounded him. It took another four to overpower him and three more to tie him up in his own chains.

'As he was led away, Lotus Blossom took Ho Hum's hand. "It's a terrible thing, Ho Hum. Are you very upset?"

'Ho Hum shivered, looking over at me. "Just as well you came with us today, Tashi. I wouldn't have wanted to be wife number six." She smiled sleepily at Lotus Blossom. "It wouldn't have been...very restful."'

Jack snorted. 'That was one mean man,' he said. 'But then, the ghosts you met were monsters too. And that white tiger – he'd have swallowed you whole.'

Tashi stood up and threw his rubbish in the bin.

'If you could choose,' went on Jack, 'would you rather be tied to a tree and eaten slowly by soldier ants or attacked by a lion?'

'Lion,' said Tashi.

'Would you rather die of cold or hot?'

'Cold,' said Tashi after a moment. 'Because you just fall asleep. Fifth Cousin almost went that way. They found him all curled up in the snow with a smile on his face. When they thawed him out he said it was just like dreaming.'

As they wandered back to the classroom, Jack and Tashi discussed what they would do if they ever met anybody as monsterish as Bluebeard again.

'We could make a book of handy hints,' said Jack. 'Call it *A Survival Guide to Monsters*.'

'Would there be a man as evil as Bluebeard in it?' said Tashi.

'You bet!' said Jack. 'But we just won't mention his name.'

The THREE TASKS

'Hi Jack,' called Mum from the laundry, 'how was your day?'

'Good,' Jack called back, flicking off his shoes and opening the fridge.

'Did you show Tashi the letter you got from his grandfather?'

713

'Yesh,' said Jack.

'Jack? Are you eating that pie for tonight's dinner?' Mum marched into the kitchen and dumped the washing on the table.

'You know the three tasks that Grandfather wrote about in his letter?' began Jack.

'Yes,' nodded Mum. 'He said to ask Tashi about them. So did you hear the whole story? And why did Grandfather ask if you had a dog?'

'Well, Tashi said that after his family, Grandfather's favourite creature in all the world was this dog called Pongo. And Grandfather's favourite Tashi adventure was about Pongo.'

'What, did the dog have to perform the three tasks?' said Mum.

'No,' sighed Jack. 'Do you want to hear the story? I've written most of it down in my *Survival Guide*.'

'So tell me,' said Mum, as she sorted the socks into pairs.

'Well, it was like this,' said Jack. 'One day Tashi was poking about behind Granny White Eyes' house, weeding her garden, when he came across a clump of mandrake plants. Wise-as-an-Owl will be pleased, he thought, and he set out to tell him.'

'What's so good about mandrake plants?' asked Mum.

'Be patient and you'll hear,' said Jack. 'As I was saying, Tashi set off and as he was going through the square he met Lotus Blossom and Ah Chu. "We'll come with you!" they both said, and Tashi agreed. It was a good excuse, of course, to peek inside the wise man's house and have a look at all those strange plants and bubbling beakers.

'But when they arrived it was his son Much-to-Learn who opened the door.

'"You didn't try to pick them I hope?"
Much-to-Learn asked anxiously as Tashi
told him about the mandrake plants.

'"Of course I didn't," said Tashi. "I
knew it would be much too dangerous for
anyone but Wise-as-an-Owl to pull them
up, although I expect you will be able to
do it soon, Much-to-Learn," he added
politely.

'Wise-as-an-Owl came in then and offered them all tea. Tashi said it had an odd taste – spicy, with a kick to it that tingled at the back of your throat after you swallowed. But it was nice and left you feeling calm. Anyway, just as they were leaving, Wise-as-an-Owl drew Tashi aside. He thanked him for coming, and he gave Tashi a little present wrapped in brown paper. Tashi tucked it in his hair, where he often carried precious things.

'As they left, the children could hear Much-to-Learn listing all the magical and important parts of wild mandrake root.

'It was a fine day, so they dawdled along, enjoying the sunshine. The way home took them past the Baron's house and they could smell the delicious scent of flowers on the breeze. The Baron had a beautiful garden – it was a pity no one was allowed to walk in it.

'Tashi said, "Why don't we stop for a moment. The Baron isn't here and we could see that new peacock he has been bragging about."

'"Yes," agreed Lotus Blossom. "I heard him in the village yesterday. He says it's the most magnificent bird in the world, and he's bought a peahen as well. He was boasting that soon he'd be making another fortune breeding the most splendid birds in the country."

'They wandered around the garden, sniffing the orange and lemon blossoms, but there was no sign of the peacock. A joyful bark made them jump and they swung around to see Pongo bounding towards them. Tashi was just bending to throw a stick for him when the Baron came walking up the path.

'"Where is my peacock?" the Baron shouted.

'Pongo barked and as all eyes turned to him they saw that his jowls and teeth were covered in blood. Nearby, lying on the lawn, were two crumpled feathers.

'The Baron roared again with rage and whipped the dog savagely. Then he dragged the whimpering Pongo to the cellar and shut him in. Tashi couldn't help following a few paces behind and he heard the Baron shouting, "You've made a meal of my peacock, Pongo, now let's see how many meals you miss before you *die*!" And he slammed the big iron door with such force that Tashi's ears were ringing.

'Well, you can imagine how Tashi felt going home that night. He couldn't stop thinking about poor Pongo. Tashi's mother wanted to know why he wasn't eating his dinner but when he told her about Pongo, she said no, they couldn't bring him home.

'"Pongo is the Baron's dog, Tashi," she said. "If you take him it would be stealing."

'The next morning Tashi and his friends sneaked down into the cellar to bathe Pongo's cuts and give him some food and water. Tashi had found some left-over chicken necks and egg noodles.

'Ah Chu was sighing – he found it very difficult to watch anyone else eating when he was not. Even a dog. Even if it was a bowl of cold scraps. "Goodness, listen to that," he said thankfully as they heard the clock strike twelve. "It's lunchtime already."

'Tashi grinned. "That's all right. You two go. I'll just stay a few minutes more to give Pongo a bit of friendly company."

'After checking to see if the coast was clear, Ah Chu and Lotus Blossom slipped away home.

'Tashi scratched behind the dog's ears and patted his soft tummy. Pongo made low moaning sounds in his throat and licked Tashi's knees.

'Only a moment later, the door banged open. The Baron glared down at Tashi. "Interfering again, I see, Tashi. Don't you know that once a dog has tasted a live bird you can never trust him again?"

'"Oh Baron, what can I say to make you change your mind?"

'A crafty look came into the Baron's eyes. "Well now, let me think. You are supposed to be so clever, Tashi. If you really want to help this cur we'll see what you can do. I will set you three simple tasks. If you can carry them out, the dog is yours. What do you say to that?"

'"And if I *can't* do the tasks?" asked Tashi. "What then?"

'"Then *you* will have to kill Pongo yourself."

'Tashi shuddered, but he nodded. What else could he do?

'The Baron paced about the empty cellar. "Let's see now," he chuckled. "Yes, that's it! Task number one: When I return to this room after lunch, I will expect to *hear* you but not see you." He paced some more. He sniggered again as he warmed to his work. "Task number two: I will find Pongo no longer bleeding all over my floor and those ugly cuts will be healed. Task number three – " The Baron's face grew red with rage again. "And THREE: My peacock will be back in my garden ALIVE!"

'The door clanged behind him.

'Tashi sank down on the floor beside Pongo. He gently put the dog's head in his lap and frowned as he stroked the silky ears. It was quite impossible. He sat for an hour staring in front of him, seeing nothing, and then his gaze dropped to his feet. A smile crept over his face.

'"That's task number one," he whispered to Pongo. He leaned back against the wall and looked about the room. His smile grew broader.

'Tashi ran to the far wall where
cobwebs hung thickly in the corner. He
carefully pulled a web down and took it
over to Pongo. It covered his hind
quarters. One by one, Tashi brought the
cobwebs from the wall to the trusting dog
until he was completely covered.

'The bleeding stopped. The thick
cobwebs lay like a bandage on the poor
dog's back. "Now we're getting
somewhere, Pongo!"

'Tashi pulled the little parcel that
Wise-as-an-Owl had given him from his
hair. As he had hoped, it was a teaspoonful
of crushed mandrake root. He popped it
into Pongo's mouth and stood back.
Before his eyes the deep cuts began to
close and heal. In another minute faint
pale scars appeared under the fur – the
only sign of those dreadful wounds. Tashi
gave a shout of joy, but then his smile
faded. He looked into Pongo's trusting
brown eyes and his heart shivered. "How
can I possibly bring the peacock back?"

'Tashi sat down and rested his chin on his knees. The minutes ticked by. He went over the events of yesterday afternoon again and again. He and his friends had come into the garden, the gate had been closed but the peacock was missing. Pongo had bounded over to meet them...

'Later, when the Baron's footsteps sounded outside the cellar, Tashi was ready...

'The Baron stood in the doorway. The room was empty except for Pongo cowering against the far wall. "Big brave Tashi couldn't help you after all, eh mutt? Scampered off home, has he?" sneered the Baron. He peered behind the door. He poked his stick under the bunk bed.

'"No, not at all," a voice answered.

'The Baron spun around and looked behind him. "Wha– where?"

'"See, I'm up here," Tashi called, "having a little walk across the ceiling."

'The Baron's jaw dropped as he looked up and saw Tashi but he quickly recovered and strode over to the dog. He prodded the cobwebs covering Pongo.

'"What's this? Trying to cover up the blood with – Good heavens!" The Baron had another shock as he pulled away the cobwebs to expose the completely healed body of his dog. He swung back to face Tashi. "Well then, smart boy, that just leaves the peacock. Are you going to bring him back to life as well?"

'Tashi bowed. "If you will come with me, Baron, perhaps we will solve the mystery."

'"There's no mystery here," snarled the Baron. "My greedy dog gobbled up a prize peacock and he's going to pay for it."

'But Tashi went out into the garden
and began to search around the spot
where he had first seen Pongo yesterday.
He examined the grass, the fallen leaves
and the bushes nearby. He led the Baron
down a path past the pavilion to a large
thorn bush. And there, caught fast in the
branches of the bush, was the peacock.
Beside it lay a dead serpent, its body
covered in bites.

'"You see, Baron," Tashi said quietly, "Pongo must have seen the snake slither towards your peacock, which ran away, trying to escape. The snake followed for the kill but Pongo must have run up and bravely fought him to the death. He risked his life to protect your property."

'The Baron swallowed and shuffled his feet.

'"But all's well that ends well," Tashi beamed, "because now I have a wonderful loyal dog to take home to my family. Don't I?"

'The Baron nodded glumly. Even he had to admit that a bargain was a bargain.'

Mum threw a pair of socks up in the air and caught them. 'Clever Tashi – he saved that dog's life! I hate it when people are cruel to animals!'

'What dog?' cried Uncle Joe as he
walked in the door with Dad. 'Have you
got a new dog? Where is it?'

'No, no,' sighed Jack, 'I was just telling
a story about one that nearly lost his –'

'Oh I see. That reminds me of the dog
I rescued once from the back of a truck
heading for north Queensland –'

'Were you telling a Tashi story, Jack?'
asked Dad. 'Did I miss out?'

'Yeah, but I've written it down so you can read it.'

'So Tashi brought Pongo home and all Tashi's family were thrilled, I suppose?' asked Mum. 'Particularly Grandfather?'

'That's right. He called Pongo his "Serpent-Slayer" and he saved the best bits of his dinner for him every night. Grandfather said that dog was just about the pluckiest creature on earth, right after his grandson, Tashi.'

'That's true,' agreed Uncle Joe. 'Dogs are brave but then he probably hasn't come across the courage of the well-known African mountain ape. Now when I was in the deep jungle of the Limpopo River I had the opportunity to...'

TASHI and the
STOLEN BUS

Tashi knocked on Jack's door. 'Let's catch the early bus today,' he said when Jack came out. 'We can play soccer before school.'

Jack looked down at his pyjamas. 'Okay, but instead of taking the bus let's just *walk* really fast.'

'Why?'

'I'll tell you on the way.'

When they were walking really fast
to school, Jack said, 'You know how
Dad and I caught the bus to the city
yesterday?'

'Oh yes,' panted Tashi.

'Well, this giant of a man got on at the
next stop. He stomped up the back, sat
down and then, you know what he did?
He barked like a dog!'

'Wah! What did everyone do?'

'Well, two old ladies got off quickly but
a little boy laughed and barked right back
at him.'

'Hmm,' said Tashi, as they took the
short cut through the park, 'bus trips can
be tricky. Why, I remember a bus trip
back in my village–'

Jack looked at Tashi. 'I didn't think there *were* buses in your old village.'

'Well, it was like this,' said Tashi. 'When I was very small there *weren't* any cars or buses in our village, it's true. If we had to go somewhere, we walked. So we were really excited when Teacher Pang called a meeting to tell us we might be able to start a valley bus line.'

'But how – did he win the lottery?'

Tashi grinned. 'No, Mr Pang had been talking to Can-Du, the father of a new boy at school. He told us that Can-Du was a wizard at fixing engines. He could find a broken-down rattletrap and make it go like a racing car.'

'But where would you find a bus?'

'Well, everyone knew about the old one dumped down by the river, at the edge of the forest. It had been abandoned by robbers years ago, left to the weeds and spiders. So the next day, we all pitched in to clean it out and fix the seats and fill up the holes in the floor.

'In a short time Can-Du had the engine purring, and when he put his foot down on the accelerator, it roared like a lion! We painted it a bright yellow and after a lot of argument we agreed on the name: *The Valley People's Very Own Bus Service.*

'I couldn't sleep the night before the first trip to the city. The bus was going to the markets, taking all the people who had something to sell. Grandma was making moon cakes. "You can come with me and help to sell them if you like," she said to Lotus Blossom and me.

'Well, people were already loading up cherries and apples and chickens onto the roof of the bus when we arrived.

'Can-Du had the bonnet up, checking the engine one last time. I peered in. He had already taught me about the rotor and the fan belt. I wanted to know more... But there wasn't time because, just then, two strangers moved up to talk to him. As I stepped away, I heard Can-Du arguing with them but their voices were too low for me to catch.

'The strangers didn't look like any of the villagers I knew. They wore dirty long coats and wide-brimmed hats.

'When one took his fist out of his pocket and shook it at Can-Du, I was shocked by how hairy it was. A prickle of fear flared in my chest. Wasn't there something familiar about these men? But Can-Du was standing aside now, letting them climb aboard.

'It must be all right, I thought. And wasn't this *The Valley People's Very Own Bus Service* after all? Everyone should be allowed on, hairy or not. But then, just as Grandma was about to take her seat, the two strangers pushed her aside and swaggered down the bus ahead of her.

'"No manners," muttered Not Yet, but he was careful to mutter it quietly.

'A nasty smell was coming from the men. It was like stale water in a vase when the flowers have been left to rot. Didn't I know that smell? I leant out into the aisle to get a better look and that prickly feeling in my chest exploded into panic: as one stranger swung into his seat I saw him tucking something under his coat. *A tail!*

'I looked around wildly. I tried to think what to do but the bus was packed to the brim now with people and baskets and piglets escaping, oinking up and down the aisle. And everyone was so happy, cheering and clapping each other on the back as Can-Du turned the key and the bus roared into life.

'The bus bounced beautifully along the roads and Teacher Pang shouted *"Congratulations!"* to Can-Du at the wheel. But Can-Du just hunched his shoulders and stared ahead. Maybe he knows who the mysterious strangers are, I thought. But if so, why did he let them on the bus?

'Then I noticed Mr Pang sniffing the air and wrinkling his nose. He was staring at the strangers. "I know you two!" he cried. "You're–"

'Oh Jack, his words were like a signal for everything to go wrong. Can-Du suddenly swung the wheel and veered off the road to the city, taking the track leading into the forest instead!

'"Where are you going? What are you doing?" we all shouted. Grandma's face was white and Not Yet had his face pressed against the window.

'But Can-Du seemed to have gone deaf.

'The strangers stood up and, as they did, they whipped off their hats, showing their horrible faces. "QUIET!" they bellowed. "SIT *STILL!*"

'Teacher Pang didn't obey. He leapt up and grabbed one of them by the arm. But the second stranger turned and lazily pushed him over. Teacher Pang crumpled at my feet.

'I knelt down and whispered, "You know these two, don't you?"

'"Yes, they're the demons! They raced you last year for the new school-house."

'I nodded. I could hardly breathe. "What do you think they want?"

'Before Mr Pang could answer there was a loud explosion and the bus came to a sudden stop.

'"What the *dill*blot has happened now?" The demons hurried down the bus to Can-Du.

"'I'll have to look at the engine," Can-Du answered. He opened the driver's door, but before climbing down, he beckoned to me. "I couldn't help it," he whispered. "The demons are crazy for buses! When I wouldn't hand this one over or teach them how to drive it, they kidnapped my son. They told me I would never find him again if I didn't drive the bus into the woods."

'"And if you want to see your boy
again you will hurry up and fix this
rattletrap," hissed the older demon, as he
pushed Can-Du out of the bus.

'The younger demon turned to us. "This
is the end of the line, you dillblots! This
is where you get off because we're on our
way to Xin–"

'The older demon leapt back and
poked his brother hard in the back.
"Hold your tongue! *You're* the dillblot,
you DILLBLOT!"

'It was starting to rain and although it was still early morning the thick branches overhead and the purple sky made the forest dark and spooky.

'Grandma called out, "You can't leave us here so far from any help. We have babies amongst us and there are wolves in the forest!" Not to mention ghosts, I thought.

'The monsters shrugged; such things mattered nothing to demons. When they got out to see what Can-Du was doing, I moved over to the front window and listened hard. Soon I heard Can-Du say, "All fixed." There was just a split second to decide if I dared to do it–'

'What? What?' cried Jack.

'Well, I was in the driver's seat, wasn't I? So I turned the key in the ignition and the bus revved into a roar. Not Yet was right beside me. "Quick, Not Yet," I cried, "my feet won't reach the pedals. Can you press them down for me?"

'Not Yet crouched down and I pointed, "clutch down!" I put the gear into the first position and released the brake. We shuddered and rolled forward. I could see the demons pulling at the door, swinging like gorillas up the side. Grandma and Lotus Blossom and Mrs Wang held onto the handle with all their strength.

'"Clutch!" I cried and we moved into second gear and went a little faster.

'"Hurry!" cried Lotus Blossom. "We can't hold them off much longer!"

'"Clutch and accelerator together!" I
sang as we jerked and bumped and rocked
in a wide circle to point the bus back in
the right direction. When we shot forward
the demons went flying off the door like
buttons bursting from a ripped seam.

'There was a stunned silence and then a
great cheer went up from the passengers.
They hung out the windows, jeering at the
demons. "I didn't know you could drive a
bus, Tashi," giggled Mrs Wang.

'"Neither did I," I said.

'I was sweating so much the wheel was slippery in my hands. How different it had been going for cosy little test drives with Can-Du than actually doing it myself!'

'And escaping from demons at the same time!' shivered Jack.

'Yes. You should have seen those monsters jumping up and down in the dirt, shaking their fists with rage, and hitting each other! Everyone was so busy yelling at them – and I was looking at the road ahead, of course – that we didn't notice Can-Du had flung himself on the spare tyre at the back of the bus. And now he climbed up and in through the window.

'Well, when we were at a safe distance from the demons I stopped the bus and turned around to face Can-Du. "What will we do now?"'

'Everyone had an idea. But most agreed with Mr Wu. "Let's go straight to the city," he said. "I have vegetables to sell. Soon they'll spoil."

'"And my piglets won't last much longer without water."

'"And my chickens will drown up there in the rain."

'"But what about my *son*?" cried Can-Du.

'The villagers told him they would look for Little Can-Du but first they had to get to the city. So that is where we went.

'When we'd dropped most of the passengers at the markets, Grandma, Lotus Blossom, Mrs Wang, Mr Pang and I stayed behind with Can-Du to figure out how we could find his son.

'"Let's tell each other everything we know about the demons," said Mr Pang. "You start, Tashi, you're the one who has had the most to do with them."

"'We mightn't have to do all that," I said slowly. "Remember in the bus, one of the demons said that they were on their way to Xin-something? Where could that be? Is there anywhere starting with 'Xin' around these parts?"

"'What about Xinfeng?" cried Mrs Wang.

"'Of course, it's beside the mountain in the next valley," Teacher Pang agreed excitedly.

"'Which is riddled with caves – perfect places to hide something, or someone," Grandma finished up.

'We were all really pleased with each other until Lotus Blossom said, "But if it's riddled with caves, how will we find the one where Little Can-Du is hidden?"

'"Let's just get there first, and see," pleaded Can-Du, and we all agreed.

'The first creatures we saw when we reached Xinfeng were the two demons.

'"How did they get here so quickly?" I whispered.

'"They're demons," Grandma answered gloomily.

'They didn't see us because they were already busy climbing up the mountain. I cautiously followed, leaving the others waiting in the bus. There was only a thin track winding around the mountain and just as Grandma had said, the steep sides were scooped out as if a ghost monster had taken enormous bites from the rock.

'I crept along at a good distance, backing into the shadows if the demons stopped or turned around. But they hurried on, past dozens of shallow caves. Suddenly, they dived into a wide deep cave. I waited. Soon they ran out again, carrying an empty water jug. I watched in the shadows until they were out of sight and then slipped into the cave.

'It was black as night inside and I had to shut my eyes for a moment to get used to the dark. How would I find anything in this gloom?

'"Who's there?" a trembly little voice
threaded through the darkness. I took
a couple of steps towards the voice and
made out a small bundle tied up against
the wall of the cave.

'Little Can-Du cried with joy when
he saw me but I told him, while I was
undoing his ropes, that there wasn't any
time to lose. Already demon voices were
floating back. What to do?

'I spied a tall oil jar in the corner.
"Quick! Jump into this," I said, giving
him a leg-up and stuffing the ropes in
on top of him. "When the demons leave
the cave again, rock the jar till it tips
over and run down the path outside.
Your father will be waiting for
you in the bus."

'There was no time for any more. The demons were standing at the entrance of the cave. "Tashi! What are you doing here?" cried the first demon when he caught sight of me. "Where is Little Can-Du?"

'"The Grand Vizier of, er, of Zenadu took him home to his father. The Grand Vizier is very annoyed with you."

'Then I took a piece of ghost cake out of my pocket, popped it into my mouth and walked through the demons and out of the cave.

'Outside, I ducked down behind some
rocks, listening to the demons argue about
what to do. When I saw them charging
out and up the mountain, searching other
caves, I whistled softly and Little Can-Du
crept out. We tore down the hillside and
scrambled into the bus.

'"Let's go!" I cried, and so we did.

'Little Can-Du had a cuddle from Grandma and Mrs Wang while Teacher Pang and Lotus Blossom asked again and again for the story of our escape. And do you know, we were back just in time to pick up our passengers in the city.

'"Just don't expect every trip to be as exciting as this one." Can-Du smiled grimly at me, as we dropped our last passenger off.'

Jack jumped as they heard the school bell ring across the park. 'Whew! That was the strangest bus trip I ever heard of,' he panted as they began to run. 'But you know, ship cruises can be even worse.

'I mean, you can't get off a ship until you reach port, not unless you want to be eaten by sharks. My Uncle Joe had to swim for ten kilometres once, when pirates attacked his boat in the Caribbean. Imagine, he had to swim to Jamaica!'

'Now that would be a good story,' said Tashi as they hung up their bags. 'When did you say your Uncle Joe is visiting again?'

But Jack didn't answer because he'd just realised they'd left the soccer ball at the park.

The MYSTERIOUS THIEF

'Has anyone seen my sunglasses?' asked Mum as she picked up her keys, ready to walk out the door.

Jack and Dad burst out laughing.

'They're on your head!' crowed Jack, collapsing onto the sofa.

'You think you're so funny,' sniffed Mum, whipping the glasses into her bag, 'but you weren't laughing when you lost your skateboard last week.'

'That's right, Jack,' said Dad. 'You were about to ring the police, remember, when I found it under your bed.'

'Yeah well, you didn't find it on my *head*, did you?'

Mum giggled. 'Now that would have looked funny.'

'I know a story about mysterious disappearances,' Jack said slowly.

'Oh, do you now!' said Dad. 'Well, I'm ready for a mystery. Pity you have to go out, darling.' Dad winked at Jack.

'A Tashi mystery?' asked Mum, flinging her bag down on the table. 'Why should *I* miss out? Just because *I'm* the woman here, *I* have to go out and do the shopping.' Mum glared at Dad. 'Well, I'm just not having it!'

'No, neither am I,' agreed Dad. 'It's plainly unfair. Think how many women in history have missed out on fabulous stories—'

'Fascinating conversations—'

'Really good jokes—'

'Just because they had to go out shopping,' finished Dad. 'So, sweetheart, why don't you sit down here beside me and we'll change the course of history right now.'

'Deal,' said Mum.

'So,' began Jack, 'the whole thing started with Ah Chu.'

'Oh dear,' said Mum reaching for the tissues, 'are you getting a cold?'

'No,' sighed Jack. 'Remember Ah Chu, Tashi's friend back in the old country?'

'Ah yes, Ah Chu,' grinned Dad.

'Well, things had been mysteriously disappearing in the village. One morning Ah Chu stumped up the path to Tashi's house and spluttered, "You'll never believe what was taken from our place last night – my old *undies*! They were hanging on the washing line!"

'Ooh, yuk,' said Dad. 'Who'd want to steal second-hand undies?'

'Exactly,' said Jack. 'Then Lotus Blossom ran up close behind and said, "Guess what – the thief came to Precious Aunt's house last night and took her painted silk fan!"'

'They were all quiet for a moment, thinking. "We'll have to put a stop to this," Tashi said at last. "Two visits in one night and there's no pattern to what is taken. It's always a mixture of valuable and useless things, like your broken spinning top last week, Lotus Blossom. People have started buying locks for their doors; we've never had to do that before."

'"I think it could be someone like the Foo brothers – they'd do it for a dare," said Lotus Blossom.

'"Maybe, but I don't think those boys would take things that people treasured. Like your grandfather's gold watch," Tashi argued.

'"I don't know," said Ah Chu. "Some of their friends would dive in first and think later."

'"All right," said Tashi, "for the next few days we'll play with them after school. There would have to be a great pile of things in their room by now, too much to hide easily."

'Four days later, the three friends met
again. "Well, that was a waste of time,"
said Lotus Blossom crossly.

'"It was your idea," Ah Chu reminded
her. "And I don't know what Ping's
mother thought when she came in and
found you looking through her cupboards.
Just as well Tashi was able to think of a
good excuse."

'"Anyway," Lotus Blossom went on as
though Ah Chu hadn't spoken, "I think
we have overlooked the obvious person."

'"Who?"

'"Your Uncle Tiki Pu. He's the most dishonest person in the village."

'Ah Chu looked uncomfortable but Tashi didn't mind. It was true. "But why would he take underwear and broken toys?"

'"To put us off the scent!" Lotus Blossom cried triumphantly.

'Tashi wasn't sure, but he agreed to go to Tiki Pu's house that afternoon because he knew his uncle was out playing cards with some visiting merchants. After an hour's rummaging through the mess that Tiki Pu lived in, they did not find one thing that had been stolen.

"'Now I suppose we'll have to put all this jumble back," groaned Ah Chu.

"'I don't see why," said Lotus Blossom. "He'll never notice the difference." As she spoke she turned towards the door. Standing there was Tiki Pu.

"'Looking for something?" he asked in a nasty, silky voice.

'There was a long silence. Tashi swallowed. "I came to ask you to dinner tonight, Uncle, and we were just tidying your room for you while we waited."

'Tiki Pu didn't believe a word of it, but he gave Tashi a false smile and said, "Tell your mother I'd be delighted to come and that she mustn't go to too much trouble."

'"That means he'll expect all his favourite dishes," groaned Tashi as they walked home. "My mother will kill me."

'A few minutes later Tashi was running up his garden path. He popped his head in the kitchen window and called, "Tiki Pu said he'd love to come to dinner tonight, Mum, and you mustn't go to too much trouble."

'"What? Why–" She dropped her pan.

'"I'll be back soon," said Tashi quickly, as he ran after the others.

'They walked on in silence until Ah Chu said suddenly, "A funny thing happened last night. I woke up just before first light and felt a bit empty. So I went to the kitchen to look for a little snack. I was just eating a bowl of cold noodles at the window when I saw your grandmother go past. She was walking along as if it was bright daylight, not hesitating, although she didn't have a lantern and it was black night."

'"Where did she go?"

'"I don't know. The darkness swallowed her up as soon as she left the light from the window."

'"The path from your house only leads to the forest," said Lotus Blossom quietly.

'Tashi felt a shiver of fear. "We'll take turns to keep watch," he said quickly. "I'll start tonight."

'Tashi's eyes grew heavy during the long night and every now and again he had to creep about the house to stay awake. Even so, his head was nodding when the sound of a door clicking shut jerked him to his feet.

'His grandmother was already moving down the path towards the village. Tashi followed, his heart like lead as his beloved grandma stopped at Hai Ping's house. She came out a moment later carrying a copper kettle and walked briskly on, past Ah Chu's door and into the forest.

'Just as Ah Chu had said, she didn't seem to need a lantern and Tashi almost had to walk on her heels so he would not lose her in the dark.

'And so, when she stopped suddenly at a small cave opening in the mountainside, Tashi ran into her back.

'"Tashi! What are *you* doing here?" She looked about her. "And what am *I* doing here?"

'"You were sleepwalking, Grandma,"
Tashi told her gently, and took the copper
kettle from her hand. "And I'm afraid it
is you who has been taking all the things
from the village."

'Together they pushed aside the bushes
in front of the cave and by the light of the
rising moon they could see all the missing
things.

'"There's Mrs Wang's carpet," cried
Grandma in horror.

'"And Not Yet's hammer."

'"And Luk Ahead's ebony ruler,"
moaned Grandma.

'"AND MY RED POTTED ORCHID!"
bellowed a great voice behind them.

'They spun around and there was the
Wicked Baron filling the opening of the
cave.

'"Grandmother didn't know she
was taking things, Baron," Tashi cried
desperately. "She's been sleepwalking. We
were just about to take them back to the
village."

'"Of course you were," scoffed the
Baron, "and I'm a tiger with purple
stripes! Well, now you've been caught."

'Grandmother began to plead with him, but Tashi cut her short. "Don't bother with him, Grandma, just pile everything onto this bed cover–"

'"Third Aunt's beautiful quilted bed cover!" wailed Grandma.

'"Never mind, Grandma, now fold the two corners like me and we can carry it all back with us tonight."

'Out of the corner of his eye, Tashi saw the Baron stoop to pick up a golden cup and slip it into his pocket.

He said nothing, but tied the quilt corners together and turned to the Baron. "The village will know we aren't thieves when they see how we have brought everything back."

"'Not if I get back first and tell them you're only returning their goods because I caught you red-handed!'"

"'Then we will just have to make sure that you don't get back first,'" Tashi said evenly.

'Grandmother touched the Baron's sleeve. "Please, Baron, you must know I didn't mean any harm. I couldn't help it.'

'As the Baron turned to flick off her hand, Tashi poured a cupful of sand and pebbles into his boot (using Hai Ping's good copper kettle!).

'The Baron strode ahead, but soon he slowed up, limping a little, then stopped and loosened his boot.

'"Are you having trouble, Baron?" Tashi ran up and poured some more sand and pebbles into the other boot while the Baron was emptying the first.

'"Not as much trouble as you are going to have," the Baron gloated.

'They set off again, but soon the Baron had to stop and see to his other boot. Again Tashi ran up with his kettle. The Baron was so busy cursing "these stupid stones" and "this despicable dirt" and "that lazy dolt of a shoemaker, Not Yet, who couldn't make a decent boot to save his life" that he didn't see what was going on right behind him.

'This all happened several times, with the Baron never getting very far ahead, until at last he realised what was happening.

'"You can't stop me, Tashi. I'm going to wake the village and tell them what you have been up to. Your family will be run out of town and at last I will be free of your meddling."

'The sky was beginning to lighten and down below in the village Tashi could see people stirring. The Baron was hurrying along the path. He would soon be reaching the village, raising the alarm, shouting from the square that Tashi and his family were thieves. No one would want to live beside a family who stole. They would have to leave the village that had been the family home for a hundred years.

'"Where will we go?" Grandma cried as she sank to the ground in despair.

'Tashi had just one last trick to try. He put his fingers to his lips and gave a piercing whistle.

'He didn't have long to wait. Very quickly there was a crashing through the trees and out leapt his dog, Pongo.

'"Come, Pongo," Tashi called as he ran after the Baron. The Baron looked over his shoulder when he heard them coming and smiled scornfully.

'"Guard him!" Tashi ordered. "Pongo, stay!"

'The Baron sneered. "That animal was my creature, you don't think he will obey *you* now, do you?" He glared down at Pongo. "SIT!"

'"Guard!" Tashi repeated desperately.

'Pongo looked from one to the other. He hesitated, his pink tongue lolling.

'"*SIT*, YOU IDIOT DOG!" the Baron shouted.

'Pongo made up his mind. He bounded over to the Baron and barked. He circled him, snarling, until the Baron dropped to his knees.

'"Good boy, Pongo," Tashi beamed. "Guard!"

'Tashi ran back to Grandmother. "Come on, Grandma. We're nearly there."

'It was amazing how quickly Grandma revived once she saw the Baron cowering before Pongo the Brave. "Make yourself comfortable, Baron," she crowed. "You'll be there for some time."

'As soon as they arrived at the village square, Tashi rang the Magic Bell. When everyone had gathered around, he showed them their missing treasures and explained what had happened. People tutted and looked at each other in wonder but they were all so pleased to see their goods again, they were soon smiling and nodding to Grandma. Someone noticed how exhausted she was and brought over a chair. Another gave her a cup of tea.

'This was too much for Grandma and she had a little weep. "She'll feel much better after that," said Third Aunt, who knew about such things.

'Tashi thought it was probably time to release the Baron. So he gave three sharp whistles. In a flash Pongo came bouncing up, but the Baron wasn't far behind. He pushed importantly through the crowd.

'"Quiet everyone! I have something to tell–"

'"Good morning, Baron," Tashi stepped up beside him and smiled at the villagers. "The Baron met us coming down the mountain but his heels were so sore he told us to come on ahead." The Baron tried to push in front of Tashi and started to speak again.

'Tashi raised his voice. "I was just about to tell everyone how you helped us and how you put Wise-as-an-Owl's golden cup in your pocket so it wouldn't fall out of the quilt. Your left pocket," he added helpfully.

'"The Baron looked down at Tashi with furious eyes. Slowly he put his hand into his pocket and pulled out the golden measuring cup. He and Tashi stared at each other long and hard.

'"Just so, Tashi," he said stiffly, as he handed the cup to Wise-as-an-Owl with a little bow.

'They all had a party that night to celebrate getting their things back. And Grandma tied a string around her ankle and hooked it up to a bell on her door. But she never did sleepwalk again.'

Jack stretched and nudged his dad. 'Don't tell me *you* are asleep.'

'Huh? No, no, I was just thinking. Your Uncle Joe was a bit of a sleepwalker when he was young. Sleepwalked right into the girls' dormitory one night at school camp.'

'Yeah?' said Jack. 'So, how about we *all* go out shopping, and while we're there, we could get me an ice-cream?'

'Yep,' said Mum, standing up, 'and don't forget the organic broccoli.'

'How could we?' said Dad, and went to find his shoes.

TASHI and the
MIXED-UP MONSTER

'Do you ever remember your dreams?'
asked Jack.

'Sometimes,' said Dad, 'when they're
scary.'

'Me too,' agreed Jack. 'Take last
night. I was being chased through the
jungle by a monster with two heads –
one was a lion and the other a goat. The
lion-head kept roaring "*rip, tear, kill!*"
and the goat-head kept saying "stop and
smell the grass why don't you?"'

'Gosh. Which jungle was this? The African or the Amazon?'

'Oh Dad, what does it *matter*?'

'Well there's completely different animal life for a start. Take your typical Amazon forest–'

'Did it catch you in the end?' put in Mum.

'The monster? No. The two heads were so busy arguing, it got kind of paralysed. Then a python slid down from a tree and strangled it.'

'Must have been the African jungle,' said Dad, 'what with the python and all.'

'That's not true, pythons are everywhere,' said Mum. 'We had one in our back yard when I was a girl.'

Dad shuddered. 'You never mentioned *that* when I came to visit.'

'You know, Tashi had troubles with a mixed-up monster,' Jack said. 'He was telling me about it yesterday.'

'A*ha*, maybe that's why you had the dream!' said Mum. 'What happened? Go on, we want to know everything.'

'Well, see, it was like this. It was
a sunny Sunday afternoon and Tashi,
Ah Chu and Lotus Blossom were sprawled
on the grass behind Wise-as-an-Owl's
house. They'd just had a big lunch and
felt a bit sleepy – especially Ah Chu.'

'Ah, that one!' cried Dad. 'He'd eat the
bottom off a porcupine if it stood still for
long enough!'

'Yeah. Well, they could see Wise-as-an-Owl nodding over a book in his garden workshop, and his son, Much-to-Learn, puttering about behind him at a table. Ah Chu was yawning, almost asleep, when suddenly Tashi put his head to the ground. "Listen," he said, "can you hear something rumbling?"

'A second later, Wise-as-an-Owl burst out of the workshop. "Tashi, children, *run*! – no, it's too late. *Hide*!" He pulled them over to some thick bushes.

'"What is it?" Tashi asked.

'Wise-as-an-Owl groaned. "Oh dear, I should have seen it coming. Much-to-Learn has been reading ahead of his lessons in the Book of Spells. It seems he's found the chapter on how to create a Chimera."

'The three friends looked at each other anxiously. "What is a Chimera?"

'"It's a creature from the past – a fearsome, fire-breathing monster with the head of a lion, the body of a goat and the tail of a serpent."

'"Wah! How big is it?" Tashi wanted to know.

'Wise-as-an-Owl's voice quavered. "This one is almost as big as the workshop."

'Suddenly the workshop walls split
apart and the roof shot up in the air.
A huge snarling lion's head appeared
above the skyline.

'"Or maybe even a bit bigger," Wise-as-
an-Owl faltered.

'The head sent out a thunderous roar
that rolled out, echoing and re-echoing
across the fields.

'"Do you think Much-to-Learn got
away?" Tashi asked in a small voice.

'"No. I left him hiding under the table."
Wise-as-an-Owl's face quivered and his
eyes filled. "I don't know how long he can
stay out of sight." The old man's knees
suddenly folded beneath him and he sank
onto the grass. "Help me up, Tashi. I must
go back to my son."

'Tashi and Lotus Blossom put their
arms around him and looked at each other
fearfully over his head.

'"What can we do, Wise-as-an-Owl?"
Tashi asked. "How can we get rid of this
creature?"

'"I can't say for sure," Wise-as-an-Owl moaned. "There is a magic formula somewhere for dealing with the monster, but it's not the sort of thing you study every day. And I couldn't stop to take the Book of Spells before leaving."

'"No, of course not," Tashi agreed. "I wonder what a Chimera eats. Do you know, by any chance?"

'"Well, lions eat animals and people, and goats eat grass and cardboard," Wise-as-an-Owl sighed. "It will be one or the other, I suppose. Help me up, would you?"

'"That roar didn't sound like a grass-eater to me," Ah Chu gulped. "And it sounded hungry."

'"You can't go just yet, not while that... thing is there!" Tashi said.

'But Wise-as-an-Owl climbed back through the bushes. He had only taken two shaky steps when the shell of the workshop fell away and the Chimera rose to its full height, unfurling a pair of monstrous wings.

'"You didn't say anything about *wings*, Wise-as-an-Owl!" squeaked Lotus Blossom.

'"That's because they shouldn't be there," the old man sighed. "Much-to-Learn has got it all wrong again."

'They clutched each other as the Chimera tested its wings, and then flew out across the rice fields.

'"Do you think it will come back?" Ah Chu whimpered.

'"Yes, I think it will," Wise-as-an-Owl nodded. "This was its birth-place after all. But I must use this chance to bring my son out."

'"And get the Book of Spells," Tashi added. "I'll come with you."

'Ah Chu took a deep breath. "We'll wait here and keep watch."

'"To warn you if it comes back," Lotus Blossom promised.

818

'Tashi heard Much-to-Learn before he saw him amongst the splintered planks and shattered glass of the workshop. He was moaning and cursing, trying to wriggle out from under the broken table.

'"My son, thank the gods, you're *safe*!" cried Wise-as-an-Owl.

'While he lifted the wood away, Tashi searched for the Book of Spells, his ears pricked anxiously for the sound of flapping wings. He found the book under a pile of rubble, undamaged except for a sooty hoof print right over the page *Mixed-Up Monsters*.

'Wise-as-an-Owl was gently
examining his son. "*Ouch!*" Much-to-
Learn yelled as he tried to move his right
arm. It was broken; Tashi could see it
dangling and useless. But they had no time
for making slings, Ah Chu's urgent whistle
told them that. Much-to-Learn flung his
good arm around his father's neck and
they hobbled back to their hideaway.

'Two heartbeats later, the Chimera glided down to its birth-place amongst the ruins of the workshop.

'Safely back in the bushes, Wise-as-an-Owl flipped through the Book of Spells until he found the page he needed: *How to Destroy the Chimera*. Tashi tried to peep over his shoulder. It was too hard to read the ancient writing in the dusky light, so he turned to help Lotus Blossom. She was making Much-to-Learn as comfortable as she could with a sling and a splint.

'Soon the old man lifted his head. "Yes, it's quite straightforward. Once we get the ingredients from my library–"

'Ah Chu choked. "Go back down there, do you mean?"

'"Just give me a list," Tashi said quickly. "I know where all your potions and mixing bowls are kept, Wise-as-an-Owl. I'm quick and light – it will be easier for me to clamber over all that wreckage. Look," he went on, "it's nearly dark and the Chimera has been quiet for ages. I'll creep down and see if it's asleep."

'Tashi wished he felt as brave as he had sounded. A droning noise greeted him as he drew near. He thought his pounding heart would surely wake the Chimera as he felt his way over the smashed walls and windows. The monster slept, eyes closed, wings furled amongst the wreckage. Only its great tail lay slowly twitching, gleaming through the grass.

'Tashi tip-toed to the library in the main house where the moonlight poured through the windows, lighting up the shelves of beakers in its cold, eerie beam. Working silently, Tashi found the ingredients on his list, one by one, and put them into a large mixing bowl. He was almost finished when he heard something move behind him.

'He stood, terrified, his insides churning.
The sound came again, slithering towards
him across the floor. The hairs on the back
of his neck prickled. He looked down and
saw something glittering in the moonlight,
beside his heel. The tip of the monster's
tail!

'Tashi tried to slow his breath, to make
his hands still. Maybe the creature would
think he was a statue, or a piece of wood.
But the tail was sliding over his foot!

'He dug his toes into his boots. He imagined he was a tree, rooted to the ground. The serpent tail was heavy, like the weight of two men.

'Tashi was melting with fright. But the tail came to rest over his feet. Oh *please*, thought Tashi, *please stay asleep*! He counted to one hundred, and still the tail didn't move. Then slowly, smooth as honey dripping from a spoon, Tashi slid one foot then the other from under the tail.

'When he was free, Tashi bolted back
to the hideaway. Wise-as-an-Owl told
him they'd have to wait until it was light
before mixing the potion. They all tried
to get some rest but twigs and stones stuck
into their backs and Ah Chu's stomach
was grumbling like thunder. When the sun
finally came up Ah Chu said it looked like
a great fried egg and that made everyone
even hungrier.

'But it was time to get to work. Wise-as-an-Owl checked every item, asking Tashi to tick each ingredient as he added it to the bowl. Much-to-Learn sniffed, offended by his father's choice of helper. "*I* could have done that, better than young Tashi," he said, "only my arm–"

'"If you hadn't played the fool with the Book of Spells, we wouldn't have to do any of this," his father growled.

'He turned to Tashi. "We'll wait until the Chimera goes hunting for its next meal and then take this bowl to his den. We'll just have to keep our fingers crossed that he drinks it when he returns."

'Finally the Chimera woke and left to look for food. When he was out of sight Tashi, with Wise-as-an-Owl close behind, carried the bowl of precious mixture down to the ruins of the workshop. He was just deciding where to put it when the air was suddenly filled with the screams of a terrified pig.

'"Quick Tashi, let's go!" Wise-as-an-Owl swung round, twisting his ankle on a loose board. He staggered and fell, hitting his head on the edge of the table as he went crashing down.

'Tashi's breath stopped in his chest. The old man's face was still. Tashi tugged at his arm and called his name, but there was no response. He wasn't dead, was he? You couldn't die from a fall, could you?

'He tried to drag his old friend across
the rubble. Wise-as-an-Owl was frail and
thin, but now he seemed as heavy as a
sackful of bricks.

'And then, Tashi looked up to see the
Chimera flying across the fields towards
him. So this is it, he thought. This is how
I'm going to die.

'He felt a sharp shove in the middle of his back and Much-to-Learn said, "Quick, take my father's feet, Tashi. You two, whatever your names are–"

'"*LOTUS* BLOSSOM is my name!" said Lotus Blossom, "and this here is AH *CHU*, if you *don't* mind, and as if you *wouldn't* know our names, when we've both followed you into this death-trap, risking our very *lives* for a mistake *you*–"

'"Oh just get on with it," panted Much-to-Learn. He was dragging the workshop door across the floor with his left hand.

'"What are you doing with that?" asked Lotus Blossom. But then she said nothing more as she watched him lift the door and prop it up against a broken chair.

'"Bring him over here, quick, and hide!" cried Much-to-Learn.

'They ducked down behind the door just as the Chimera dropped to the ground. It looked around warily and moved over to sniff the bowl. Four pairs of eyes watched it without blinking.

'It slurped the potion.

'Out of the corner of his eye, Tashi noticed that Wise-as-an-Owl had lifted his head. The old man looked around, dazed, and rubbed his forehead.

'*CRASH!* The door suddenly banged down, *WHUMP!* on the floor.

'The Chimera sprang up with a snarl
and faced its enemies. It spread its wings
wide, scales glinting like fire, cutting like
glass. Its teeth were bared, its nostrils
flared in fury. It pawed the ground with
its terrible hoof and opened its mouth and
roared a thousand times louder than the
Magic Warning Bell.

'The children clapped their hands over
their ears and squeezed their eyes shut, and
still the grinding roar went on and on and
on until...

'"Open your eyes. Look!" cried Tashi.

'"No, I can't!" wailed Ah Chu.

'As the Chimera sprang towards them, Tashi could suddenly see through it, to the chair behind. The fiery scales were growing dull, wavering in the air like puddles after rain. The dripping teeth were fading with every second. Something hot stung Tashi's cheek, leaving a small wet patch. And then, as the children all opened their eyes wide, the monster dissolved like a bubble in the air and there was nothing left to see, at all.

'"What? How?" Ah Chu was rubbing his eyes as if he couldn't believe them. The others just stood silently, feeling their hearts thumping.

'"Well done, Father. Brilliant! I knew you'd find the very potion we needed! Let's–"

'But you know, they never did hear what Much-to-Learn was going to suggest because there was suddenly a dreadful yelling and cursing coming from the field below. Wise-as-an-Owl tottered off to find out what it was.

'He came back with Mr Ping from the village. Much-to-Learn was still beaming. "Well, as I always say, all's well that ends well!"

'"Yes you always do, my son," Wise-as-an-Owl said dryly. "Perhaps you would like to explain that to Mr Ping. He says that someone has stolen his prize pig."

'Well,' said Dad, getting up to make
a cup of tea, 'it just goes to show you
should always listen to your father. Isn't
that right, Jack?'

'I suppose,' said Jack. 'Especially if your
father is as wise as an owl.'

'That's right,' said Dad happily.
'Absolutely right.'

GUILTY or NOT?

'That's *so* not fair!' exploded Mum when Tashi finished telling her the story.

'What?' asked Dad, walking into the kitchen.

'Well,' said Tashi, 'it was like this. At school today, Arthur Trouble drew a rude picture on the board with chalk but Angus Figment got the blame for it–'

'That's ridiculous!' said Dad. 'Angus Figment – as *if!*'

'Yeah,' agreed Jack, 'but see, Angus came into the classroom with chalk on his hands. The teacher wouldn't listen when he explained he'd just been drawing up handball lines in the playground, plus he wouldn't even *know* how to draw a naked mermaid because he's much more interested in Ancient Egypt and, by the way, did she know that the priests used to pluck out every hair on their bodies, even their eyelashes?'

'It's true,' said Tashi. 'Angus is only interested in Egyptian mummies. He draws them all over his books, and people's arms. Although sometimes he draws jackal masks, which look quite spooky.'

'Well, anyway,' Mum turned to Jack, 'you said you actually *saw* Arthur Trouble drawing on the blackboard. Why didn't you go and tell?'

'It's not that simple. Arthur's already in so much trouble and he's got a mean temper, and anyway I don't like dobbing.'

'But it's not fair on Angus!' cried Mum.

'That's right,' said Tashi. 'Something like that happened to me once, over a ball game.'

'Really?' said Dad. 'What did you do? Wait a sec, I'll make the tea – oh boy, I'm just in the mood for a story!'

'Well,' Tashi started, when the water
had boiled, 'one day Ah Chu and I were
playing a game of Catch when our ball
flew over a wall and into Soh Meen's
courtyard. And there was a loud splash.
Wah!

'We had to run then because this furious
man came barrelling out of the house.
It was Soh Meen, chasing us with his
broomstick. "Who did that?" he shouted.
"Who threw that ball into my fish pond
and very likely killed my precious carp!"

'"We're very sorry, Soh Meen," Ah Chu called over his shoulder. "Tashi didn't mean to do it." I gave Ah Chu a dirty look and stopped running.'

'I would have given him more than a dirty look!' said Dad. 'I would–'

'You would have sat him down,' said Mum, 'and talked to him about what it means to be a friend, and sharing responsibility.'

'How did you *know*? You took the words right out of my mouth!' cried Dad.

'Well, I didn't have time for that unfortunately,' said Tashi, 'because Soh Meen was shaking his fist at me.

'"It was a bad mistake, Soh Meen," I said. "Could we come in and see if the carp are hurt?"

'Well, thank goodness the fish were swimming about quite happily, but still Soh Meen gave us each a good whack with his broomstick and refused to return our ball. Apart from a sore bottom, that was the end of the matter, I thought.

'Until the next day.

'When I went to the square the following morning a crowd was gathered there. They were listening to a loud and angry speaker. I knew that voice.

'Someone let me through and I moved up to the front while the voice raged on, shouting "And then I saw them. My beautiful golden carp, lying upturned, dead, in a pool of stinking oil!"

'The murmur of the crowd was like a wind whooshing through the rice paddies. My heart sank.

'"And there is the culprit!" Soh Meen roared, pointing right at me. "Yesterday he attacked my carp with a ball. Then last night he sneaked back and finished my poor fish off! He poured bad oil into my beautiful clean pond!"

'"I didn't! I didn't! The ball was an accident..."

'But it was no use, Soh Meen went on and on until people started to believe him. The next few days were terrible. Ah Chu tried to explain what had really happened but Soh Meen wouldn't let him be heard. I kept turning the question over in my mind. How do you prove that you *didn't* do something?'

'I know, I know!' Dad cried. 'By proving that someone else *did*.'

'That's exactly right. But that was the easy bit – finding the real fish-poisoner would be the hard part. So I made a list of all the people who had a grudge against Soh Meen. There were quite a few, actually, but that didn't prove anything. And then my mother poured a glass of lemonade for me and there, suddenly, was the answer. "I have to go and see Wise-as-an-Owl straight away," I told her.

'Wise-as-an-Owl looked at me calmly over his spectacles, just as he always does. He said, "Sit down, Tashi, and get your breath. Now, why do you need the Truth Potion? You know I don't use these magic brews without serious thought."

'When I explained my problem to him he chuckled and shook his head. "I would really like to be a cricket in the corner of your kitchen tomorrow evening, Tashi. You must be sure to tell me what happens when they all find themselves speaking the honest truth."

'So my family invited all the people on my list to come to our house that evening to discuss the situation. My mother told each one that their advice would be really important. Besides Soh Meen and his wife there were: the Wicked Baron, Mrs Ping, Mr Ping, Not Yet, Teacher Pang, Granny White Eyes, Tiki Pu and Luk Ahed.

'As soon as the guests arrived my mother poured them a glass of her delicious lemonade, which she had mixed up in a big jug, together with a cup and a half of Truth Potion.

'"This is very good," said the Baron, surprised, as he held out his glass for another helping.

'"It's the best I've ever had," agreed Mr Ping. "What's your secret?"

'"*I* know the secret of this lemonade," crowed Mrs Ping. "I peeked through the curtain one time while it was being made. They use limes as well as lemons, you know."

'My mother looked annoyed but Grandma poked me in the ribs and whispered, "It's working! Now we'll see what they *really* think about each other."

'My uncle Tiki Pu joined us at the table and nodded to Luk Ahed. "You haven't come along to our card evenings lately, Luk Ahed."

'"No, and neither will any of the others if you keep cheating like you did last time, Tiki Pu," growled Luk Ahed.

'Before Tiki Pu could answer, Granny White Eyes said quietly to herself, "I wonder why the Baron always smells so unpleasant. He has plenty of money for hot water."

'The Baron went red and jumped to his feet, but my father quickly spoke up. "We were wondering if you would all be so kind as to tell us where you were on Saturday night? Someone might have seen or heard something that would help. Tiki Pu?"

'Tiki Pu shrugged. "I haven't been near Soh Meen's house for a week."

'My heart sank. Tiki Pu had been my surest suspect.

'Not Yet suddenly piped up. "Teacher Pang and I were in Soh Meen's garden that evening. We were keeping watch because we're sure he's the one who has been dumping his rubbish in other people's garbage bins. He's too mean to pay for a big enough bin for himself."

'Soh Meen choked on his lemonade.

'"But he didn't leave his house that night," Not Yet went on gloomily, "so it was a waste of time."

'"How dare you talk about me like that!" shouted Soh Meen.

'"No, I never would have dared to before," said Not Yet. "I don't know what came over me."

'Teacher Pang turned to the Baron. "Did you see anything odd or unusual that evening, Baron?"

'The Baron cleared his throat and was surprised to hear himself say, "No, I was at the other end of the village smashing Mrs Yang's best melons. I am determined to win the prize for the biggest melons at this year's harvest festival, you see."

'Everyone gasped and looked at their hands, or the floor.

'"I didn't see anything either, I'm afraid," said Mrs Ping after an awkward pause. "I only went outside once during the evening because Mr Ping made the most dreadful smell and I had to get some fresh air."

'"I think he's just done it again," said Luk Ahed, who was sitting closest.

'"He thinks, just because they're silent, no one will notice," Mrs Ping said confidingly to Luk Ahed.

'"The silent ones are the worst," said Teacher Pang.

'"Well, I never knew that," said Mr Ping wonderingly. "You should have told me, dear. Next time we have beans, *I'll* be the one to step outside."

'Mrs Ping smiled and patted his hand across the table. "Thank you, Ping dear."

'There was a silence as everyone looked
at the only person who hadn't explained
where they'd been. "Well, *I* certainly didn't
kill any fish," Luk Ahead said angrily.

'"No, I know you didn't. I did,"
whispered Mrs Soh Meen.

'"YOU!" thundered her husband.

'"Yes. It was all a terrible accident. I dug a hole at the bottom of the garden near the fish pond to get rid of some bad oil. It must have leaked into the pond overnight and killed the fish. It was wrong to let Tashi take the blame," she went on dreamily as the lemonade did its work, "but I knew I would never hear the end of it if I told my husband that it was *my* fault. He really is an awful bully. And Tashi, well, he doesn't have to *live* with him."

'No one spoke. Soh Meen cleared his throat and rubbed his nose.

'"It really is a strange smell. Perhaps it's bad breath," said Granny White Eyes, nodding at the Baron.

'"Or the terrible tobacco he smokes," Mrs Ping replied. "At least Mr Ping doesn't do that."

'"I'm not listening to any more of this," shouted the Baron as he stormed out of the house. "I was expecting a pleasant evening deciding about Tashi's punishment, not insults."

'My father thought he had better bring
the meeting to an end before anyone else
said something they would later regret, but
he didn't close the door quickly enough
to stop the Baron hearing Mrs Ping say
to Granny White Eyes, "That *was* an
interesting evening. Why don't we call in
on Mrs Yang and see if she knows what
happened to her melons?"

'Hmm,' said Jack, taking another cup-
cake. 'I wish we had a Truth Potion at our
school.'

Just then there was a knock at the door
and Angus Figment walked in. 'Guess what
everyone. Trouble confessed about the
mermaid!'

'How come?' asked Mum. 'Did you talk to him about what it means to be a friend and how he has to take responsibility?'

'Yeah, a bit, but you know how he's always pestering me to lend him my book *Secrets of the Tomb*? Well, I said he could have it for the weekend if he owned up. Plus I said I'd draw a really spooky jackal on him if he confessed straight away. So he did. You know, he's not so bad, Arthur Trouble, when you get to know him. May I have some cake, to go with the tea?' He shot a worried glance at Tashi. 'They're not Ghost Cakes or anything though, are they?'

TASHI and the
PHOENIX

'There's a surprise for you in the garden,'
said Mum, when Jack and Tashi walked into
the kitchen.

'Good or bad?' asked Jack.

'Sometimes it's hard to tell,' sighed Mum,
mysteriously.

There was a loud bang from the garden,
then a roar. Both boys jumped.

'That could be a lion tamer with a gun,'
whispered Jack, peering out.

'Or a warlord with a temper,' said Tashi
nervously. But he straightened his shoulders
and went outside with his friend.

A thump came from inside the shed, followed by a crash and a very bad word. The boys opened the door just as a big hot hairy creature shot out.

'Uncle Joe! You've grown a beard!' cried Jack.

'You come back right now and put your tools away!' came Dad's voice from the shed. 'Always the same, ever since we were kids!'

'What were you doing in the shed?' asked Tashi.

Joe hugged the boys and put a hand on their shoulders. 'I'm inventing an absolutely fantastic musical instrument for my dear friend Primrose. Unfortunately my hammer slipped and caught your father's thumb.'

'Have you come to stay?'

'Well, a few days, that's if…'

'Then maybe you should get back in there,' suggested Jack, 'and help clean up.'

When Joe had disappeared inside the shed, Jack grinned. 'I like it when Uncle Joe comes to stay. But he never gives us much warning.'

'In my experience,' said Tashi, 'surprises can be tricky things. Especially surprises with uncles in them.'

'Oh, like that uncle of yours, Tiki Pu!' frowned Jack.

'Yes, he used to make me *so* angry –'

'Wait a sec, tell it when Dad comes out. A story will put him in a good mood.'

When everyone was sitting comfortably, and Dad had stopped muttering at Uncle Joe (even passing him the biscuits), Tashi began.

'It was like this,' he said. 'One day I was so angry I thought I was going to explode! I ran out of the house, across the fields and into the forest –'

'What made you so mad?' asked Jack, his mouth full of biscuit.

'Did someone go into your shed and mess with all your tools and hit your thumb and then run *off*?' asked Dad. Joe hid his face in his cup of tea. When he looked up, his beard was dripping.

'No, it was worse than that,' said Tashi. 'My Uncle Tiki Pu had been up to his old tricks again. He wasn't just annoying – no offence, Uncle Joe – he was *dangerous*. And this time, he put our whole family at risk.'

'So what did he do?' asked Uncle Joe.

'He's *coming* to that,' said Dad. 'Let him tell the story *his* way.'

'I was only saying –'

'Well, there I was,' Tashi put in, 'boiling with fury, running blindly, when suddenly I found myself at the entrance to a small cave.

'The air was very still, and at my feet were the embers of a fire. Two logs still glowed red and their branches were furry with ash. As I watched, the ash beneath the logs began to stir. Flashes of colour glowed through the grey: red, gold, purple, emerald, like jewels. Was treasure buried under there?'

'Well, was there?' cried Joe.

'Wipe your beard,' said Dad. 'Every time you shake your head, drops fall on my plate. In fact, why have you stopped shaving? You look like a werewolf.'

'What was under the logs?' asked Mum.
'*Treasure?*'

'No,' said Tashi. 'Or at least, not the usual
kind. Something was moving in the embers.
A bird with a tail like sunrise! I watched it
step right out of the dying fire and preen
itself.

'"Oh, how beautiful you are!" I cried. "Why weren't you burned in that fire?"

'The bird looked at me thoughtfully for a moment. "I am a Phoenix," he said calmly. "We Phoenix don't burn. In fact, every five hundred years we are born again in flames." He smoothed an emerald feather lovingly, turning this way and that to get a good view of himself. "Don't you *love* the new me?"

'"Yes," I told him, because it was true. Already I was thinking that perhaps here lay the answer to my troubles. "You are a miracle," I said. "You're as magnificent as fire itself! I remember Wise-as-an-Owl telling me once about you. Did you know that you have your own page in the Book of Spells? It says *Phoenix have eyes of crystal and tail feathers of gold*." I couldn't help my own eyes opening wide. His unearthly beauty made me feel strangely hungry, with a longing for some taste I would never have. "Oh fabulous Phoenix, you could be the very person to help me with a terrible problem."

'The Phoenix instantly drooped. He closed his eyes with boredom. "Why should I?" he asked.

'"As an act of kindness?" I suggested. The
Phoenix hunched his wings disdainfully.
"You are so beautiful," I coaxed, "that I
would like to call you Glorious One – or
Glory for short."

'"As you like," he said, "but I still haven't
time to help you. That's not what we
Phoenix are for. Anyway, I'll be leaving in
the morning, as soon as my colours have
deepened."

'I decided right then to stay by his side all
night. I knew my mother would be worried,
but she'd understand if my plan worked the
way I wanted.

'In the morning I made one last try. "Glory, what do Phoenix like best?"

'"Hmm, I can only tell you what I would like above all else."

'"Yes? What?"

'"To feel a mother's love."

'I drew a deep breath. "If you help me with my trouble, Glory, I promise that you will have your wish."

'The Phoenix settled down in the ashes. "Tell me," he said.

'"Well, it's like this," I began. "I have an uncle, Tiki Pu, who will say anything to get out of a tight spot. This morning he came sidling into our house looking guilty, as well he might. We knew straight away that something was wrong."

'"What have you done now, Tiki Pu?"
my father sighed.

'"There's no need to look at me like
that," sniffed Tiki Pu, "as if I'm *always*
making trouble. It's just, see, I was asked
to spend the evening with the Warlord and
his friends. They were all boasting about
how many splendid horses and houses they
had. I simply couldn't stand it." He stopped,
embarrassed, and then went on with a rush.
"And so I told them that on my last voyage
to Africa I had captured the most dazzling
creature in the world. That was good – they
all looked crestfallen."

'"But then the Warlord said, 'Where is this creature? I want to see it!' Well, I hadn't thought of that, and in my confusion, I'm afraid I told him that I had given it to my dear family. Well, you know the Warlord. He said, 'I want this creature brought to me by tomorrow at noon, otherwise –' Tiki Pu didn't say what *otherwise* was, but you can be sure it will be the end of my family. Glory, we don't have anything like this dazzling treasure to give the Warlord. I don't know what we can possibly do."

'The Phoenix cocked his head to one side as I began to explain my plan. Then he interrupted crossly. "We Phoenix are not born to be some Warlord's plaything. We must be free to soar the heavens and dazzle the stars. What you are asking would be very undignified, Tashi." His feathers ruffled in outrage.

'"It would only be for such a little while," I explained, and I told him the second part of my plan. He quite liked the idea of astonishing the Warlord with his beauty. His feathers calmed as I talked and finally he agreed to come home with me. Besides, he was curious to meet Tiki Pu.

'I sat myself on his back amongst those
fabulous feathers and a few minutes later we
were sitting beside my amazed family at the
dinner table. Tiki Pu revived like a thirsty
plant when he saw the Phoenix and heard
my plan. He showed not a moment's worry
for the danger he had brought to the family,
and could only talk of the riches the Phoenix
would bring to him. Glory looked at him in
wonder. "He is even worse than you said,"
he whispered in my ear.

'We found a large cage for Glory and spent some time coaxing him to step into it. "This is not at all the sort of thing we Phoenix are used to," he said, looking down his beak.

'At noon the next day we were in the Warlord's Great Hall. When he saw Glory, the Warlord jumped up from his gold chair and clapped his hands. He threw Tiki Pu and me a coin each and waved us away. He could look at nothing but the flame-coloured feathers of the Phoenix. As we were leaving the hall I said to the Warlord, "You do understand, my Lord, that my family has given up a great prize for you?"

'"Yes, yes," he replied. "In fact you and your uncle must stay for the banquet I'm holding tonight. I'm going to show off this fabulous creature to all my friends and enemies."

'That evening, Glory in his cage was the
centre of attention in the Great Hall. He
preened and bowed as the guests marvelled
and told each other tall tales of Phoenix
they had almost met. His feathers glowed
so intensely, he looked like a small trapped
sun. It hurt my eyes, and my heart, to look
at him. I checked once more for the small
package wrapped in silk in my pocket.

'Towards the end of the evening, I bent under the table, pretending to look for something I'd dropped. In the darkness, amongst people's fine leather boots, I drew out my silk handkerchief. I undid the knot and took out the squashed piece of ghost cake. Then I stood up and strolled over to Glory. Quickly, quietly, I dropped the ghost cake on the floor of Glory's cage.

'He nodded to me and gobbled it up with his ruby-red beak. Then he stepped through the bamboo bars that melted away at his touch. I couldn't help laughing with relief as I watched him.

'But what was he doing now? He froze, looking back at the cage in wonder. He was entranced by the magic of the ghost cake. To my horror he stepped back into the cage and out again through the bars – in and out, again and again.

'And then, instead of flying straight for the
open windows as we had planned, he glided
up to the heavy gold chandelier hanging over
the Warlord's chair. From there he dropped
a deposit on the Warlord's head! That's the
kind of bird Glory is – he just has to show
off and make mischief!

'The Warlord sat shocked and silent as something white and smelly trickled down his cheeks and into his ears.

'Glory dived and tipped a flask of wine over one tipsy guest, and knocked a large bowl of vegetables over another. He was having such a good time, he didn't notice the Warlord and his men hurry over to lock all the doors and windows.

'Too late, Glory realised what he had done. I had told him the magical effects of ghost cake did not last long. He flew wildly around the room, pushing in vain at the high windows. He flashed me an anguished look. *Serves you right!* I felt like shouting, to teach him a lesson. *I warned you to be quick!*

'The Warlord and his guests were rushing about the hall throwing cloaks and tablecloths in the air like washing flapping in the wind, trying to bring the Phoenix down.

'I made my way over to the far wall and felt in my pocket for ghost cake crumbs. Nothing. Panic was making me hot all over. Breathe deep, I told myself. Carefully I drew the scrunched handkerchief out of my pocket. I smoothed it in my palm. There! One last crumb, tucked into a fold of silk. Just then someone grabbed my arm, jerking me off balance. "Quick, give me the cake!" hissed Tiki Pu.

'My fist closed tightly over the crumb. "No, I promised Glory no harm would come to him." I pulled away, waving my hand to Glory, and threw the crumb up into the air.

'Glory wheeled back but the crumb was falling faster. He dived right down like something about to crash, his beak pointed at the earth, then suddenly up he swooped.

Oh, he was so beautiful, like a shooting star.
He caught the cake in his beak and then,
without a check, he sailed on through the
great stone wall and out into the freedom of
the frosty night.

'The Warlord stormed over to us. "You cheating bamboozlers!" he raged. "You have shamed me in front of my guests! You'll pay for this!"

'Tiki Pu sank to his knees, whimpering. He was going to be no help, as usual.

'"But, Sir, there is no shame," I cried. "You have given your friends – and enemies – a night to remember! Just look about you!" The Warlord turned. Indeed, his Great Hall had never been so lively. People were laughing and shouting and pointing, waving their arms in the air as they described to each other what they had just seen. "This will be a story to tell their children and grandchildren in years to come."

'Just then a guest slapped the Warlord on the back. "Well, old friend," he gasped, "What a night this has been! You have shown us not only a fabulous Phoenix, but a Phoenix who flies through walls!" And he slurped another glass of wine to celebrate.

'The Warlord looked stunned, but he smiled stiffly and nodded to the guards to push open the doors and windows. He glared at Tiki Pu, but made no move to stop us as we quickly made our way outside where Glory was waiting in the branch of a plum tree.

'When we reached home, Glory looked around expectantly. "Well, what about your promise, Tashi?"

'I glanced over my shoulder at my mother, who smiled shyly. "I promised you would feel a mother's love," I told him. "Well, this is a mother – *my* mother – and believe me, Glory, she is so grateful for what you have done for us that she will love you like her own for the rest of your days."

'At that, my mother held out her arms and Glory flew right into them.'

Dad cleared his throat. He wiped his eyes. 'Ah yes, family. Nothing like it.' He looked at his brother Joe. 'Can't get used to the beard though. Suppose it will just take time.'

Joe blew his nose. 'Like a few days?'

Dad grinned and Mum got up to clear away the tea things. Jack saw her lean down to whisper in Tashi's ear, and kiss his cheek.

'What did she say?' Jack asked Tashi when they were outside.

'She said the Phoenix might have been *my* treasure, but I happen to be *hers*.'

'Well, you're mine too,' said Jack, standing up and spreading out his arms, 'and this whole family's, and this whole *world's*!' He went running around the garden until Tashi tackled him and Jack flipped Tashi over with an ancient wrestling move taught to him by his father, who'd been taught by *his* father, the famous World Champion Suburban Lawn Wrestler.

The UNEXPECTED LETTER

'What a surprise!' said Mum, as she opened
a letter telling her that she'd won a luxury
car from a lottery in Nigeria. 'Especially as I
didn't even buy a ticket.'

'Life is full of surprises,' Uncle Joe told Jack.

'But they can turn out well or not so well,'
said Jack, 'depending on what you *do* with
them.'

Uncle Joe scratched his head. 'How do you mean?'

'Well, Tashi was talking about that very thing today.'

'Ah, I would have liked to have heard *that* conversation,' said Uncle Joe.

'Me too,' said Dad, coming into the kitchen.

'And me,' said Mum, handing him a tea towel.

'Well, it was like this,' said Jack, settling himself on a stool. 'There was a letter for Tashi. An unexpected letter –'

'*That's* not surprising,' said Uncle Joe. 'I get letters all the time. Mostly from the bank, which is bad news.'

'Well, it was surprising for Tashi. Nobody
could remember such a thing happening
before. The postman got off his bicycle and
waited to hear what it said. All the family
crowded around to see. But when Tashi had
read the letter, all he said was, "I'm sorry,
I can't tell you about it now. This letter has
already taken four days to get here and a
friend of mine is in terrible trouble. I have
to go straight away."

'His mother picked up the envelope that Tashi had dropped on the table. It was of the finest paper and was addressed in rich black ink by a delicate hand. The handwriting belonged to Princess Sarashina. And it looked like it had been written in a hurry.

'Tashi read the letter again in his bedroom.

Dear Tashi, it said. Something dreadful
has happened. My father the Emperor has
suddenly announced that my sister, Princess
Hoiti-Toiti, must marry Khan! You may not
remember him, Tashi. He is the son of the
Master of Revels, and for all the years
we have known him he has been sneaky
and cruel — I could tell you such stories!
Besides, Hoiti-Toiti loves Cha Ming, who is
good and kind, and loves her back.

My father won't talk about it anymore.
He just keeps saying Khan will do very
well — and the wedding will be held next
week! I know that you and Hoiti-Toiti have
not always got on together in the past, but
you are the only person I can think of, dear
Tashi, who might find a way to help. Please
come quickly!

'Tashi shuddered as he put down the letter. How could he forget the Master of Revels? He'd met him only the year before, and –'

'Nearly lost his feet!' cried Dad, almost dropping his tea towel. 'That villain was going to chop them off!'

'That's right,' nodded Jack. 'But Princess Sarashina sounded so worried that Tashi felt he must go to her. Quickly he stuffed some ghost cakes into his pocket, together with a balm for spider bites, plus a new herb Wise-as-an-Owl gave him for calming snakes. Then he put on his dancing shoes and told his family he would be back as soon as he could.

'When he arrived at the Palace, Tashi went looking for the Princess Sarashina and her sister. As he stole through the ornamental gardens he heard a voice he knew well: it was the Master of Revels. He was talking to his son Khan, and what Tashi heard next filled him with anger and dread. He moved closer, holding his breath to hear better.

'"I don't know," the Master of Revels was saying. "If the Emperor should find out…"

'Khan interrupted sharply. "He won't know a thing until it's too late, Father. I have already spread stories around the Palace that the Emperor is growing feeble-minded. People are talking. As soon as I am married I will declare that he is no longer fit to rule, and the throne will be mine – I mean ours," he quickly corrected himself.

'The Master of Revels shook his head. "We'll need more men. Too many of the Palace guards will stay loyal to the Emperor."

'"Yes, I know," Khan said impatiently. "That's why I have written this letter to General Xeng telling him to come at once with extra men."

'A troop of guards came marching past, and Khan told one of them to get a horse and deliver the letter. When the guard asked the way to the General's fortress, Khan shouted, "You fool! They'll tell you at the stables." Then he kicked the man in the bottom to hasten him on his way.

'Tashi, treading softly, keeping to the shadows, followed the guard. While he crept along, a cunning idea came to him. By the time the guard arrived at the stables, Tashi had worked out a plan. He bowed politely before the guard, and told him what was in his mind.

'That done, he hurried back to the Palace, searching through hallways,

skirting around piles of wedding presents
that guests had sent ahead, listening at doors,
until he finally heard the Princesses' voices.
Their door was locked. Of course – they
were in disgrace.

'Tashi swallowed a piece of ghost cake
and glided into the room. There was a loud
argument going on.

'" – and so there's no point in your trying to escape," Princess Sarashina was crying. "You'd be brought back to the Palace before you could say fried chicken feet, and Cha Ming would probably lose his head."

'"Then what do you suggest? Just sit here, waiting for the wedding and a life of misery with Khan?"

'The sisters jumped when they noticed Tashi standing beside them.

'"Where did you come from?" gasped Princess Hoiti-Toiti.

'"Tashi, at last!" cried Princess Sarashina, leaping up to hug him. "The wedding is tomorrow. Can you possibly help us?"

'Tashi blushed and glanced over Princess
Sarashina's shoulder at Hoiti-Toiti. She
was rolling her eyes. Still bossy and proud,
thought Tashi. She had a fine sense of her
high place in the world, and didn't really like
her sister's friendship with Tashi, who had a
lot of relatives but not one at the Palace.

'Tashi sighed. "Look, this is what we could
do," he said quietly. And he told the sisters
of the conversation he had overheard that
morning in the garden, and about Khan's
plans for the Emperor.

'"But how can we prove it?" Hoiti-Toiti objected. "My father would never believe a common boy like you over the son of his most trusted adviser."

'Tashi's ears flushed red and he wished yet again that this Princess had a nicer way of talking, even if he had to admit that she was right. "I spoke with a Palace guard on the way to the stables," he managed to answer calmly, "and persuaded him to let me have Khan's note to General Xeng."

'Princess Sarashina's eyes opened wide. "How did you do that?"

'"It wasn't very difficult. The guard had already decided to look for a new master, and when I explained how grateful the Emperor would be to have this warning about Khan's plan, he was only too happy to leave the note with me."

'"I knew you would think of something, Tashi!" Princess Sarashina beamed. "Now we must find a way for you to get close enough to speak to my father. There is to be a big pre-wedding dinner tonight, you know."

'"Yes, but Khan and his guards would never let me into the Banquet Hall." Tashi looked thoughtfully at the sisters. Then his eyes dropped to the beautiful carpet on the floor. He smiled. "I've just had another little idea. But first you must tell me where I can find Cha Ming."'

'Cha Ming had never eaten ghost cakes before, and he was very surprised when Tashi pulled him through the Palace wall. Princess Hoiti-Toiti ran to her beloved Cha Ming. "Not now," said Tashi. "Cha Ming and I have some arrangements to make. We'll be back in time to escort you both to the banquet."

914

'The girls were dressed ready for the evening when Tashi and Cha Ming returned. Princess Hoiti-Toiti tugged Cha Ming's arm. "Make him tell us what is going to happen," she cried.

'Tashi's eyes twinkled. He flopped down on the silken carpet at his feet. "All right, Cha Ming, roll me up." The young man took one end of the carpet and rolled Tashi right up in it. "You see," Tashi's voice came from deep inside, "Cha Ming is going to deliver a beautiful last-minute present to the Emperor for his daughter."

'And that's exactly what happened. They went ahead to the Banquet Hall, where five hundred guests were already waiting. Cha Ming followed, with Tashi tucked inside the carpet like a prawn inside a dumpling. At the huge iron doors they were met by two Palace guards with swords gleaming at their sides. But one of them smiled quickly and looked down at the carpet, giving it a nod. Cha Ming smiled back. The guards waved them inside and then went before them, calling, "Make way! Make way!"

'When Cha Ming stopped in front of the Emperor's chair, he slipped the carpet from his shoulder and unrolled it across the

floor with a flourish. Out popped Tashi, like
a seed from its pod.

'The air was almost whooshed from the
hall as five hundred guests gasped. Khan
sprang up and signalled to his men. Tashi
was ready. He stepped forward and bowed,
holding out the letter to the Emperor.

'"Gracious Majesty, your friends at the Court have heard that your life is in danger. Please read this letter."

'The Emperor's face froze as he read Khan's letter to General Xeng. Khan's hand clutched at his sword. His jaw clenched hard as steel. But he was too late. Tashi's new friend, the Palace guard, had already doubled the Emperor's troops and they were surrounding the hall. Khan and his father were seized and marched outside.

'The Emperor shook his head. "I can't believe it. He seemed such a fine young man." He looked over to Princess Hoiti-Toiti. "I'm sorry, my daughter. You were right and I was wrong." He gave a sad laugh. "And all the wonderful wedding preparations wasted, all the beautiful presents must be sent back…"

'The Emperor shrugged, and cleared his throat. "Well, young Tashi, once again I must ask how I can reward you for such a great service to me and my family."

'Tashi took a deep breath. "Thank you, Majesty. What I would like most of all would be to see the Princess Hoiti-Toiti marry the man she loves – Cha Ming." And he added in a rush, "The wedding could still take place tomorrow, and all the preparations would not be wasted and the presents not sent back."

'The Emperor looked startled. Then he gave a reluctant laugh. "Is that what you really want, Hoiti-Toiti?" His daughter nodded, her smile gleaming wide in the lamplight.

'"Then let the celebrations begin … *again!*"

'Later that evening, Princess Hoiti-Toiti pulled Tashi aside. She took a magnificent gold medallion from her neck and clasped it around Tashi's. "I want you to wear this, Tashi, as a token of my gratitude and as a sorry from me for all the times I spoke unkindly to you in the past. I am very lucky that you have such a generous heart."

'Tashi found it hard to speak just then. There was a lump in his throat – it was the first time Hoiti-Toiti had ever been kind to him.

'He was saved from answering by Cha Ming, who laughed, "And if you were wondering what to give us for a wedding present, Tashi – there's nothing we'd like more than one of your special ghost cakes!"'

Jack's family was quiet for a moment, thinking.

'So what's the message here?' said Uncle Joe. 'The next time I get a bad surprise, I should roll myself up in a carpet?'

Dad was frowning. 'I can see how the ghost cakes were useful, but what about the balm for spider bites and herb for calming snakes? Where do they come in?'

'That's another story, I bet,' said Mum.

'Or,' said Dad, his frown clearing, 'they're like the extra cash I put in my pocket when I go out for the day – a just-in-case Tashi thing.'

'A you-never-know Tashi thing.'

'A Tashi weapon-against-bad-surprises!' cried Uncle Joe, leaping up with satisfaction and dashing out to the shed.

'No, you'll see, they'll turn up in another story,' Mum whispered to her teacup. 'And it'll be a surprise.'

TASHI and the
GOLEM

'Anybody sitting here?' Frank Fury squashed down between Jack and Tashi. He peered into Tashi's lunchbox. '*Erk*, what d'you call *that*?' And he stuck a big dirty finger right into the middle of a sandwich.

'Dragon egg,' said Jack, helping himself to one. 'And get your paws off it.'

'Who's gunna make me?' said Frank, and shoved Jack just under his ribs so that he dropped his sandwich on the ground.

'Hey, look out, you *dill* blot!' cried Jack.

'*You* look out, dog breath,' Frank held
up his fists, 'or you could hurt yourself
on *these*.'

Tashi finished his sandwich and gazed
at Frank's fists. 'Strong hands. Good for
working in the fields, or digging a well. Big
Uncle could have done with hands like yours
when we were digging for treasure.'

'What? Who's Big Uncle?' Frank's voice
was gruff but a small smile pricked at the
corner of his mouth. He laid his left hand,
fingers splayed wide, on his knee for
everyone to see.

'Now *that's* a story you'll never hear,' said Jack, 'because you can't even appreciate dragon eggs.'

Frank went red. He leapt up and loomed over Jack, his fists up.

'Not many people in the world have heard of dragon eggs,' Tashi went on. 'Let alone tasted one. It's a shame because they're delicious. My friend Ah Chu likes them even better than giants' dumplings.'

Frank stared at Tashi, confused. He looked at his fists hovering in the air, as if he didn't know what they were doing there. Then he shook his head in a scornful way, and stumped off.

'What a loser,' muttered Jack. 'He's only been here a day and already everyone hates him. I bet he'll thump someone and kill them and then he'll have to go to *jail*.'

'Hmm,' said Tashi. 'People do change, though. You can't be sure what they're going to do next. It's like the weather. Something could happen in between today's rain and tomorrow. The sun might come out!' Tashi gazed off into the distance.

'Are you talking about someone in particular?'

'Well, I'm thinking of Bang Bang, right now. But a minute ago I was thinking of Soh Sorry, Soh Meen's son.'

'So start with Bang Bang, who was he?'

'Someone you might say would end up in jail.' Tashi took a bite of his apple. 'Bang Bang rubbed everyone up the wrong way. Including me. But Ah Chu was the first to come up against him.'

'What happened?'

'Well, it was like this. One day Lotus Blossom and I were walking to school and we met Ah Chu. He was kicking along his bag, instead of carrying it, and muttering some really bad words. I was amazed because the bag was very special to him, and inside there might be dumplings or fish cakes getting all bashed up.

'As soon as he saw us he growled, "Did you know the Baron's nephew, Bang Bang, has come to stay with him?"

'"What's he like?" I asked.

'"What would you ex*pect* a nephew of the Baron to be like?" said Ah Chu.

'"Oh, greedy," Lotus Blossom shrugged, "a bit of a bully, just like his uncle?"

'"Not necessarily," I said. "Look at Soh Meen's son, who isn't mean at all, but tries extra hard to make up for his father. My grandma says it is a terrible burden for a young man to carry and that's why Soh Sorry went away. You have to see someone for who they are, not where they've come from."

'"That's all very well," Ah Chu cut in, "but Lotus Blossom is right about Bang Bang. I met him while I was unwrapping a sticky rice cake that your mother had given me, Tashi, when he grabbed it and ate it and tipped me upside down to see if I had any more in my pockets. Then he said he'd beat me with his bamboo cane if I told anyone."

'"What a pig!" This is just the sort of thing that makes Lotus Blossom boil. "I hope he doesn't stay long."

'That afternoon I saw Bang Bang for myself. He was swaggering through the village as if he owned it. When my Auntie Tam didn't move out of his way quickly enough, he pushed her so roughly she fell into a basket of beans waiting ready for market.

'I helped her to her feet and said to Bang Bang, "Look what you're doing. You could have hurt her!"

'Bang Bang grabbed my arm and twisted it up behind my back until the pain took my breath away. Then he spun me around and, poking me in the chest with each word, hissed, "I've heard about you, young Tashi. You stay out of my way or we'll be having these arm exercises every day." He lifted me up so that his face was right in mine. "Did you hear me?"

'I nodded and he dropped me, *flop*, on the ground. Then he strolled away, well pleased with himself.

'I stood still till my heart stopped hammering. No one had behaved like that to me before. As if I was a bag of old fish heads. Even the Baron treated me like a respected enemy. I could see why people were frightened of Bang Bang. It was as if he didn't understand other people had feelings at all.

'I was still sore and troubled the next day when we bumped into Much-to-Learn coming out of Not Yet's shop. He was bursting with news and rage. But it wasn't because his shoes weren't ready.'

'No, it was that bully Bang Bang, wasn't it?' Jack burst out. 'What's he done *now*?'

'Well,' said Tashi, 'Much-to-Learn said Bang Bang had called around, saying that he and the Baron had decided the spring bubbling up at the back of Wise-as-an-Owl's house really belonged to the Baron. "We own the field next door and we say that fence was put in the wrong place. The spring is on the Baron's land, and we are going to take it over."

'"He can't do that!" I shouted. "Your father uses that special spring water for his medicines. Besides, it has belonged to his family for hundreds of years."

'"Yes, but my father just won't take him seriously," Much-to-Learn fretted. "Really, I think Bang Bang is a very dangerous young man. I'm afraid that he and the Baron will just march in and take over the spring."

'That's just the kind of thing Frank Fury would do,' said Jack. 'If he wants something he'll get it, and look out anybody who's in his way.'

'Well, so you can imagine how we felt. Something had to be done quickly. We were standing in the square, thinking, when Much-to-Learn said nervously, "I learned a new spell the other day, Tashi, that might just be useful."

'Lotus Blossom caught my eye and shook her head. I knew she was thinking about how Much-to-Learn's last spell, the mixed-up monster, had turned out. But he was so much more careful these days. I didn't think he'd make a mistake like that again.

'So I listened closely while he explained that he had been reading in the Book of Spells about a little creature called a golem. "You make it from clay and then, when you chant a spell, you can bring it to life."

'"*Wah!* Have you actually done it, Much-to-Learn?" we wanted to know.

'"No. Not actually *done* it, not yet, but–" Much-to-Learn took my arm and led me a few steps away to the gloomy lane behind Not Yet's shop. In a whisper, he repeated the spell three or four times until I knew it by heart.

'"That's it!" I cried when we came back to the others. "Only we won't make a little golem, we'll shape a great big one!"

'Much-to-Learn looked still more anxious when he heard this and seemed sorry he'd ever mentioned the spell. Even Lotus Blossom said, "And then what? What happens when it comes to life?"

'But Ah Chu was excited. "If you bring it to life, it would have to be your servant, wouldn't it?"

'I wasn't so sure, but if Wise-as-an-Owl wouldn't see the danger we were facing, it seemed the best thing to do. So we told Much-to-Learn not to worry, we would be careful, that he should go back and keep Wise-as-an-Owl occupied.

'Then we ran home, collected our buckets
and met at the river bank. All afternoon
we trundled loads of mud up to a grassy
clearing and when we had a really huge pile,
we began to shape the Golem.

'Pale pink was seeping into the sky when we sat back and looked at what we had done. A cool breeze suddenly sprang up, and as I gazed at the Golem lying in the grass, I wasn't sure if it was the sudden chill in the air or my own uneasiness that lifted the hair on my neck.

'The Golem was about three metres long, with arms and legs like trunks and a huge block of a head.

'Lotus Blossom shivered. "I don't like the look on his face." She smoothed over the grim mouth and turned up the lips in a smile.

'"That's better," I said. "He looks friendlier now. And just to make sure, we'll give him a heart. There's a pine cone behind you, Ah Chu."

'I took from my pocket a piece of paper with the sacred word *LIFE* written on it and put it under the Golem's tongue, and then, with a fine stick wrote the word once more on his forehead.

'"We have to light three fires now: one at the head and two at the feet, using cedar branches," I told them. I was getting nervous again. It was all very well for Lotus Blossom and Ah Chu – they hadn't heard the incantation, so haunting and mysterious in the shadows of that lane. They didn't know how Much-to-Learn had tried to keep his voice hushed and low on the ground, but even so the spell had tugged at the air and risen up with a life of its own, flickering between us.

'Yet as we went about lighting the sticks, I felt a little shudder of excitement, too, thinking of how Bang Bang might change from a swaggering bully to a – a what? What would he do when he saw the Golem?

'We each stood by a fire and I lifted my
voice, repeating the chant I had learned.
And with every word the sun slipped further
into the river, and the long shadows of the
willows rippled out from the bank. And as
I spoke, the scented smoke thickened and
danced around the Golem.

'The breeze dropped as we waited, and
the river was still. We watched the drifting
smoke and the hulking clay figure hidden
inside it and it seemed the whole world was
holding its breath with us. Slowly, through
the haze, we saw two lights shining.
We stood transfixed: the Golem had
opened his eyes.

'A tremor passed over the huge body
and the giant sat up. Lotus Blossom gasped.
Ah Chu sank to his knees.

'The Golem turned his great head. "Who
are you?" His voice was rough, like grinding
gravel.

'I quickly explained what we had done,
and why.

'The giant frowned. "The Golem does
no man's bidding."

'Ah Chu found his voice. "Oh, but you must. We brought you to life, so that makes you our servant … doesn't it?" His question dribbled away to a squeak.

'The Golem surged to his feet and towered above us. He was tall as a ship. "I am hungry," he said. He plucked Ah Chu up and sniffed his arm, hastily dropping him back.

'"What do I like to eat?" He looked at us reproachfully. "You have given me a heart but no memory."

'We offered him some nettles and a dead lizard but he didn't like them. Then Ah Chu remembered the fish balls and the honey cakes in his bag. Sadly, he watched the Golem devour them. "What golems like are fish balls and honey cakes," Ah Chu sighed.

'There was a sudden loud gurgle from the Golem's stomach and a gulp from his mouth. "What was that?" he asked, surprised.

'"That was a burp," Ah Chu told him. "It's because you ate too quickly. The wind comes up and out your mouth."

'The Golem did it again. "I can taste the food I just ate," he said wonderingly.

'"That's right!" Ah Chu cried excitedly. "It happens to me all the time." He stood beaming at the Golem until he noticed we were grinning at him.

'"We could bring you some more food tomorrow if you will just give a *certain person* a good scare," I told him.

'"The certain person is called Bang Bang," added Ah Chu, just in case.

'"I'll think about it," the Golem replied. "But now I have a strong feeling that it is time for me to have a little rest. This living business is very tiring for a golem." And he lay back down, *whumpff*, on the flattened bushes to sleep.

952

'"We gave him a lovely smile," said Lotus Blossom with satisfaction.

'"And he has a noble forehead," said Ah Chu gruffly.

'The Golem opened one eye, "And good burps." We waited. "So, this Bang Bang you were talking about," he went on, "what do you want me to do to him? Tear him apart?"

'"No!" I shouted.

'"Throw him across the river?"

'"No, no!" Lotus Blossom went white.

'"Stand on him?" We shook our heads. "*Lean* on him?" His eyes twinkled. I could swear that he was enjoying himself.

'We walked home very quietly, I can tell you. There was just a sliver of moon and the dark hung between the trees like a curtain. We jumped at the sudden hoot of an owl. "Yesterday I didn't think we would be worried about looking after Bang Bang, did you?" whispered Lotus Blossom as we reached the empty square. Before parting we agreed on the food we would bring to the Golem, and then we each made the sign of the dragon, for luck.

'The next afternoon after school we arrived at the river bank, but there was no Golem. We ran along the bend of the river, searching, and then into the forest, and we were wishing we had never heard of golems and wondering what harm such a creature would do in the village when we heard heavy steps and snapped branches coming towards us.

'But it wasn't the Golem. It was Bang Bang.

'"Hah!" he cried. "Tashi and his little friends! I'm on my way to tell our men where to put the new fence. I'm going to–" but he noticed that we weren't looking at him any longer. We were staring over his shoulder at something else.

'The Golem had been lying among the bushes right behind Bang Bang and now he sat up. Bang Bang turned and gasped. He looked back at us in terror as the Golem slowly rose to his feet.

'"Is this the Bang Bang you were talking about?" the Golem asked.

'I nodded and went over to him, reaching up to take his hand. "This is our friend, the Golem," I told Bang Bang. "And you are – what? Our enemy? Friend?"

'"Oh friend, your *friend*," stammered Bang Bang and he searched frantically in his pockets, finally pulling out a piece of bamboo shoot. "Here," he said, offering it to the Golem as if he were a savage dog. The Golem took the bamboo, cautiously nibbling an end of it. A pleased smile spread across his face.

'"*This* is what Golems like!" he said.

'"It came from across those mountains,"
Bang Bang told him eagerly. "Not far from
where I grew up. I could draw a map to
show you where." He pulled out some paper
and a pencil from another pocket but after
a few minutes the Golem said impatiently,
"I can't read those squiggles. You'll have
to come with me and show me the way."

'Bang Bang looked stunned. "On second
thoughts, it's a rather lonely forest where
those shoots grow, a long way from any
village or people."

'"Good," said the Golem, "that's just what I like – not all this talking, talking, talking, just the wind in the trees and the birds singing." He looked around, surprised and pleased. "That's what I *like*!"

'"But first we'd have to get some food for the journey," Bang Bang pointed out anxiously.

'"Here you are," we all cried together, holding out the food that we'd brought for the Golem.

'"Fish balls," beamed Ah Chu.

'"Honey cakes," I cried.

'"And plenty of carrots," Lotus Blossom added.

'Bang Bang glared at us but he couldn't think of any more objections. The Golem bent and scooped him up under his arm. He gave us a little smile and a wave as he strode off along the path. "Tell my uncle–" Bang Bang began but the rest was lost as they passed into the forest.

'Much-to-Learn was overjoyed to hear the news of what had happened. He hadn't had a moment's peace since he'd taught me the spell, he said, and he would rather we didn't mention it to anyone else.

'A few days later I heard the Baron talking to Luk Ahed in the village. "Young people today have no manners. That nephew of mine was supposed to be making a long visit with me but he just took himself off without a word of thanks or goodbye. I had a letter from his father this morning saying that he doesn't know what I did with him, but he's a different boy, obedient and polite and helpful to his mother. He can't get over it, but you can be sure I won't be asking Bang Bang to come and stay with me again!"

'I wish *we* had a Golem,' said Jack, watching Frank snatch Angus Figment's tennis ball and put it in his pocket.

'What you looking at?' said Frank, as he swaggered past.

'A Bang Bang in need of a golem,' said Jack.

'What? You guys talk rubbish.'

'You'd understand if you'd heard Tashi's story. Could be the story of your life,' said Jack.

'Oh yeah?' Frank held up his fists. 'Well these could be the end of yours!'

'Bang Bang had a brother, you know,'
Tashi said. 'But that's another story.'

'Yeah?' said Frank. 'How does that one go?'

'Well,' said Tashi, 'it was like this.'

'Like what?'

'Oh, let him get on with it,' said Jack.
'He always starts this way.'

'Can I have my ball back, Frank?' Angus
Figment crept up, looking down at his shoes.
'If you're quite finished with it?'

Everyone looked at Frank.

'If you give the ball back,' said Tashi, 'then
I can start the story.'

'Tell me what's in it then,' said Frank.
'And I'll see.'

'Oh, kidnappings and river pirates...'

'Okay, here's your ball, Figment. It was a
dumb ball anyway.'

'Oh, thanks so much!' said Angus, and he
sat down on the bench.

'So, okay, *start* then,' said Frank. He
smirked. 'Anybody sitting here?'

'Yes *I* am,' said Jack. 'Can't you see? Find
your own seat for once.'

'Well, it was like this...' Tashi began.

THINKS-TOO-LATE

'Remember, Jack, how disgusted the Baron was with the rude way his nephew Bang Bang left him?'

'Who's this Bang Bang?' Frank interrupted.

'A rude guy, a bully just like you,' said Jack.

'Hey, who are you calling a –'

'Shut up, Frank, you might learn something,' said Angus suddenly. Everyone stopped talking and looked at him. He smiled, 'That's if you don't mind.'

'Well,' Tashi went on, 'as Jack explained, Bang Bang was a bully, and he'd made everyone's life a misery, so you can imagine how surprised they were in the village to hear about the Baron's next visitor. It was Bang Bang's young brother! Their father had written to say that the Baron had done such a good job with Bang Bang, he was hoping that the Baron might take his other son in hand.'

'Ha, the *Baron* doing a good job, what a joke!' said Jack.

'*What* joke? I'm not laughing,' said Frank.

'Just listen, and you'll get it,' said Angus.

'Well, this younger brother, he was like
a hurricane, stirring up trouble wherever he
went. By the time he was five, his family had
named him Thinks-Too-Late because he was
always doing terrible things without thinking
what the results would be.'

'At least he *did* stuff,' said Frank. 'I mean,
he didn't just sit around on his bum all day
doing *nothing*.'

'Go on, Tashi,' said Angus.

'Well, he certainly looked a completely
different sort of person from Bang Bang.
He was a cheerful, smiling boy, interested
in everyone he met and full of suggestions
for what they should be doing.'

'See?' said Frank, slapping his knee, 'what did I tell you? A helpful guy, handy to have around!'

'On the very first day that he bounced into our village, he persuaded three small boys to jump off the schoolhouse roof to see which one would land first.'

'Yeah,' said Jack, 'such a *help*ful guy!'

'Then he talked Little Wu into seeing if you could spark a fire by striking a piece of metal on a brick. You can, and it was just luck that Not Yet's storeroom didn't go up in flames before he found out what they were doing.

'Thinks-Too-Late couldn't see what all the fuss was about, and soon he turned his attention to the problem of Granny White Eyes. Everyone had been worried about her since Mrs Ping had found her dazed and sore after a fall in her kitchen. It wasn't the first time this had happened, and now lots of people wanted her to go and live with them.

'But Granny White Eyes wouldn't even think about it. "I can manage perfectly well on my own. It's what I like and I would miss my own little house and my garden too much."

'Thinks-Too-Late didn't take part in these discussions, but later he caught my arm. "I know how we can convince her that she can't live alone anymore. We can give her frights. No, listen, it'll be interesting – and it's for her own good."

'I heard him out in silence. He suggested we could pretend to be burglars and ghosts and make phantom door knocks at her cottage in the evenings. Lotus Blossom, who had come up in time to hear this, was speechless for once, but I couldn't help angry words exploding out of me.

'"Listen you, if you so much as go *near* Granny White Eyes, we will see that no one in the village speaks to you again."

'But Thinks-Too-Late didn't mind.
"Okay," he said cheerfully, and with a breezy
wave of his hand, he set off to call on Wise-
as-an-Owl. He sneaked around the house
to the back window and listened as Wise-
as-an-Owl was listing for Much-to-Learn
the ingredients of a new medicine they
were mixing.

'The next thing they knew, poor Mrs Yang was covered in huge purple and red blotches. "That awful boy told me it was Wise-as-an-Owl's new cure for backache!" she moaned.

'But Thinks-too-Late didn't mind being scolded. Particularly when he heard Soh Meen loudly complaining around the village about how bad his cold was. "I know what you need!" he cried, and ran off to fetch a capful of dark green plants.

'"What have you got there?" asked Soh
Meen suspiciously. He was even more
doubtful when he saw Thinks-Too-Late take
off his socks and pull them over his hands
before picking up the plants.

'"This is just what you need," beamed
Thinks-Too-Late. "Open your shirt."
He rubbed the plants vigorously into
Soh Meen's chest.

973

'The next moment Soh Meen was running around in circles, tearing off his shirt. "I'm stinging and burning and stinging!" he cried. "Those were nettles you rubbed into me!"

'"Yes, but haven't they made you lovely and warm?"

'"I said I *had* a cold, you stupid boy, I didn't say I *was* cold! Oh, my skin feels like it's on fire!"

'"Anyway, it's taking his mind off his cold." Thinks-Too-Late winked at me.

'By now everyone in the village had heard about the trouble Thinks-Too-Late had caused. Even so, no one was prepared for what he did next.

'What?' said Frank. 'What did he do?'

'Well, it was like this. One day Lotus Blossom and I called on Ah Chu to ask him to come down to the river for a swim, and to see the River Pirate's new sampan. I'd spotted him that morning pulling in for supplies. Ah Chu said he couldn't go because he had to mind his baby sister. But as we moved on down the road, Ah Chu came running after us. "On second thoughts, Little Sister can come with us. She is eight months old after all – it's time she had her first swim."

'We took turns carrying Little Sister, babies can be quite heavy after a while. We were watching her splash her hands and feet in a shallow pool by the river when Thinks-Too-Late came along.

'Little Sister smiled sweetly at him and offered him a wet bun. It was so pleasant there, talking and joking and rolling in the cool water and out again, the time passed quickly. Until Ah Chu looked around. "Where is Little Sister?" Dread clanged in the air.

'"And where is Thinks-Too-Late?" I cried.

'Ah Chu, his face as white as flour, dived and dived, searching the river. Lotus Blossom and I raced up and down the river bank, calling. It seemed hours before we caught sight of Thinks-Too-Late sneaking back to the village through the trees.

'When we caught up with him, he stammered, "Oh, L-L-Little Sister? I gave her to the River Pirate."

'"You did *what*? What were you thinking of? Can't you imagine how Little Sister's parents will feel? And that little baby without her mother?"

'Thinks-Too-Late shrugged. "I didn't think, and anyway, I had to give her away. See, I took her down to the sampan to show her what a boat was like and the River Pirate saw her. He and his wife don't have any children, and he said his wife told him not to come back without a baby this trip. So he gave me this jade horse to keep me quiet until they'd got away. He said he'd cut me into little pieces with that great sword of his if I told."

'I didn't stop to hear any more of his sniffs and excuses. I grabbed the horse and shouted at him, "*Run!* Run faster than the wind and bring Little Sister's mother down to the boat." Then, "Come on!" I told Lotus Blossom and Ah Chu, and we raced down the path to the landing stage, just in time to see the pirates casting off the ropes from the dock. We leapt onto the boat and swarmed over the pirates, tripping them up, re-tying the ropes, ducking and dodging the big tattooed arms flung out to catch us.

'"Captain Drednort!" we called. "Come out!"

'"What do yer want, fish-bait?" growled the River Pirate, coming up on deck. When we told him there had been a terrible mistake and he had to give the baby back, he just laughed. But he didn't sound amused. He sounded angry. His face closed over like a big iron trap. "A deal is a deal," he snarled. "Pirate's code. Now get off my boat or I'll chop you up like sardines and feed you to the sharks."

'Ah Chu let out a moan. He was watching Little Sister struggling against the shoulder of a big hairy sailor. "But you can't, you don't even know—"

'The River Pirate drew out his sword.
It flashed silver fire in the midday sun.
We couldn't stop looking at it, even though
it hurt our eyes. Ah Chu started to weep.
Oh, what to do? And then, out of the corner
of my eye, I saw something. Someone was
flashing past the stacks of lumber, leaping
over coils of rope, *flying* along ... Thinks-
too-Late racing to reach us! And on his heels,
Ah Chu's mother! As she spotted us she took
a heart-stopping leap and sprang on board,
holding her arms out for her child.

'Little Sister wanted her mother. She began to wail.

'"Listen to that," I said quickly. "How will you and your men enjoy the trip home with that baby screaming in your ears all day?" His men looked very impressed with this argument, but the River Pirate just shrugged and said a good smack would keep him quiet.

'"Him?" said Mrs Chu, grabbing her child, "Little Sister is not a *him*."

'"It's not?" bellowed the River Pirate. "Do you mean to say I have bought a girl?"

982

'Lotus Blossom's chin jutted out, like it always does when she's in a temper. "What's wrong with being a girl? We're just as good as boys any day."

'The River Pirate brushed her aside and turned to Mrs Chu. "As well as returning my jade horse," he said as he lifted it from my hands, "I will need some compensation from you for my trouble."

'Poor Mrs Chu looked at me in despair.
She had no money or jewels to give the River
Pirate. None of us did. And wasn't that the
only thing that would satisfy him? But as
I watched her wringing her hands, an idea
popped into my mind. There was no time to
look at it from all sides as I usually do.
It just had to work, and it was the truth.

'"You will need to go and ask the Baron
then," I said to the River Pirate, "seeing that
it was the Baron's nephew, Thinks-Too-Late,
who sold the baby to you."

'A strange smile broke out on the River Pirate's face. "Oh ho, he is, is he?" And the pirate grabbed Thinks-Too-Late by the scruff of his neck. "Then let's go and visit your *uncle*, my little blabbermouth," he spat. "We'll see what he has to say about the way his nephew does business. He'll pay a tidy sum to keep this matter quiet, I think."

'As we watched him march Thinks-Too-Late down the path to the Baron's house, Mrs Chu snuggled Little Sister into her. "When the Baron has to open his money bags, he won't be wanting to keep Thinks-Too-Late with him much longer," she said with satisfaction.

'Lotus Blossom did a little dance. "Granny White Eyes will be pleased."

'And the baby laughed in agreement, sucking her mother's nose.

'Er yuck,' said Frank. 'Babies are disgusting.'

'Is that all you can say?' cried Angus Figment. 'Little Sister nearly got kidnapped forever!'

'Well, would *you* want to suck someone's nose?' said Frank. 'Even for fifty bucks?'

The boys were quiet a moment, considering.

'I dreamed my little sister got kidnapped once,' said Frank. 'It was an amazing dream. It had all the features of a great adventure: pirates, quicksand, bugs living in your ears, sea snakes.'

Everyone stared at Frank.

'Let's hear it!' said Tashi.

'Yeah!' said Jack.

'Maybe tomorrow,' said Frank. He grinned at them all. 'Sometimes it's good sitting round doing nothing, hey?'

The Amazing

Tashi

Activity Book

Come and play with Tashi!

In *The Amazing Tashi Activity Book* you'll find
puzzles and games and Tashi's very own board
game. And there's a brand new adventure story
called 'Tashi and the Strangers'.

What will you make first? A boat? A dragon?
The tiger pop-up card? Or you could try Tashi's
Treasure Chest of Words or his Tricky Word
Puzzle. Can you find the Baron's gold with the
treasure map? Or help Tashi rescue the children
in the Warlord's maze? How will Tashi
escape from the dungeon?

The Amazing *Tashi* Activity Book

Play Tashi's Board Game

Solve all the Puzzles

Learn to Draw Tashi

Make Fabulous Things

Read a New Tashi Adventure

Anna Fienberg
Barbara Fienberg
Kim Gamble

Climb aboard with

Minton!

Minton loves anything that moves and
he's always ready for action. His friend Turtle
is not so brave but together they have
wild adventures.

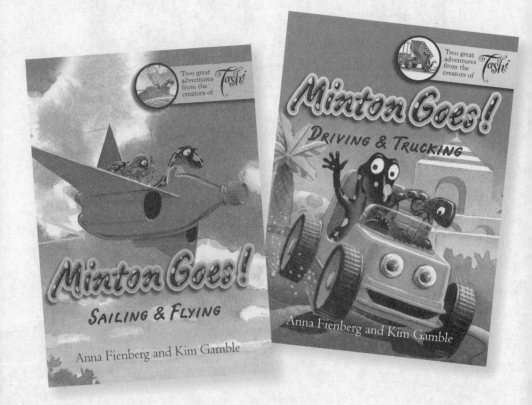

Two great stories in each book.
Perfect for L-Plate readers and fun to read
aloud. Plus you can make Minton's boat, plane,
car, truck, hot-air balloon and submarine!

The
Hottest
Boy
Who
Ever Lived

A Minton Adventure by
Anna Fienberg
and Kim Gamble

The Hottest Boy
Who Ever Lived

Another fantastic Minton adventure!

The first time Minton saw him, Hector was
shooting right out of a volcano. No one can
come near him, except Minton, the fire
salamander. So Hector is unbearably, bone-
achingly lonely. Until one day a storm sweeps
Hector and Minton far away to the cold snowy
lands, where they meet Gilda, a cool
Viking adventurer…